Praise for Deb Kastner and her novels

"A Daddy at Heart is well-written…"
—*Romantic Times BOOKclub*

"Debra Kastner treats readers
to a breathless romance…. *A Holiday Prayer*
is a riveting book that proves that fairy tales
do indeed come true and have a place
in the inspirational market."
—*Romantic Times BOOKclub*

"Deb Kastner creates two very likeable characters
with her seemingly effortless writing style
in *Black Hills Bride.*"
—*Romantic Times BOOKclub*

DEB KASTNER

The Forgiving Heart

A Daddy at Heart

Steeple
Hill®

Published by Steeple Hill Books™

STEEPLE HILL BOOKS

Steeple
Hill®

ISBN-13: 978-0-373-65266-2
ISBN-10:   0-373-65266-6

THE FORGIVING HEART & A DADDY AT HEART

THE FORGIVING HEART
Copyright © 2000 by Debra Kastner

A DADDY AT HEART
Copyright © 2001 by Debra Kastner

CONTENTS

Books by Deb Kastner

Love Inspired

DEB KASTNER

is the wife of a Reformed Episcopal minister, so it was natural for her to find her niche in the Christian romance market. She enjoys tackling the issues of faith and trust within the context of a romance. Her characters range from upbeat and humorous to (her favorite) dark and brooding heroes. Her plots fall anywhere from a playful romp to the deeply emotional story. When she's not writing, she enjoys spending time with her husband and three girls and, whenever she can manage, attending regional dinner theater and touring Broadway musicals.

THE FORGIVING HEART

"I was in prison and you came to Me." Then the righteous will answer Him, saying, "Lord, when did we see You...in prison, and come to You?" And the King will answer and say to them, "Assuredly, I say to you, inasmuch as you did it to one of the least of these, my brethren, you did it to Me."

—*Matthew* 25:36-40

To my sister Amy.
I'm blessed to be your relative,
but so much more to be your friend.

Keep chasing the wind,
and don't ever let anyone talk you out of it!

Chapter One

The young man set his jaw, his throat corded with strain. Surprisingly dark eyebrows scrunched grimly over wide blue eyes, a shady contrast to his closely cropped golden-blond hair. Long, muscular arms with hands tightly fisted crossed over a chest just beginning to show a hint of breadth.

He looked angry. Resentful. Bitter.

Scared completely out of his wits.

Officer Callie Brockman felt an unfamiliar wave of emotion she could only classify as maternal instinct, however misplaced and foreign.

She quickly masked it with her usual armor, her way of getting by in the world. Anger.

Fortunately, even that was easily hidden. Callie Brockman was an expert in concealing her true feelings. She'd learned early that it was best to reveal as little as possible about what she was thinking and feeling. Life was safer that way.

"What's the kid in for?" she asked Bobby, the middle-aged dispatcher sporting a paunch and a bald spot. She nodded toward the benched teenager, who had unfolded his arms and was clenching his hands together and glaring a hole in the floor.

Who, she wondered, could leave a youth to fend for himself like this, though her acrimony didn't show in her tone. Unfortunately, she had a pretty good guess about the boy's parents, or lack of them. She just hadn't expected to deal with this so soon.

Not in such a small town. Why had she moved to John Day, Oregon, if not to slow down and find a more deliberate way of life?

Bobby stretched back in his oversize office chair and ruffled the short, spiked ends of his black hair—what was left of it, anyway—with the tips of his fingers.

"Shoplifting. Classic case."

"Yeah?" As the newest police officer on the force, it was her job to take on the juvies. She shook her head in reluctant acceptance of this part of her job. It was unavoidable, she knew, but still...

This was only her second night on the job, and already, a *classic* case to handle. She sighed under her breath.

Couldn't she have gone for at least a week without a *classic* case? She'd hoped for better in a small town, having come from fast-paced, crime-ridden Portland where juvenile crime was at an all-time high.

But this wasn't Portland. Everyone knew everyone in John Day, most from several generations. More than likely, she'd met this kid's parents already; if not at the post office, then perhaps in line at the grocery store or the local deli.

If somehow she'd missed out on meeting them already, though, the slight was about to be remedied, and not in pleasant circumstances, either. It wasn't a thought she wished to dwell on, so she turned to the paperwork Bobby shoved at her.

She ran down the teen's file in short order. There wasn't much to see.

Brandon Wheeler. Sixteen. First time offender.

Wheeler. The name sounded familiar, though she couldn't immediately place it.

"Oh, man," said Bobby, whistling under his breath. "His old man's going to pitch a fit when he finds out about this." He punctuated his sentence with a negative grunt.

"Wheeler?" she asked, hoping he'd clue her in. The more she knew about this kid's parents, the easier processing the criminal would go. And as far as Callie was concerned, the easier, the better. She wasn't big on tough cases.

"Everett Wheeler. Goes by Rhett. Community service agent," Bobby supplied.

Rhett Wheeler. *That's* where she'd heard the name before. The kid in question was the son of the community service agent.

It figured. It just figured.

Bad luck followed her around like a little black rain cloud hovering directly over her head. She'd hoped changing locales would help her lose the shady veil, but obviously she'd been mistaken.

A woman couldn't run from herself.

Her gaze returned to the young man slouching on the bench, looking increasingly miserable with every tick of the clock. She could only imagine what had gone through that boy's mind, what would prompt a handsome kid like Brandon Wheeler to break the law.

Actually, she *could* imagine why a seemingly typical teen would commit a crime. She remembered all too well.

She blew out a breath and turned away, unwilling to revive memories she thought had been laid to rest.

It hurt to be a cop and have to face these kids and their parents. The pain of it scratched black marks in her heart. She'd run away from it if she was able, but that was beyond her capabilities.

Whatever internal wounds she incurred as a police officer, it hurt far more to stand around and do nothing.

With effort, she reined in the empathetic sting of bitterness she felt at seeing Brandon Wheeler shuddering in his tennis shoes.

She was a cop. A juvenile cop, at the moment. And she had work to do, however distasteful.

"He's been booked and fingerprinted," Bobby said, answering her unspoken question. "You can call his dad to pick him up, or you can take him home yourself, if you'd like."

Her gaze snapped up in surprise. "Take him home?"

Bobby chuckled and patted his ample midsection. "Sure. There's not a whole lot else going on here tonight, in case you hadn't noticed."

Callie pressed her lips together, leaving her thoughts unspoken. *Portland* police didn't escort their young criminals home. Many young people stayed in jail overnight—or sometimes even longer—when uncaring or absent parents didn't respond.

Who was she to say this small-town police department was making a mistake? Maybe they were right, giving a little personality to their police department. Especially for the kids' sake.

She paced toward Brandon Wheeler until she stood directly in front of him. He avoided her eyes, glaring unseeingly at a point near his knees.

"You want me to give you a lift? Or should I call your mom to come get you?"

"No!" The towheaded youth came alive, bounding to his feet. "I mean, yes, ma'am."

He reached for her arm, then appeared to realize what he was doing and dropped his hand, stuffing it in the pocket of his blue jeans. He looked up at her, and then down at the floor again, toeing the tile with the tip of his sneaker. "I—I guess I'd..." He paused, continuing to toe the tile. "I'd rather have you drive me home."

He shrugged as if he didn't care one way or the other. "If you don't mind." And then as an afterthought, he added, "Ma'am."

Ma'am? Her eyes narrowed speculatively on the boy. This was certainly the first time she'd been called *ma'am* by a juvenile delinquent, at least without prodding.

This kid was too polite by far, setting off warning bells in Callie's head, which she studiously ignored.

Brandon Wheeler wasn't any of her business.

"First offense?" she barked at Brandon, though of course she already knew the answer.

She'd worked with hundreds of teenage offenders in Portland, kids no different from Brandon except they'd been born on the wrong side of the tracks in a city that didn't give second chances.

This kid was probably nothing more than the small-town version of the big-city type. Same song, different verse.

She gestured the youth ahead of her, then studied him on the way out to her patrol car. Brandon Wheeler was too soft for crime.

Real crime, anyway.

He was clean-cut. A mom-country-and-apple-pie kind of small-town kid, the brand of youth Uncle Sam dreamed about. Unfortunately, she already knew the tune this kid was playing. She'd heard it before, and not just from her work as a police officer. It hit too close for comfort. *Way* too close.

Seeing Brandon safely into the netted back seat of the car, she slid in behind the steering wheel and turned the key in the ignition. It was a mere three-minute drive to the address Brandon provided. Not much time to chat.

Besides, the youth was still surly, though he

was reluctantly cooperative to the few requests she'd made of him.

She glanced in the rearview mirror, taking further assessment of her charge. One thing was certain—he was going to end up with a killer headache if he kept gritting his teeth.

It occurred to Callie to provoke him into speech, but he looked as if he might cry, though she knew he'd deny it vehemently if she voiced her concern.

Give this kid a break, she prayed silently, awkwardly. She and God weren't exactly on a first-name basis, but this seemed as good a time as any to make an exception.

She'd do just about anything to keep from having a crying kid on her hands, especially one that was tugging at her heartstrings.

She was a little frightened she might cry, too. For whatever reason, her carefully maintained dam of emotions appeared to have been compromised.

She wondered if she ought to attempt to strike up a conversation with Brandon, to take his mind off his trouble, if that was possible. At any rate, *she* could stand to think about something besides the unfortunate first meeting to come, with the social worker who'd be taking her caseloads.

Brandon's father.

She'd be working closely with Rhett Wheeler, and the very first time they were introduced, it had to be when she was bringing his own kid home to him from the police station on a shoplifting indictment.

Maybe she'd get lucky and Rhett wouldn't be home. Maybe she'd be able to put off the inevitable, at least for the moment.

Yeah, and maybe pigs would fly.

"Hang in there, kid."

The moment the words left her mouth, she wanted to bang her forehead against the steering wheel. How idiotic could she be? In her experience, teenage boys did *not* like to be called *kid,* and she'd just flunked Juvenile Cop 101.

Brandon, who'd been staring grimly out the window, whipped his head around front, the whites of his eyes gleaming in the reflection of passing street lamps.

Callie held her breath, waiting for him to tell her what he *really* thought of this situation.

He cleared his throat, licked his lips and uttered a single word. "Thanks."

What?

Surprise jolted through her, which was no doubt the instigator of her next words, which were every bit as idiotic as her first.

"You want to talk about it?"

"No."

Short, sweet and to the point. She chuckled. "I figured."

The boy grunted.

She glanced in the rearview mirror, catching his wide-eyed gaze, which reminded her of a deer caught in headlights. Again, Callie found herself feeling for Brandon, wondering why he'd committed a crime.

"Just one question."

"Do I need a lawyer?"

The kid cracked a joke under pressure. Callie grinned despite herself. She liked him more and more by the minute. Too bad there were only a few minutes left between them.

"This is strictly off the record."

"Yeah?"

"Yeah."

To her surprise, he smiled, making his face turn from surly to downright cute. He'd be a knockout when he grew into his shoulders.

"What's a kid like me doing in a place like this?" he quipped.

Astounded, she laughed out loud. "I'll admit the question crossed my mind once or twice." A hundred times, she amended silently.

A kid like Brandon didn't just put a department store T-shirt on over his own and waltz out in direct view of everyone unless he had good reason. Even rookie shoplifters had more sense than that.

Especially rookie shoplifters.

Which could only mean Brandon had another reason for breaking the law, and Callie's guess was that he was doing it to get attention—most likely his parents' attention.

Anger flared a familiar fire in her chest, but she tamped it back. It really wasn't any of her business. Not beyond doing her civic duty.

She'd drop Brandon off, go home to her tiny cottage and spend the night screaming into her pillow if that's what it took.

What she would *not* do—could not do—is crack the facade she'd taken so long to acquire.

Pulling onto Brandon's street, she parked in the driveway he indicated and shut down the motor. She took two deep breaths before speaking.

"You ready?"

She wasn't.

He shrugged, his eyebrows a grim line again. "Guess so."

"Think your dad is home?" she asked, holding her breath for the answer.

She *really* didn't want to know. She *really* didn't want to do this.

"Yeah. The light is on."

"Couldn't that be your mother?"

His jaw clenched as he swallowed hard. "She checked out when I was eight."

"Checked out?" replied Callie, scrambling to backtrack, feeling as if she'd taken the first step off a dangerously high cliff.

Checked out. The words made her shiver.

"Left. You know. Took off. To find herself, or whatever."

She felt it when he punched the back of the front seat, but she didn't draw attention to the fact. She'd punch something, too, if she could.

"She didn't come back. Dad said it was because of her health, but…" He slammed his jaw shut as if he'd said too much already.

"I'm sorry," she murmured, not knowing what else to say.

And she *was* sorry. Brandon's revelation explained, in part, anyway, what was bothering him.

Losing a mother was a traumatic experience, especially if she abandoned her family first.

What kind of a mother left an eight-year-old kid on his own and didn't look back? Callie reminded herself there were two sides to every story, but she couldn't help but toss her own judgment into the ring.

Brandon just shrugged, his eyebrows making a dark V over his nose. "No big deal. She died a little while after that, so I guess it didn't matter much either way."

She cringed inside, wishing she had some words of wisdom that would make Brandon feel better. But what could she say? How could she express her sympathy to a boy she barely knew?

Taking a deep, calming breath, she released Brandon from the back seat and gestured for him to precede her to the porch. Her mind spun with questions.

Why would Brandon break the law? And why now, and not last year, or next year? It wasn't as if his grief over his mother were fresh fodder. It had been years since she died.

Years for resentment and bitterness to grow and fester. Years for Brandon's self-esteem to wither to the point where he'd try to get his deficit father's attention by shoplifting.

The youth seemed bright enough on the outside, but he was obviously hiding a great, deep hurt—something he couldn't settle on his own.

How, she wondered, did Rhett Wheeler fit into this near-violent turbulence? Had he run Brandon's mother off? Was he an absentee father? Cold? Abusive?

Reluctantly, she raised her hand to the door and knocked. Her stomach quivered as a chill washed over her.

She had the strangest feeling she was going to find out exactly what was wrong, why Brandon had acted the way he had and how Rhett Wheeler fit into this picture.

She was an unwilling victim. Truth be told, she didn't really want to know.

Chapter Two

Brandon!

At the firm knock on the front door, Rhett bolted out of his leather easy chair, and blitzed toward the entry, his slippers scuffing lightly on the carpet.

Brandon had a key. Why wasn't he using it?

Rhett didn't have to look at his watch to know his son was four hours late getting home from school, even if he'd stayed to play a game of football with his friends.

And he didn't have to look too deeply into his heart to know why.

Guilt edged through him. They hadn't been

getting along very well lately. He and Brandon hadn't been getting along at *all*. He had no idea what had gotten into his teenage son—or maybe it was just a stage teens went through.

How was he supposed to know what to do with a boy who thought he knew everything and disagreed with everything Rhett said?

If he said the sky was blue, by golly, Brandon thought it was yellow, and said so quite adamantly. If Rhett threw on a classical CD, Brandon countered it with a loud, thumping bass that made Rhett's head ache just thinking about it.

And he was thinking about it.

He'd been sitting in the den in the half dark, with only the desk lamp on low, wondering where things had gone wrong. More to the point, how could he fix it?

What had happened to the closeness he'd shared with his son as a child? Now, he might as well be speaking a different language, for all Brandon listened to him. Rhett was stunned by the change.

Maybe if Kayla was still alive he wouldn't be having all these problems with Brandon. The poor kid hadn't had the benefit of a mother's influence during the rocky teenage years.

No.

What good did it do to wish for something that couldn't be? Where was his faith? Hadn't God placed him in this situation? He wasn't the world's first single father, and he wouldn't be the last. Or the worst. Of that, he was certain.

"What did you do, forget your—" Rhett's words slammed to a halt in his throat as he encountered the glint of a police badge reflected off the porch light, and then caught up in his breath when he looked at the serious, silver-blue eyes of the woman wearing the uniform.

As the community counselor and social worker, he knew every officer on the police force. But he *sure* hadn't seen this lady around.

He might be an early widower, but he wasn't blind.

She was tall, five-eight or five-nine, he guessed, with short blond hair that glistened in the moonlight. She was slim, with womanly curves in all the right places despite the ill-fitting polyester uniform.

Her classic profile created quite an entrancing

silhouette, what with her high cheekbones and a long, straight nose.

All this he appreciated, as only a man can appreciate a woman. But what drew him most, what made him do a double take inside and out, was the sparkle in her eyes.

She noticed him notice her and lifted one frosty eyebrow, her lightly glossed lips pressed in a firm, straight line.

Flustered, his gaze slid to the right of the policewoman and landed squarely on his son. At the same moment Rhett realized the urgent nature of the situation, Brandon tipped his chin defiantly in the air, though he didn't quite meet his father's now serious gaze.

"What...?" Rhett croaked, his stomach cinching tight. He didn't know what was going on, but it wasn't good, not with the way Brandon clenched and unclenched his fists, looking like he wanted to dig his way to China if given half the chance.

The cop pierced him with a thinly masked glare, and he took two mental steps backward. She sized him up in detail before answering his half-question, her gaze probing his.

Uncomfortable with the intensity of her scrutiny, he swallowed hard and slid his gaze back to his son, who had neither moved nor spoken in the interim.

"Mr. Wheeler," the flashy lady cop began, her voice, soft and silver-toned, belying her tight expression. "I'm afraid your son has visited us at the precinct. He's been caught..."

She paused and pinched her lips even more tightly together, looking decidedly uncomfortable, as if her thick polyester uniform had suddenly become too tight.

"What?" he demanded, his voice low and coarse.

"Um..." she shrugged "—shoplifting."

She'd said the word so softly it was as if she hadn't wanted him to hear. But he'd heard. Loud and clear.

"Brandon *stole* something?" he roared, narrowing his furious gaze on his son, who shifted from one foot to the other and looked at the ground.

He shifted his gaze back to the officer, demanding an explanation with his expression if not his words. Her eyes sparkled with what he thought might be amusement, which only served to up his emotional ante.

"That's the generally accepted definition of *shoplifting*."

Rhett's blood went from hot to boiling, pounding through his veins. His temper fared no better, and her idea of a joke did nothing to alleviate his fury. If she thought this was funny...

"Brandon Adam," he bellowed, grabbing his son by the collar of his coat, "Get your sorry carcass in this house *now*."

Brandon tensed and pulled against his grasp, the boy's gaze darting to the left and right as if he were considering making a mad dash down the darkened street. Rhett was good and ready to follow him.

One more look at his father clenched the matter, as Brandon appeared to think better of it, and slipped quickly past Rhett and into the house, running as soon as he made it through the door.

Rhett listened to the pounding of Brandon's footsteps on the stairs leading up to his bedroom, but didn't relax until he heard the door to the boy's room slam closed.

Brandon would stay put, if he knew what was good for him. He was in a heap of trouble, and he had a world of explaining to do.

Rhett felt a light grip on his forearm, and looked down to see the officer's hand resting on his bare skin, which prickled as if touched by an electrical current under her gentle touch.

He stepped back, as outraged by the fact that he noticed—no, *responded*—to the attractive lady police officer holding on to his arm, as he was that she was still standing on his porch in the first place.

She'd obviously stuck around to watch him bluster through this whole pathetic attempt at fatherhood, and a sorry attempt it was.

Was she judging him on what she saw?

Her next words confirmed the worst. "Go easy on the boy, Rhett. It's his first offense."

Her tone was soft. Kind. Filled with genuine concern.

And completely out of line. He didn't want, or *need,* her suggestions or her interference.

Does the word privacy *mean anything to you?* He bit the inside of his lip to keep from saying the words aloud.

"Look Ms.—" he paused, his gaze sliding to her name plate "—Brockman."

"Callie," she correctly softly, in a voice that would have otherwise engaged him.

"Whatever."

He blew out a breath and jammed his fingers into his thick, light-brown hair. He wore it a good inch longer than the typical businessman's, an inch and a half over the buzz-cut cops he worked with. He might not be in fashion, but then, Rhett rarely was. Nor did he care.

"Look, I appreciate your bringing Brandon home and all. Thank you for the extra effort. However—"

She cut him off midsentence—before he'd attempted to get her out of here. He wanted to be upstairs with his son, but courtesy dictated he get rid of Ms. Brockman first. And fast, hopefully.

"It was no trouble," she said, flashing him a quick, bright smile. "I was glad to do it."

"Again, Ms. Bro—uh, Callie. Thank you."

Anyone else would have recognized his words as the dismissal they were, Rhett thought, incensed, but Officer Callie Brockman was either uncommonly imperceptive or acutely stubborn. Looking into her fixed gaze, Rhett was inclined to believe the latter.

"It's his first offense," Callie repeated, her voice at once intense and uncertain.

"You don't have to tell me that," Rhett snapped. It wasn't as if he hadn't heard her the first time. *Or* that he wasn't aware of his own son's lack of a criminal record—at least until tonight.

Still, he gave her the benefit of the doubt. She could legitimately be trying to be helpful.

Nevertheless, Rhett wanted her gone. Now.

Softening his voice, he continued. "I know he'll be facing a court date and all, but I'd appreciate it if we could discuss Brandon's situation some other time. Right now, I have a son to rake over the coals. Hot coals."

It was the wrong thing to say. He knew it—and regretted it—the moment the words passed his lips, especially when Callie took a quick step backward and inhaled sharply, as if she'd been struck.

Exasperation quickly replaced any guilt he might have harbored had she not glared daggers at him. It wasn't as if he were going to take a stick to Brandon, though heaven knew the boy deserved whatever he got.

He was a social worker, for pity's sake, not to mention a Christian. He knew the rules of the state—and the love of God.

There was one other thing he knew for certain. What he did or did not do to—or with—his son *sure* wasn't any of *her* business.

"Good night, Officer Brockman." This time, he purposefully chose the formal use of her name, in case she was a little slow taking a hint. Which, of course, she appeared to be.

Determined to put an abrupt end to any further arguments she might pose, he stepped backward and swung the door closed.

To his surprise, it bounced back open a few inches from the doorjamb.

With an audible sigh, he looked down through his dark scowl to find a dainty foot, albeit clad in county-issued dress-black shoes, blocking the door's natural progress.

Silver-blue eyes glared at him through the crack made by her foot, and then she moved closer, stabbing him with her now one-eyed gaze. All he could see besides the eye was one scrunched blond eyebrow and half a frown.

What was he supposed to do now?

Several distinctly un-Christian thoughts crossed his mind. But in the end, he groaned and stepped back, allowing the door to swing open another foot—*exactly* one foot. That was *all* he was going to give.

"Are you going to listen to me or not?" she demanded, her voice a high squeak.

It occurred to him he might find humor in the situation at a later occasion, once he cooled off. Come to think of it, this whole night would make a good story to tell around the family campfire years from now.

But at the moment, he was as mad as a hornet ready for the sting. Angry at Callie, at Brandon, and most of all, at himself.

Somehow, it always boiled down to *him* in the end.

"Well?" she asked, sounding not only annoyed, but impatient.

"What choice do you leave me?" he muttered irritably under his breath.

She caught his sarcasm anyway, and even had an answer. "None whatsoever."

He mentally nixed *uncommonly imperceptive* and ran the flag up for *acutely stubborn*. Callie Brockman was quite possibly the most stubborn woman he'd ever had the *dis*pleasure of meeting.

And he a social worker and psychologist. A people person. Was he simply missing the point?

Callie obviously thought so.

He frowned and tried to think about the situation from her perspective. She was a cop, and new in town, to boot. Didn't lady cops have to be bad to the bone to survive against their peers? Not to mention the criminal element.

He'd give her one more tiny chance to redeem herself, he decided quickly. Maybe she had something worthwhile to say behind all that bluff and blunder.

"Make it quick," he growled, continuing to hold the door open exactly one foot and not an inch more.

"Your *son* put a department store T-shirt on *over* his own shirt with the plastic surveillance tag not only still attached, but in plain sight. He walked right out the front door."

Rhett's heart dropped like a stone into the pit of his stomach—that is, if he had any heart left at all after her callous pronouncement.

What was this, some kind of teenage prank or double dare? Gang initiation?

But this was *Brandon* they were talking about. His own son, his flesh and blood.

And Rhett *knew* better.

Still, he couldn't help but blurt the question aloud, almost as if Officer Brockman weren't still standing on his doorstep staring him down. "Get to the point. What are you trying to imply?"

She frowned and looked him up and down. "You're a smart man. You figure it out."

She jerked her foot out of the threshold so suddenly that Rhett's weight, as he leaned against the door, had the effect of literally slamming in his own face.

Fury tore through him as he ripped the door back open, heaving it back until it banged against the wall.

"This is none of your business!" he yelled at the receding figure, only afterward realizing the interesting scene he was creating in the neighborhood for the eyes and ears of all his friends and neighbors.

Even then, he couldn't stop himself from having the last word. "You don't know anything about Brandon! *I'm* his father."

Callie froze halfway down the walkway and visibly tensed, but she didn't turn around.

"You want to be a father?" Her words were barely more than a whisper, and filled with so much agony Rhett immediately regretted his unkind words and actions, the way he'd blown her over like a mortar shell.

He was halfway down the walk, preparing to make things right and apologize for his previous words and actions, when she spoke again, bringing him up short.

"A father isn't born." Her silvery voice had transformed into cold steel, matching the crispness of the evening air. "He's made. Do Brandon a favor and act like a *real* father."

Chapter Three

Rhett leaned his forearm on the back of the closed door and blew out a breath. He'd been standing motionless for at least ten minutes, his gaze locked frozenly on the doorknob. Anger, frustration and resentment warred within his chest, causing an almost physical pain.

He slammed the flat of his hand against the back of the door. He didn't make a fist only because he didn't want to have to replace his door.

With an audible huff of breath, he spun around and started up the stairs. He'd made a complete mess of the incident. From start to finish, and every minute in between.

In what was definitely among the most memorable moments of the evening, he'd killed the messenger. Not a pretty sight.

It was bad enough he couldn't reach his own son with God's love, not to mention his own. But to take it out on an innocent bystander—God forgive him.

He slumped against the door frame of his son's room, deflated. Yelling at innocent bystanders wasn't his style, and it certainly wasn't God's style.

As if that weren't enough, he'd actually been attracted to the woman inside the uniform, something that not only surprised him, but threw him for a loop.

Uniforms were supposed to do something to a man's image, but in his experience, uniforms didn't usually do much for the ladies in the force.

At least until tonight.

He had a suspicion Callie Brockman would look good in a gunnysack.

But he wasn't about to go there. Besides, as he'd so succinctly pointed out to Callie earlier, he had a kid to rake over the coals. He wasn't looking forward to it, but he'd put off the inevitable long enough.

He straightened, his fist paused, ready to knock. Yet he hesitated.

He hadn't the slightest idea what to say. Until this moment, Brandon had been the epitome of the ideal student—a player on the varsity football team, popular with the girls and grades good enough for the Ivy League, not that Rhett could afford Ivy anything on his fast-food budget.

How could something like this have happened in John Day? What was the point of living in a small town if it wasn't to avoid bad influences on his kid?

He'd moved here hoping for a new start. How foolish. Trouble followed him like stickpins to a magnet. All he'd done was change the background scenery.

He'd have to talk to Brandon sooner or later, and sooner was probably preferable to later. He knocked crisply, but received no reply.

Consciously controlling his anger, he knocked again, but when the room continued to be silent, he barked out Brandon's name and let himself in.

Brandon was sprawled on his bed, ostensibly engrossed in a sports magazine, though Rhett could tell his attention was elsewhere.

"Brandon Adam," he began in his sternest voice. "We need to talk. Now."

Brandon rolled away from Rhett and tucked one arm under his head, continuing to stare at the slickly glossed magazine and hum to the tense beat of the music on his stereo.

Rhett's mind was whirling, trying to solve the riddle of how to approach his son, who was obviously not going to cooperate. His music only added to the pounding in Rhett's head.

Personally, he was inclined to let the incident slide with just a stiff lecture and a warning not to do it again.

Not only was it Brandon's first offense, but it was clearly done with the intention of getting caught, if Callie's assertions were correct.

"C'mon, kiddo, let's talk this out," he said, amazed at how calm his voice sounded, at odds with the furious pounding of his heart in his head. Until this moment, he'd never realized how difficult parenting could be, and he prayed desperately for the right words to say.

Pray. That was a good idea. "Do you want to pray about it?"

"Don't call me kiddo," Brandon snapped.

"Excuse me?" Rhett barked back, despite his best intentions. "I don't believe I heard you correctly, young man."

"Not like *that's* anything new."

"What?" Rhett was practically screaming now, at least on the inside. His voice was low and cold on the outside. Proverbial steam poured from his ears, and all his good intentions with it. Raw anger sprinted through him, and for a moment he lost his capacity to speak.

"Just leave me alone." Brandon's words met Rhett like a bombshell, and rejection exploded through him. Those were the words Brandon's mother, Kayla, had said to him just before she left him.

Brandon wanted to be alone?

Fine. Rhett could concede to that.

"You're grounded for a month, kiddo," he growled between clenched teeth.

Brandon just grunted in response.

"That means," he continued, pacing the room, "you are to be home directly after school is out for the day. I'll be checking on you at three-fifteen, and you'd better be here. In your room, doing your homework. No exceptions.''

''I've got football practice.''

''No. You don't.'' Rhett caught his breath, realizing only after the words were out of his mouth what he had said.

Brandon rolled to his feet, his red face a stark contrast to his white-blond hair. ''You can't do this to me!''

In for a penny, in for a pound, Rhett quoted to himself with an inward sigh. What was done, was done. He couldn't very well back off now.

''Yes, I can. And I have. Do we understand each other?''

Brandon didn't answer.

''Do we understand each other?'' Rhett asked again, enunciating every syllable.

''No way. No way are you going to ruin my life,'' Brandon screamed. ''If I don't go out for varsity football this year, there's no way I'll make the starting squad in my senior year.''

He pounded his fist into his open palm, but Rhett didn't budge through the outburst.

''It's my only chance to get into a decent college on a football scholarship.'' Somewhere along the way, his son's tone had turned to pleading.

Which made what had to be done every bit more difficult for Rhett. He clenched his jaw and shook his head. "You have your grades. That'll have to be good enough."

Brandon snorted. "You *know* this is my only chance. You *know* it!"

He threw the magazine at Rhett, who ducked around it, clamping his jaw shut to keep from reneging, or worse yet, reacting to his son's anger in kind.

"You better watch it, mister, or you'll find yourself packed off to a military boarding school. Serve you right for throwing things at me. Maybe military training will teach you some respect."

"I hate you. I *hate* you." Tears poured down Brandon's cheeks as he tore from the room, slamming the door behind him.

With a tired sigh, Rhett slumped onto Brandon's bed, holding his suddenly aching head in his hands. The pounding had turned to a dull, throbbing ache. "I've really done it this time, God," he prayed aloud. "How on earth am I going to get out of this one?"

Chapter Four

Callie hadn't darkened the door of a church in years—not since Colin had been sent away to military school when they were both sixteen. Churches made her nervous, and she wasn't sure she should be here now.

Which explained why she was still in her SUV and not in the chapel. She gripped the steering wheel tightly with both fists and pushed her weight back into the bucket seat until her forearms ached from the tension.

Going to church shouldn't be a big deal. But it was. At least for her.

Her mind flashed back to when she and Colin

were seven, and they'd given their hearts to Jesus during vacation Bible school. How simple faith in God had seemed back then.

But that was then. When God took Colin away from her for good, she couldn't bear the thought of going to church without him.

Like most fraternal twins, Callie and Colin had bonded in a special way. Even now there were times when she felt saddened for no apparent reason, or elated or frightened.

It was her only link to Colin, and she treasured those moments, knowing in her heart her twin was alive and well somewhere in the world. Only God knew where.

And He wasn't sharing His knowledge with her. Then again, she wasn't asking for His help.

She didn't know who she was angriest with—God, Colin or her father, for running Colin off in the first place. If only...

But there was no *if only*. She hadn't stood up to Father then, and Colin had disappeared. One youthful prank, and Father had packed Colin off to boarding school.

For his own good.

Even now, her father's dismal words echoed

in the recesses of her mind. That memory haunted her to this day, though Father died years ago.

She shook her head. She couldn't imagine Colin in uniform. He'd been kind and sensitive. Full of laughter and spontaneity. Not someone who could handle the tough, impersonal world of the military.

But Father hadn't seen that. He hadn't cared. Sending Colin away was probably the easiest thing he'd ever done.

And when he refused to attend Colin's graduation, and wouldn't even allow her to go…

She should have bucked her father's authority and gone to see her brother as her heart had begged for her to do. Maybe if she had, Colin wouldn't have run off without letting his family know where he was going.

For eleven long years a part of her heart and soul was missing. Would she ever feel whole again?

She doubted it. She really, truly doubted it.

Chimes pealed from the belfry, announcing to one and all the service at St. James Community Church was about to start.

Callie blew out a breath and called in every last bit of her courage. She'd come here to apologize to Everett Wheeler, and she wasn't leaving until she'd accomplished that task.

It hadn't taken much prompting for Bobby to tell her where to find Rhett on a Sunday morning. Apparently he and Brandon faithfully attended the small church.

It was worth her having to sit through a church service if it meant the opportunity to talk to Rhett. And that's what she was here to do.

He was going to get his apology *today.*

The last thing Callie needed in her new life in John Day was to start off on the wrong foot with the admittedly handsome community service agent. Becoming the leading lady in the *Taming of the Shrew* wasn't exactly what she had in mind.

Bolstering her determination, she locked her car and walked toward the nearest door, head held high and shoulders squared. Her police academy training was holding up in good stead at the moment. No one looking at her would guess she was quaking in her shoes at the thought of entering God's house.

She realized belatedly that the door she'd approached didn't appear to be the main entrance, and she wondered briefly if she ought to walk the perimeter of the church building to look for something more accessible.

"Six of one, half-dozen of the other," she quipped to herself, trying the handle on the door in front of her. If she couldn't find the sanctuary on the first try, at least she might find someone to point her in the right direction.

The handle gave way easily under her touch, and she stepped into a large, echoing, wood-floored room. It was immediately obvious she'd found the gym, and not the sanctuary. Still, she'd gained access, and the sanctuary couldn't be far away.

She was halfway to the hall door when a peculiar thumping sound caught her ear. Her police training took over, and she moved in to investigate.

In the far corner of the room, a boxer's punching bag swayed in the rapid, methodic rhythm of the pounding noise. Someone was obviously trying to work off a bad mood.

Maybe she should invest in a punching bag,

given her recent history. The corner of her mouth quivered into a half smile.

Squinting toward the swaying bag, she hesitated, caught between her natural curiosity and desire to help, and the hard-earned knowledge that help was rarely desired or asked for. People liked their privacy, and guarded it jealously. She might be—probably already was—intruding on someone's personal moment.

She was on the verge of leaving for the second time when an off-center punch threw the bag to the side, and she caught an eyeful of the young man behind the series of angry strokes.

Brandon Wheeler.

Her skin prickled with nervous energy even as her body switched into confrontational mode. Her gaze darted around the room, looking for the striking green eyes of Brandon's father.

Thankfully, he wasn't around. She let out a sigh that was half relief and half annoyance that she'd mustered her defenses for no good reason.

At least she knew Rhett was around someplace, probably worshipping in the sanctuary, joining in song with the others. She should be finding the sanctuary, as well, if the organ music in the background was any indication.

But she needed a minute to compose herself against the emotional roller-coaster ride that got her here in the first place. The congregation joined their voices in a sweet, familiar hymn of praise.

Rhett would be there, his honey-coated tenor blending into the heavenly meter. That thought was almost enough to coax her into joining the service. Was she being sacrilegious to think that way?

Probably. Mentally ducking bolts of lightning, she consciously switched her gaze to Brandon. It couldn't hurt her position any to patch things over with the kid.

"Hey, Brandon," she called in a loud voice, wanting to give fair warning before she approached. Her voice sounded low and scratchy in the echo of the gym. A byproduct of her dry throat, no doubt.

Brandon didn't appear to hear her. Either that or he was purposely ignoring her. He didn't miss a punch, and appeared singularly devoted to mutilating the punching bag in front of him.

Sweat dripped off his chin and onto his neatly ironed button-down white oxford shirt.

A sixteen-year-old kid who knew how to iron? Now *there* was a contradiction in terms if she'd ever heard one. She grinned.

"I think it's dead," she offered, slowing the punching bag with the flat of her hand.

Brandon didn't look amused. Startled, maybe, and a little scared. But definitely not amused.

"Hi," she said, focusing on keeping her grin steady. He didn't have to know she was shaky on the inside despite her brave exterior.

"Hi," he responded, his voice squeaking up an octave halfway through the syllable, a most revealing trait in an adolescent boy.

"Remember me? Callie Brockman."

"*Officer* Brockman."

She shrugged, not missing the emphasis on his words. "The one and only."

Did she imagine it, or did the corner of his mouth creep the tiniest bit upward? Suddenly, it felt very important to make the boy smile.

She threw a playful punch at the bag.

"Ouch!" The punching bag was harder than

it looked, yet Brandon had been swinging at it bare-handed.

She shook her hand out, then assessed it for bruises. "Nothing broken, at least."

She noticed Brandon's knuckles were scraped and bloody, but she continued the one-sided conversation without making mention of his wounds.

"What's in this thing, rocks?"

This time when she hit the bag, she was prepared for the impact.

At long last, Brandon smiled. The rivulets of sweat—possibly, Callie suspected, mixed with tears—poured down his cheeks, sweeping around his mouth and tunneling through the cleft in his chin that was remarkably similar to Rhett's.

Now that she'd had the opportunity to study him in the daylight, she realized just how much he really did look like his father, except that Rhett's hair had darkened with age. She'd bet a month's paycheck Rhett's hair had once been the same golden blond that made Brandon such a cute kid.

"You're supposed to wear boxing gloves," he said gruffly.

"Oh." She shook her hand out again. "But you're not wearing them."

Brandon merely shrugged, then dashed his forearm against his temple in a vain attempt to wipe the sweat away.

"Let me guess. Dear old dad?" She gestured toward the bag. "I can find a black marker, if you'd like to draw a face on it."

She frowned and stroked her chin, pretending to seriously give it some thought, and was rewarded with Brandon's light chuckle.

"If, however, this bag is supposed to represent that sweet, friendly police officer who drove you home from the station the other night, I definitely don't want to know about it."

She paused and winked at the youth. "And no Magic Marker faces. I don't look good in black."

That earned her a full-blown laugh, but it didn't last long. Brandon's brows soon went back to their original position, creased low over his forehead.

She felt awkward, and was certain she looked that way, as well. She leaned against a gymnast's horse and tried to act casual. But how, exactly, did one look casual with a teenage boy? "Want to talk about it?"

He licked his lips in preparation to speak, and Callie could tell by the expression on his face he was going to refuse to give more than a cursory answer.

"No pressure, kid," she said hastily, charging in before he could come up with a way out. "I just figured I already kind of know what's going on, so you wouldn't have to bring anyone else into this—" she paused and ran her fingers through the hair at the base of her neck "—*delicate* situation. I've been told I'm a wonderful listener. And since I'm definitely not going to jabber to your friends, I think I'm a pretty safe bet, confession-wise."

"Or talk to my dad?" he asked sharply.

She zipped her thumb and forefinger across her mouth. "My lips are sealed."

He blew out a frustrated breath. "Dad won't let me go out for the football team this year."

He punctuated his sentence with a quick *one-two* of his fists against the rough vinyl covering the bag. "Just because I stole one stupid shirt, he's going to ruin my whole life."

Callie knew his bruised knuckles must be really bleeding by now, and she inwardly cringed in sympathy, simultaneously amused by the teenager's overexaggeration of his dilemma. Then again…

"He's still pretty mad about the other night, huh?" She couldn't blame Rhett for being angry, but no one knew better than she that there were two sides to this story.

Brandon nodded.

Every sensitive nerve within her mind demanded she ask him why he pulled such a stupid stunt in the first place, but she was certain Rhett had already asked those very questions, possibly a number of times.

She doubted if he'd received a plain answer back. If his own father couldn't get anywhere with Brandon, why should she expect to? Rhett was a psychologist, for pity's sake.

Not only that, but she suspected the memory of those questions, and the disagreement that followed, were all a part of Brandon's frustration now.

She decided the best way to help everyone concerned was to keep listening, if Brandon wanted to keep talking.

It didn't take long to realize he needed, if not wanted, a listening ear.

"Dad said if I—" *punch three-four* "—don't get my act together—" *left hook to the middle* "—he's going to send me away—" *two swift right jabs* "—to a military boarding school."

Callie's stomach dropped into her toes.

Military school.

Was this some kind of horrendous nightmare, or was history repeating itself right before her eyes? She wanted to pinch herself and pray she woke up.

Her head spun, and she squeezed her eyes shut, trying to steady herself through the red rage pulsing through her.

"You okay?" For a kid, he sounded pretty mature. And pretty concerned. "You don't look so good."

If she looked as pale as she felt, there was no doubt in her mind she didn't look so good. Her mind urged her to run, but her body wouldn't cooperate, no matter how her insides screamed in panic.

"There you are," came a familiar, honey-rich voice from the hallway. "Church started a half hour ago, young man. Why aren't you—?''

Rhett cut his sentence short when he noticed the tall, shapely blonde by his son's side, meticulously and attractively dressed in a straight black skirt and an oversize snow-white sweater.

Officer Brockman.

As feminine as she'd looked in the polyester police uniform, that wasn't half what her Sunday outfit did for her, accentuating her tiny waist and long legs.

Rhett's breath caught in his chest and stuck there, unmoving. Callie Brockman was absolutely, stunningly beautiful.

He was pleased to find her at church. Naturally, it would be nice to be working side by side with another Christian when it came to the juveniles under parole. Shared faith, common goals and beliefs, would make many parts of the job easier for both of them.

It was a moment more before he noticed Callie's eyes were closed, and her face was an odd, blanched color.

''Are you okay?'' he asked, quickly moving to her side to take her arm. He gave his son a sharp I'll-deal-with-you-later warning glare. A father's look.

"Could you...I...could use a glass of water, please," she croaked.

"I'll get it." Brandon was off like a shot.

Officer Brockman's eyelids flickered open and she met his gaze briefly. Then, with a groan, she squeezed her eyes tightly shut again.

However brief the action, it was enough for Rhett to notice her pupils were wide and her eyes glassy, as if she were on the verge of fainting. He didn't know much about fainting females, and he wasn't real keen on learning about them now.

Had Brandon said or done something to make her so upset?

It had to be Brandon. Why else would his son be in such a rush to leave the scene? And if it was...

"Look, I'm sorry if Brandon did or said something to offend you," he said softly and firmly, deciding a frank apology was the best course of action.

He was preparing to dive into the side of his speech that he'd rehearsed long before he'd found Callie in the gym—the part where he apologized for his behavior the previous Friday night, and for rushing her out of his house and slamming the door on her without cause.

But she cut him short before he could get his thoughts together, her eyelids opening wide, and her silver-blue eyes glimmering in the reflection of the fluorescent lighting which filled the gym.

"If *Brandon* said something to offend me?" Her voice was unnaturally shrill, and sparks lit her eyes. "*Brandon* was a perfect gentleman, thank you very much."

Color had returned to her face, staining her cheeks a pretty pink.

"Which is more than I can say for you," she added, in what Rhett could only assume was for good measure.

"Look, I'm sorry," he began. "I don't—"

"Don't threaten your son with things you don't mean," she said, her voice softer now, though it hadn't lost its sharp edge. "You'll be so sorry if you send him away." Her eyes filled with tears.

Rhett was flabbergasted.

Send Brandon away? What was the crazy woman talking about?

Before he could say so much as another word, even to ask her what she meant by her unusual and unwarranted accusation, she wrenched out of his grasp, and dashed haphazardly, heels and all, out the side door of the gymnasium that led to the far parking lot.

Stunned into inertia, he stood agog and watched her leave, feeling as if he should do something, but not having the slightest notion what that something might be.

"Where's Officer Brockman?" Brandon had returned with a glass of water and looked every bit as surprised as Rhett felt.

"She left," Rhett answered, still feeling bemused.

Brandon's eyebrows shot up in surprise. "Why?"

Rhett bit out an astounded chuckle. "Your guess is as good as mine."

He watched the empty doorway for a moment more, then patted Brandon on the shoulder, noticing only now that his son was drenched with sweat, and was gripping the water glass he'd brought for Officer Brockman with hands that had bruised and bleeding knuckles.

As they were standing next to the still-swaying punching bag, Rhett inwardly grimaced. It didn't take a rocket scientist to figure out what Brandon was doing here.

And why.

His only question was how Callie had joined him, and for what purpose.

The insatiable guilt of fatherhood stabbed through him once again, and he prayed for wisdom and guidance.

"C'mon, son," he said gently, putting his arm around the boy's shoulders. "Let's clean up those hands, and then we can go worship God. In the smaller chapel. Alone." He paused, heaving a world-weary sigh. "I think we could both use a little prayer right now."

Chapter Five

A few days later, Callie was sifting through the mounds of paperwork left to her by the last juvenile parole officer. It was a lot to do, but her mind wasn't really on her work.

Rhett Wheeler was never far from her mind. Even if she'd wanted to, she couldn't avoid him forever. If she could, she'd bury her head in the sand ostrich-style, except that she'd be as equally obvious as the silly bird to the curious onlooker, never mind anyone involved.

She'd gone *way* beyond *open mouth, insert foot*. More like a song from her childhood that chimed through her mind, haunting her.

I'm being swallowed by a boa constric-
tor...
And I don't like it very much.
Oh, gee, he's up to my knee.
Oh, fiddle, he's up to my middle...
Oh, dread, he's up to my...

Yes, well, she got the picture. Loud and
clear. In over her head, in every sense of the
word.

For some unknown reason, Rhett Wheeler
had brought out the worst in her—not that the
best was anything to rave about, but her behavior with Rhett definitely went beyond the norm,
even for her.

It was bad enough that she was as klutzy as
a clown and twice as eye-catching. But despite
everything, even the glaring warning sirens in
her head that suggested any dealing with Rhett
wasn't going to be in her best emotional interest, why did she find her heart stirring with attraction every time he was around?

Every time she saw him arrive at the station,
she made a beeline for the ladies' room.
Chicken.

When, oh *when* would she learn to mind her own business and leave the rest of the world alone?

"Phone for you, Callie," Bobby announced from the switchboard, stifling a yawn with the back of his hand. "Line five."

Callie sighed and scooped up the receiver, punching line five more forcefully than she needed. "Officer Brockman."

"Callie, it's Rhett."

Her heart beat such a wild tattoo she wondered if it might give her away. She schooled her features, though she knew Rhett couldn't see her through the phone line. But she didn't want *anyone* to suspect what the mere honey-richness of Rhett's voice did to her insides.

"Rhett. What can I do for you?"

"We need to talk."

"Look, about the other day at church. What I said about Brandon—"

"No."

That one single, solid word from Rhett slammed her words to a halt in her throat.

"What I meant is that we need to meet and talk about my *caseload.* I'd prefer *not* to talk about my son." She heard him pause and inhale audibly. "Ever."

Any hope that Rhett had forgiven her big mouth and wanted to start over with a clean slate went skittering away like a family of mice after hearing the snap of a mousetrap. And right along with her disappearing hopes went her confidence that she could handle this situation without making another lethal blow to her ego.

She steadied her quivering hands on the edge of the desk. "Of course."

"Can you meet me at my office in an hour? It's inside the old field house at Fifth and Main."

"Sure. Okay."

"Good." He sounded gruff, and she wondered if his bad mood was her fault.

Maybe. But it *wasn't* her fault he was stubborn, she thought defensively. Or that he was, however unintentionally, driving his sixteen-year-old son down the path of no return.

She uttered a stiff goodbye and clamped the receiver down on its cradle.

"Now I remember why I'm still single," she muttered under her breath. "Men!"

Her mind brushed through to her other meetings with Rhett—and Brandon—untangling the snarls as best she could. Remembering the details about Brandon's situation was enough to strengthen her resolve against Rhett.

She wouldn't back down on her position where Brandon was concerned, for she well knew the inevitable conclusion of such a path, even if Rhett refused to see it. Brandon was too good a kid to lose to a stubborn man, even his father.

She would fight tooth and nail if it meant keeping father and son together. Single parenting was tough enough without creating extra issues, and that's exactly what Rhett was doing, whether he realized it or not.

There were differences between his situation and Colin's, to be sure. There was no doubt in Callie's mind that Rhett loved his son, or that he wanted the best for the boy. That in itself made what happened between Colin and her father as far different as east and west.

But Callie knew all too well what happened when a father alienated his son, even unintentionally.

She bit back her frustration, along with other emotions she refused to name or acknowledge, at not being able to change anything despite her best effort.

Rhett was right in one thing—it was none of her business. She shuffled the pile of papers nearest her, then sighed aloud and pushed them aside. She wasn't getting anything accomplished sitting here staring absently at her piles of paperwork, her mind a million miles away.

She might as well go see the man and get it over with. She wondered if tarring and feathering was still legal in Oregon.

"Rough day?" Bobby asked with a friendly smile.

She glared at her desk full of papers as if they were Rhett himself. "I'll say," she groaned. "I think I'll get out of here and go visit Rhett. My head is pounding like a jackhammer."

It couldn't get much worse than this, she thought, gathering her papers together and slipping them in an attaché.

Or could it?

Rhett leaned back in his chair and jammed his fingers through his thick hair, wondering absently if he ought to go in for a haircut. It was only one of a thousand distracting thoughts he'd encountered this morning.

For some reason, he found himself unable to concentrate on the case file in front of him, or anything else for that matter. Hearing the silvery alto of Callie's voice over the telephone wire was enough to drive any man to distraction, even without the clash between them.

A conflict over his *son,* of all things.

Something had set her off about him, but though he'd gone over and over their meetings in his mind, he still couldn't find a common link.

Why did she care what happened to Brandon? Certainly none of the parole officers he'd known in the past got personal with their cases, or expressed their personal opinions on what was best in any given situation.

What difference did it make to Callie what kind of father he was? Who had died and named her Royal Queen of the Universe?

He clamped his jaw until his teeth ached from being ground together. What happened between Brandon and him was all his, partly Brandon's and *no* one else's business.

Most especially not the attractive, annoying, *maddening* Officer Brockman.

As if his thoughts had caused her to appear, Callie stood leaning her back on the door frame, staring at him with a bevy of questions in her eyes, not to mention the sparkle of amusement.

He blinked and looked at his watch. "You're early."

She strode forward, carrying two steaming paper coffee cups from the espresso stand. "We didn't set an exact time," she reminded him. "I didn't know your preference, so you can take your pick. A double shot of espresso, or a rich chocolate latte."

A peace offering?

He met her gaze squarely, but all he could read in the glimmering depths of her silver eyes was a tenaciousness that made his breath catch in his chest.

Obviously she hadn't blown out her candle of resentment toward him, and he didn't know how to feel about that. Inwardly, he shook his head in frustration, but outwardly he only smiled.

What would Jesus do in this situation?

Lord, help me be the one to let go and get past the brick wall between us, he prayed silently. *Help me reach her with Your love.*

He cleared his throat. "I'll take the espresso. I could use a double shot right about now."

A wave of compassion washed over him as he left his burden of frustration on God's shoulders. It was a sure sign he was on the right track. He strengthened his resolve not to react to her anger, but rather to pierce through the stone fortress of her heart with the love of God, to find and help the woman beneath the shield of her antagonism.

Perhaps the grudge she carried on her shoulders had very little to do with what had happened thus far with his relationship with Brandon. Maybe nothing at all.

Now that he thought about it, this line of reasoning made a great deal of sense. She'd certainly come out of nowhere blasting him with both barrels.

Before she'd really had the opportunity to size him up.

Before she had time to form a rational opinion.

The psychologist in him switched into gear with a vengeance. Who'd hurt her, and why? Why was she so angry with so little provocation?

He took a sip of his espresso and sized her up, allowing this new information—a hunch, really—to affect his view of her. His mouth twitched into the hint of a smile when she dropped her gaze against his scrutiny.

"I..." she began, then faltered to a stop.

Standing to her full height and wearing a deliberate expression, she tried again. "Was there a particular reason you wanted to see me right away?"

"I'll show you what I do here, and then we can discuss our current caseloads."

He patted a foot-high pile of file folders for emphasis, every one of which was overflowing with colorful, legal-size papers.

A good foot more of juvenile delinquent activity than he wanted to see in John Day. Or anywhere else, for that matter. Juvenile justice was an odd lot at its best, and ineffectual at its worst.

The court system believed in rehabilitation of

its youngsters, where there was no such system in place for adult offenders. Yet in the same breath, they locked kids away in detention centers that were little more than overglorified prisons, where the rough learned from the rough how to major in a life of crime.

The only real hope was in community service, which was where he came in. But he was only one man, and he could only do so much in the limited hours of each day he spent with the youth here.

Maybe Callie Brockman could help.

He shook himself back to the present and gestured to the door. "If you'll follow me, I'll show you the field house."

Callie didn't miss the excitement in his voice as he mentioned his work, and she admitted curiosity as to what he actually did in this big, dusty field house. It wasn't like any juvenile justice building she'd ever seen.

At first she'd thought it might be a detention center, and grimaced at what must be unspeakable surroundings.

But there were no electric fences here, no kids in the yard. So she'd explored a little bit on her own.

Not that she'd gained much by her self-guided tour. She'd noticed a number of odd pieces of equipment that looked like it was in some semblance of order, though she couldn't figure out for what.

Some pieces looked like the fences jump horses used in competition, only they appeared too small for an equine. Large, curved tubes that looked like they belonged behind a dryer, boarded A-frame ramps and thin bridges completed the course, along with a succession of plastic poles placed about twelve inches apart in a straight row.

Definitely not anything that looked like a human could use, even if he was putting the kids through their paces, she thought, amused.

Quite frankly, she couldn't make heads or tails of it, and she waited, intrigued, for his explanation.

She followed him through the odd assortment of apparatus to the far door, which she'd missed earlier; not that it would have mattered, as the door was locked.

Rhett rustled the keys at his waist until he found the one he wanted, then led her into a noisy kennel full of barking, whining, yapping dogs.

Dogs, she discovered as she looked from kennel to kennel, that came in every breed, size, color and shape, from the sleek-looking greyhound to a box-headed bull terrier.

Her first instinct was to balk and run, and for the first time, it wasn't Rhett making her want to flee. The muscles in her neck and shoulders hardened into stone as she worked through it mentally.

"Are you okay?" Rhett stepped forward. One gentle hand went to her elbow, and the other arm slipped around her waist, supporting her as if she were about to faint.

Despite the cold sweat breaking out on her forehead, she knew she wouldn't faint. Not Callie Brockman. A memory surfaced, and she fought to press it back.

"I'm fine." She stepped out of his grasp and crouched before the first kennel, where a lanky black Labrador retriever puppy circled in excitement.

"Hello, puppy," she crooned. She set down her latte and reached a tentative finger through the fencing, conquering her innate fear of dogs by the sheer force of her will.

Hearing her voice, the pup stopped chasing his tail and licked Callie's fingers where they curled through the chain-link fence.

She chuckled. "Don't tell me this little fellow is a juvenile delinquent!"

Rhett laughed and shook his head. It was the first time he'd cracked a genuine smile in her presence, and Callie's heart did a somersault.

He went from being handsome to knock-down-drag-out gorgeous with a single upward twist of his lips. Not only that, but he looked a good deal younger when he smiled, and his grin accentuated the attractive fan of laugh lines around his sparkling green eyes that Callie only now noticed. Her mind gratefully shifted gears, away from the dogs' din.

Maybe Rhett wasn't the ogre she'd made him out to be in her mind. Maybe she'd overreacted. Maybe Brandon had made up that nonsense about military school. Or maybe Rhett was just blowing off steam, and hadn't been seriously considering sending his son away.

Had she mistaken Rhett's intentions toward

Brandon all along? With Rhett smiling down on her, it suddenly appeared a very real possibility.

For the first time all day, she relaxed, allowing the tension in her shoulders to unknot, and the coils in her stomach to unwind.

Rhett took another sip of his espresso and gestured to the Lab puppy. "Would you like me to take him out for you? His name is Merlin."

She nodded, trying to mirror Rhett's enthusiasm for his dogs. She hadn't much experience with puppies, but Merlin looked adorable. And safe. "How old is he?"

"Four months." Rhett lifted the catch to the kennel and allowed the puppy to wiggle past him.

"So he is a juvenile, after all. And so cute!" Merlin rubbed his head under her fingers, and she scratched obligingly.

"Do you show these guys?" She hadn't walked the whole length of the area, but she guessed he had a number of dogs by the noise being made by the dogs' barking. Probably begging for attention. The ruckus increased exponentially when they heard the golden tenor of Rhett's voice, coaxing Merlin to sit and stay.

She turned her attention back to the puppy, who was obeying Rhett's series of commands surprisingly well for such a youngster.

"I can't show them," he said, crouching beside her and play-wrestling with the puppy after he'd put the dog at ease. "Not a one of them is purebred."

Merlin had abandoned Callie in favor of Rhett, who was growling out of the back of his throat and teasing the pup incessantly. He spoke to the dog with the endearing, high-pitched voice men used with pets and babies, and Callie felt her throat catch in response.

"Well, I see you have one fan, anyway," she commented, punctuating her statement with another laugh.

Rhett nodded. "He knows where his next meal comes from."

He stood suddenly and touched Callie's elbow in order to help her rise to her feet. The contact was gentle and light, but it felt to Callie as if an electric current had passed between them.

She tried to swallow, then wet her dry lips with the tip of her tongue. Her heart stopped and started like an automobile with engine trouble.

He released his hold as soon as she was on her feet, but the imprint of his fingers on her bare arm remained, warm and soft.

Just like Callie's heart.

Chapter Six

Even after playing with Merlin, Rhett thought Callie looked distinctly uncomfortable within the kennel walls, and he was eager to learn why. His dogs were his world, and though Callie was polite, it was clear she was nervous. He wondered if she sensed the way the dogs picked up on her unspoken fear, making them louder and more boisterous than usual.

"You look a little nervous," he said, tentatively poking into her thoughts.

Callie grimaced and leaned against a steel post. "I am." Her gaze blanked as she became distant, then brightened when, he supposed, her thoughts regained the present.

She cleared her throat. "When Colin and I were eight—"

Her sentence dropped abruptly as the Doberman pinscher behind her lunged into the gate, teeth bared and growling ferociously.

Without thinking, Rhett bolted into action. "Baron, *platz.*" The dog immediately dropped into a down position.

Baron was the one dog in his kennel he wouldn't introduce to someone afraid of dogs, at least not without warning. He hadn't realized it was Baron's kennel Callie had been leaning against, caught up as he was in the silver-blue of her gaze. "He doesn't usually—" he began, turning to Callie with an apologetic shrug.

His words froze on his tongue as he realized he was alone in the kennel area. Callie was gone.

Abandoning all thoughts of working through Baron's outburst, he took off in the direction he guessed she'd gone. Outside, into the fresh air.

Anywhere away from Baron. He should have guessed, should have known. He'd seen the little hints she'd been giving him—the startled looks, her beautiful eyes just a bit wider than usual. Her breath increasing as she entered the kennel area.

"Callie?" he called as he exited the building, silently chastising himself as every kind of fool. "Callie? Are you okay?"

"Mmm."

He whirled around to where the sound came from, and found Callie leaning her shoulders securely against the dull, dented aluminum of the warehouse siding. Her arms were wrapped tightly around herself, and her eyes were wide with panic.

"You look like you've seen a ghost," he commented softly, moving forward until he could smell the sweet, musky scent of her hair. Wanting to comfort, he tentatively reached for her, caressing her bare arms with his palms. She shivered, though the fall afternoon was unseasonably warm.

Rhett's breath caught in his throat. He wanted to say something—anything—to reach her, to comfort her, but his mind drew a blank.

After an extended moment of silence, Callie shrugged away from his grasp. "I did see a ghost, in a way."

"How's that?" His voice sounded gravely even to his own ears, though for a completely different reason. His heart matched the beat of her pulse marking time on the tender skin at the base of her throat.

She was so beautiful. And so fragile. If his chest grew any tighter, he thought it might burst, so completely were the deluge of bewildering emotions consuming him.

"Your...dog."

"Baron?"

"The Doberman. I...he..."

She turned away from him, but he couldn't let her move away. He stepped forward and wrapped his arms around her waist, firmly but gently leading her back into his embrace. He half expected her to reject his hug once again, but though she froze in place, she didn't break his embrace.

"My twin, Colin, and I were playing out on the front lawn. You wouldn't expect for a little boy to..."

"Colin?" he queried gently, assuming her thoughts had drawn back to what she'd attempted to explain earlier.

Heart in his throat, he pictured an eight-year-old Callie playing with her twin. "Go on."

"Colin had the football, and was running across the yard. I think I'd skinned my knee or something, because I was sitting on the porch instead of chasing him.

"All of a sudden, out of nowhere, this Doberman was running down the street. Running straight toward Colin."

She swirled around and buried her head in his chest, shivering from the memory. Rhett tightened his grasp and brushed her hair away from her face with the backs of his fingers.

"I yelled, but it was too late. The dog tackled Colin. By the time my dad came and chased him off, Colin had been bitten numerous times."

She pulled in a deep, unsteady breath. "He was in the emergency room for hours while they stitched him up. He still has a scar on his chin."

"Why didn't you tell me this before?" he murmured softly. Stroking her hair with decisively slow, even caresses, he silently encouraged her to slow her breathing.

Callie responded to his touch, much more

than she cared to admit. It had been a long time since she'd been so close to a man, and Rhett wasn't just any man.

He was a man who could coax a story of her past from her, when all she wanted to do was forget. A man who was, in his own quiet, gentle way, helping her face an incident she'd thought she'd forgotten and moved beyond.

All this added up to the making of an outstanding psychologist, but Callie didn't want to think about that now, nor why he'd provoked such a response from her. She'd never been one to talk about herself, to reveal any more than absolutely necessary to get by.

For some reason, she could talk to Rhett. She looked up into his face, wanting to voice what their budding friendship meant to her, but every thought flew out of her mind when her gaze met and locked with Rhett's.

Her gaze dropped to his lips, then moved back up to his eyes, where she read the same conflict of emotions she felt in her heart. It was a thought, and it wasn't; a feeling, and more. Rhett's hint of a smile confirmed it a moment before he bent to capture her lips with his in the sweetest, warmest kiss she'd ever experienced.

His lips barely covered hers, yet they caressed her soul, reaching into her and coaxing a response. Conceding to his touch was the easiest, and paradoxically the most difficult move she'd ever made, she thought as she slipped her arms around his neck and pulled him closer.

His kiss became hers. No vicious Doberman, no memories of Colin, no fear of what was, or what might be. For the first time in years, Callie Brockman experienced a moment of true peace in Rhett's arms.

The threadbare executive office chair creaked as Rhett leaned backward, lacing his fingers behind his head and groaning aloud as he worked the kinks out of his neck and back.

He really wasn't the office type, but he compromised by promising himself a good workout after he was finished shuffling the monumental pile of paperwork that went along with his job.

With a grunt, he righted himself in the chair, the flats of his palms flush with the glass-covered desk.

It was bad enough that he was a half a month

behind on paperwork, without being side-tracked by thoughts of a certain police officer who gave the words *true blue* an entirely new meaning.

Being a community service agent to John Day's delinquent youth was his penance—the way to dig his way out of the hole he'd fallen into and reclaim his life.

Callie wasn't a part of that, yet she'd changed his world in a single afternoon. And though Rhett hadn't seen or spoken with her for days, her presence was as strong here at the field house as if she'd just walked out the door.

He didn't expect her to visit the field house any time soon, given their past history and her innate fear of dogs. He'd have to work on that—coaxing her to give him and his dogs a second chance. His dilemma with Callie never left his mind for long—not while he was sleeping, and definitely not when he was working.

Every time he'd get a good start on his paperwork, his mind would slip back to that explosive moment with Callie when his lips touched hers. How could one kiss change so much?

He was as brain-dead as a lovesick teenager,

with about as much tact. He was afraid when he saw her again, he'd drop to one knee and propose. Thank goodness there were no diamond stores in John Day, or he might just end up doing something so insane he'd regret it for the rest of his life.

It wasn't the first time the notion of marrying again had crossed his mind, but it *was* the first time he'd put a face to that vague, ghostlike image of the woman who'd fit the mold he and Brandon had made for themselves.

Callie Brockman.

What was so crazy about his thoughts was that she wasn't the type of woman he'd considered *marriage material* at all—at least not what he'd thought he and Brandon needed.

Brandon needed a mother figure, something akin to Mary Poppins, only set to the tune of a teenage boy's requirements. And Rhett needed a feminine perspective to give him a heads-up on his son's needs whenever he was blind to them. Lately, that was more times than he dared count.

Callie *had* given her very dogmatic opinion on the subject of his son on numerous occasions, but that wasn't quite what Rhett had in mind.

Rhett had—sort of—planned to remarry someday. He'd tossed the idea around a few times, but that was before Brandon got into trouble with the law.

Now, facing the rebellion of his own son and nobody on either side to run interference, it appeared doubly essential to find *Ms. Right.*

He creased his eyebrows low over his eyes.

He didn't know exactly what it is he was looking for in a woman, but Callie wasn't—*couldn't* be—whatever that was, even if the role was yet to be defined.

He pictured a plump widow woman with a cheery disposition and a sweet smile. Someone who baked her own bread and made homemade sugar cookies. Someone who'd put frilly, hand-sewn curtains in her kitchen.

And flowers. Cheerful, colorful fresh flowers, carefully and artfully arranged in a vase on the kitchen table.

Callie was nothing less than a gun-toting spitfire who turned his insides to mush. No matter how hard he tried, he couldn't picture her worrying about frilly curtains, never mind sewing them, and he didn't know why it mattered, anyway.

He chuckled at the picture forming in his mind—Callie sitting at a sewing machine, humming a hymn while she sewed the ruffles on her new gingham curtains.

True, she had a heartstoppingly sweet smile. When she smiled, which wasn't very often.

Cheery disposition? She'd hardly qualify as Mary Poppins in that category, or any other. Yet she intrigued him as no other woman had— not even Kayla, God rest her soul.

"So, like, I'm here already," growled a young man from the doorway.

Rhett swung toward the door and received a well-practiced blank stare in response to his welcome.

Don't know, don't care. That was how kids acted these days. He shifted through his papers, looking for his schedule book, which was somewhere in this monstrous pile. And even when he found the book, it took him an excruciating moment to flip through it and look up the information he needed to proceed.

"Lance?"

"Yeah. Who wants to know?"

Rhett worked to keep the tone of his voice even, to keep his expression from betraying him. He was used to dealing with teenage attitude.

Teenagers. Guys who thought they owned the world and knew everything about everything. But being king of the mountain left them a long way to fall.

He inwardly grimaced. Must be rough. He wished *he* knew everything—like how to stop these kids from getting into trouble in the first place.

Or at least how to cushion them from another fall. His own son most of all.

Rhett forced a smile as he stood, towering over the skulking youth in a conscious, if subtle, intimidation tactic. The kid might as well figure out right now where his attitude was going to take him.

"C'mon, son," he said, placing a gentle hand on the boy's bony shoulder and turning him around toward the door.

Lance shrugged out of his grasp, but Rhett continued, pretending not to notice. "We've only got an hour today. And we've got a mountain of work to do."

Chapter Seven

Callie turned the key backward in the ignition and shut the motor off, but didn't immediately exit her SUV. She stared wanly at the large, ugly aluminum-paneled warehouse and sighed.

This wasn't going to work. She leaned back, tossing her keys from one palm to the other and back again. As hard as it was to admit, even to herself, she was terrified of animals, especially dogs. She'd never owned a pet of her own, which made Rhett's obvious passion for his job something completely beyond her scope of experience.

There were cat people, and there were dog

people. And then there was Callie. As usual,
she didn't fit into any category. A paradox. An
enigma.

A complete and total mess. And thinking
about Rhett—about the kiss they'd shared—
only made things worse. None of her defenses
worked against the kindest man she'd ever met.

Had he been other than what he was, she
would assume he'd taken advantage of her during a weak moment. At least then she could be
angry, an emotion as familiar and comfortable
to her as her pair of old, broken-in running
shoes.

But that wasn't what Rhett had done, and she
didn't know how to feel. He'd offered a bit of
himself to comfort her, and she'd welcomed it
with open arms.

If there was a problem, it was most certainly
hers. How she was going to work with him on
a continual basis without wanting to kiss him
again was beyond her.

But wanting and doing were two different
things. Surely she could keep one from becoming the other, couldn't she?

She wasn't so sure anymore. Her record

wasn't good when it came to thinking before she spoke. Or kissed, in Rhett's case.

Truth.

He was a threat in a sweat suit. Or with his broad shoulders exaggerated by the cut of a sport coat like the one he wore for church, she mentally amended. Or in slacks and an oxford shirt like he wore for work.

She was in big trouble here.

Truth.

At least she could be honest with herself.

The primary reason Rhett Wheeler presented a big threat was not that he mishandled his relationship with his son, nor that they'd gotten off on the wrong foot initially. All that was child's play next to the real problem.

Rhett Wheeler made her socks roll up and down, despite her best efforts to ignore the obvious, that she was wildly attracted to the man.

She always thought she'd go for the Superman type, not Clark Kent in the flesh.

Rhett had shown her a whole new side to *Mr. Nice Guy.* Who would have known?

A laugh tickled her throat, the sound echoing through the vehicle. "You've got to laugh, or you'll cry,'' she said aloud, then shrugged her shoulders in answer.

She'd make this work, this working relationship with Rhett Wheeler. No more barbs—no matter how he set her off, intentional or otherwise. And definitely no more kissing.

As much as possible, she'd just ignore the man and do her job. Ignore him as much as a woman could do with a man like Rhett.

With a quick, deep breath of air for courage, she exited the vehicle and marched determinedly toward the front entrance to the field house, her good intentions fresh in her mind.

Her attraction to Rhett was no longer an issue.

She hoped.

Her reaction to the dogs she couldn't vouch for…but a woman could only concentrate on so many problems at once.

As she approached, she heard the muffled sounds of male voices and decided to let herself in without knocking. It was a bit unconventional, especially for the small-town western mentality of each man to his own.

Privately, she hoped she'd have the opportunity to see Rhett in action, see the fruition of the community service methods he was so excited about, not having forgotten for one moment her last time visiting here with Rhett and his kennel.

As she let herself in, she spotted Rhett walking between the dog kennels, talking to each pup in turn. A young man with long, stringy hair of an indeterminate color followed at a distance, his hands crammed into the pockets of oversize, droopy jeans, a style currently the favorite among teenage boys in the area.

Rhett called to the boy, but he continued to hang back.

"Not afraid of dogs, are you, Lance?"

The boy squared his shoulders and took an aggressive stance, though Callie noticed he still stayed a good way from the dog kennels. "No way."

She could relate. It would take a minor miracle to get her near those kennels now.

Rhett merely smiled. Callie wondered if perhaps he enjoyed ruffling a few teenage tail feathers. Or did he not realize a flat-out lie when he saw one?

"Good thing for you," he said to the boy, his sparkling green eyes squinting into laugh lines. He gestured to the largest, slobberiest dog Callie had ever seen. "Because this fellow here is your new partner."

Any doubt Callie might have had that the boy might be hanging back because he was intentionally trying to be churlish or uncooperative, however much he might have been both, flew out the window on a breeze.

That kid was scared stiff.

Rhett flipped the gate open and called the dog to him, acting and looking as if there were nothing out of the ordinary in this situation. Did he really not see?

In the same instant, the boy plastered himself against the opposite kennel, only to lunge back wildly when the dog in the kennel behind him jumped up on the fencing and barked in excitement.

Callie shivered, only marginally tempering her own fear of animals. Fear for herself as much as for the boy. Memories of Colin surfaced, along with the guilt she'd never been able to quench. She gripped her attaché case with two fists.

Rhett restrained the large dog by the collar. Callie's eyes widened as she got a good look at the monstrous, slobbery dog, if a dog was, in fact, how that animal could be classified.

It reminded Callie more of Bigfoot than a puppy, though that's what Rhett called it. At least as tall as Rhett's waist, it sported a muscular, fawn-colored body that was only superseded by his oversize head and colossal jaws.

The dog's head reminded Callie of a game she'd played as a child, where she assembled various multicolored plastic animal bodies with an equally assorted number of animal heads.

She'd spent many happy hours making Eleraphs and Rhinoroosters.

This dog was such a creature—definitely one of the most unusual of God's creations she'd ever laid eyes on. And the young man appeared to agree with her assessment.

The dog was large, slobbery and nasty. She could see the whites of his eyes even from where she was standing, and the boy was a good deal closer. No wonder the kid was still struggling to regain his composure.

What was Rhett thinking? He appeared immensely insensitive, which went against everything she knew about him. Confusion washed over her.

This massive brute was a far cry from the Labrador retriever puppy he'd introduced her to the other day. Giving the kid a taste of his own medicine, maybe?

She restrained herself once again, this time from darting forward to lend the boy a hand. This was Rhett's territory, and though it went against the grain, Callie trusted him enough to keep watching without interfering.

Whatever Rhett's strategy, it appeared to be working. In fact, it would be almost laughable, if the poor kid didn't look so terrified, *and* if she was absolutely certain Rhett meant it as a joke.

But she wasn't certain of anything at the moment. Rhett certainly *looked* serious. Determined. And calm.

"I'm not touching no dog," the youth spouted, flipping his hair out of his eyes with a jerk of his chin.

Rhett merely shrugged. "Up to you, son. You can pick up trash along the highway if you want."

The youth scowled.

Rhett met him stare for stare, then flicked his glance in her direction. Their gazes met for only a moment, but that was all she needed to see into the soul of the man, and what she saw made her world spin.

She read a myriad of emotions in his gaze. She half expected the hard edge, disillusionment or polite unconcern she'd so often seen in the social workers in Portland, but she found only gentleness. Strength tempered by compassion.

A man of steel masquerading as mild-mannered. Or maybe the best combination of what both Superman and Clark Kent had to offer.

"Lance, I'd like to introduce you to Bear, our resident mastiff." Rhett's mild tenor was as warm as honey, and Callie swallowed with difficulty.

Apparently, though, Rhett's voice wasn't quite as effective on the boy as it had been on her. Lance merely shrugged, his eyebrows a thick, dark line dashed over his eyes.

He wasn't giving an inch, whether from anger or fear. Callie suspected it was a little of both. And Rhett knew exactly what he was doing.

"So?" Lance blurted, as belligerent as ever.

To Callie's amazement, Rhett didn't bat an eye, even when she herself had, for a moment, forgotten her fear of dogs in response to the boy's antagonism.

She'd only been watching for a few minutes, and she was frustrated beyond belief. How did Rhett stay so composed? How'd Rhett know to make the right match, of dog to kid and kid to dog? There was a lot more to this therapy dog business than she'd first believed.

And with what she'd seen so far, she was admittedly impressed. Lance wasn't making Rhett's job easy on any count, but Rhett took it in stride, never missing a beat as he spoke to the boy.

Then again, the mastiff was on Rhett's side. All things being equal, she'd vote for the dog.

"Bear wants to shake your hand."

The youth's eyebrows popped up so high they were lost under the stubborn lock of hair that fell down over his eyes. "No way."

Again, Rhett merely shrugged. "Your call. If you don't like Bear, I can always…"

He left the sentence dangling, and Callie smiled. Rhett knew *exactly* what he was doing.

"No," Lance said after an electrical silence. "I'll take the stupid dog."

Rhett didn't quite smile, but the laugh lines reappeared around his eyes, which were glimmering with amusement. "I think you'll find Bear to be smart enough for you."

He ruffled the dog's floppy ears. "Lance, meet Bear. Bear...Lance."

The boy tentatively held out his hand, and was rewarded when the big dog lifted his paw for a shake.

Lance chuckled, a foreign and unexpected sound to Callie's ears.

"Well, whadda ya know?" Lance murmured, cocking his head and visually relaxing.

"You don't have a dog?" Rhett queried gently, though the answer was obvious enough.

"No," said the boy, scratching Bear under the chin, and laughing when the dog flopped over onto his back so Lance could scratch his belly.

"My mom never—" He cut himself short with a scowl, though he didn't stop scratching the dog.

Rhett nodded in encouragement, as though he'd been witness to a giant breakthrough with Lance, rather than producing a single statement that told Callie, and no doubt Rhett, much more than if the boy had completed his awkward sentence.

"Bear likes to chase sticks," Rhett said, slipping a lead on the dog's collar. "Think you can handle that?"

The boy shrugged a shoulder as if he didn't care either way, but his eyes were shining with excitement.

With a nostalgic smile, Callie wondered how long it had been since Lance had anything to be excited about. What Rhett was doing here was nothing short of a miracle.

"Out back, then," Rhett instructed gruffly. "Keep Bear inside the fence, please."

Callie's heart leapt into her throat and froze there. Was it really safe to allow the young man and the dog to be alone together? Rhett didn't appear concerned, so she allowed the thought to pass untested, though not without some effort.

"Callie," he said, waving her over as he began adjusting the chain on one of the kennel gates. "Glad you could make it today."

She smiled, her breath catching in her throat as a fluttery feeling washed over her. She supposed it had something to do with seeing another side to Rhett, a mysterious combination of strength and gentleness that was uniquely masculine.

She shifted mental gears as quickly as possible, the clutch grinding. "I have to say that was an astonishing display."

Rhett cocked his head and stopped wrapping the chain around the kennel. "How's that?"

"The boy and that...*dog.*"

He crooked a grin. "Bear will be good for Lance."

"If you say so." Callie shook her head. "Though I don't understand why you'd pair a kid who is so obviously afraid of dogs with *Bear.*"

She shivered despite her best efforts. Rhett's glance was full of compassion, and heat rushed to Callie's cheeks. Would she ever be free of her fear?

If only...

Chapter Eight

Rhett gestured toward his office. He felt oddly pleased by Callie's interest in the dogs, especially considering how frightened she was of them. "I'd be happy to explain the rationale behind my choice, but I'm sure we'd both be more comfortable in my office."

Callie nodded, looking distinctly relieved by his suggestion. He held the door and allowed her to precede him. As she passed, her gaze rose to his, a question in her eyes. He didn't know the answer. He couldn't think straight with her soft, musky scent tantalizing his senses.

"Please sit down," Rhett offered, covering his discomfiture with a gesture of courtesy. "Have you eaten? I've got some doughnuts. And there's soda in the fridge."

"Anything chocolate works for me."

"Soda?"

"Water, if it's bottled and cold."

Rhett reached into the small fridge for a bottle of water for Callie and an orange juice for himself, then flipped open the box of doughnuts on the shelf, selecting a maple bar and a chocolate éclair.

He set the éclair before her and took a bite of the maple bar, settling himself on the corner of the desk with his weight on one hip.

"I have to know why you gave that kid such a big dog," she said, gesturing back to where the teen had been, picking up the conversation where they'd left off. "I mean, it was perfectly obvious even to me that the poor boy was scared to death."

Rhett grinned, feeling like a schoolboy whose girlfriend had seen him make the winning touchdown at a football game. "I thought I'd give the kid someone his own size to pick on."

Callie laughed in delight. "You know, I was thinking that very same thing when I was watching you."

"Were you, now?" he asked, feeling oddly pleased by the notion.

Their gazes met and locked for a moment that was both a second and an eternity. He thought his heart stopped dead in his chest. At any rate, his lungs were burning from sudden lack of use.

Callie broke eye contact first, turning aside and taking a bite of éclair. He didn't know whether to feel offended or relieved. That was the problem. He didn't know *how* to feel.

He cleared his throat and took a sip of his juice, trying with debatable success to regain his equilibrium.

After a long pause, he attempted to regain the easy camaraderie they'd had minutes earlier by returning to the subject of Lance and Bear. "Bear is the least aggressive dog in the kennel."

Understandably, she looked unconvinced.

"Really," he insisted. "Mastiffs are big and rough-looking with teddy-bear hearts."

Callie gave him an odd look, a mixture of surprise and something he couldn't put his finger on. "As opposed to Dobermans?"

Rhett pursed his lips in thought. Instinctively, he knew his next words were do or die, and he wanted to say the right thing. "Callie, there aren't bad dogs. Only bad people. The Dobie who attacked your brother was probably taught that aggressiveness by his owner."

"Do you think?" Callie retorted.

Rhett chose to ignore her animosity. "I took Baron from the pound when no one else would take him."

"Why am I not surprised?"

"I won't ever be able to use Baron in the therapy dog program, but hopefully he'll mellow out enough to find a new home through the Doberman rescue foundation. He needs a lot of love and work to get over his aggressive tendencies, but he'll get there."

"You sound pretty confident."

"You'd be amazed," he said through a tight throat, "at what love can do."

Her jaw dropped in surprise, but she quickly closed it again. He plunged on while he still had the advantage. "Back to poor Bear—he was scheduled for doggie death row. Would have been a waste."

He shook his head, remembering the many dogs—and kids—he couldn't help. That was a part of his burden as a social worker, and a therapy dog worker, that he could never quite unload.

But at least he could, and did, help Bear. Eventually, he'd help Baron, as well.

And, Lord willing, Lance.

Callie appeared to be following his train of thought. "And Lance?" She spoke softly, with a hint of a catch in her throat. He wondered if she were feeling the same effects he was whenever they were together.

Again, he plunged on. "Lance is just another kid looking for attention any way he can get it." The brick in his chest softened as he looked out the window, watching a smiling Lance toss a stick for the large, lumbering dog to retrieve. "It's only a matter of time until they turn to crime, when nothing else does the job."

He shook his head, wishing he didn't sound fatalistic. "I try to give kids like Lance positive experiences with people—and animals."

Callie nodded. ''It's been my experience that those who mistreat animals often mistreat people, as well. Not that I've been around that many animals,'' she amended.

He narrowed his eyes on her as pain flitted across her face. Without making a conscious decision to do so, he reached out for her, brushing his knuckles against the sweet softness of her right cheek.

Meeting Callie had been the parallel of getting to know a tornado on a personal level—a hard-edged woman who swung defensively at every turn and wore her attitude like a turtle wore his shell.

But then, she'd probably learned from the school of hard knocks. It couldn't be easy to be a lady cop, not under the best of circumstances, and he suspected hers weren't.

Her delicate skin was like the brush of rose petals under his touch. What a shocking contrast. There was definitely more to this woman than met the eye. Not for the first time, he was interested—*very* interested—in getting to know the woman behind the emotional fortress she'd so securely erected around herself.

No time like the present.

"You sound as if you're speaking from experience," he queried gently, ready to drop the subject on the spot if she didn't feel inclined to talk about it.

For the slightest moment, she leaned into his caress, and he caught his breath at the sensation, like warm maple syrup drizzling over pancakes.

But the next moment, she turned away, standing so suddenly her chair spun on its coasters. "We weren't talking about me," she returned, her voice raw with emotion.

Apparently he'd hit a nerve.

"Right," he agreed immediately, dropping his hand to the corner of the desk.

"Lance," he murmured, more to remind himself of a safe topic than to remind her.

"Lance," she repeated, as if that lone word were a lighthouse in a storm.

"I'll train Lance with Bear for a few weeks, until he's comfortable with the dog, and vice versa. That's what all the equipment is for—dog training. And kid training."

He flashed her his most charming smile.

"When I think they're both ready, I'll take him with me to a nursing home or a hospital. Dogs are a big hit in the pediatric ward."

Callie's silvery eyes widened noticeably. "They let you take *dogs* into hospitals?"

He nodded. "Sure. My dogs make the kids smile, and forget about being in the hospital for a while."

"But isn't that unsanitary? I'd think the nurses on duty would be pitching fits."

His grin widened. "Some of them do. But not those who've studied dog therapy, or seen it in action."

She nodded, her focus completely on his words.

"Of course we don't visit intensive care or those with infections, but there are whole wards full of cancer patients, especially in the kids' ward."

"Children?"

He pinched his lips together and nodded.

It wasn't something he liked to think about, but it came along with the job. It was undeniably difficult to see those little ones suffering and dying from a terminal illness and know he could do nothing about it, except give them a moment of relief through a smile or a laugh.

He could definitely relate to the sheen of moisture in Callie's eyes, even if he kept his own feelings locked deep inside.

"I never get tired of seeing the way a surly kid destined for juvie hall can change once he's been given something meaningful to do with his time."

He hoped the sudden gear switch sounded natural, but he could tell from Callie's expression she suspected what he was doing—carrying the conversation so she could pull herself together.

In fact, Callie knew exactly what Rhett was doing, and appreciation for his thoughtfulness nearly overwhelmed her already overstimulated senses. Light and kindness blazed from his eyes, and she wondered at the source. She didn't know what to call it, but whatever it was, she liked it.

"I'd never heard of therapy dogs until I met you—er, I mean, moved to John Day," she commented, sliding over her blunder.

He nodded enthusiastically. "The use of

therapy dogs is a relatively new practice in the field. The great part about it is that it benefits everyone involved, from the elderly ladies and gentlemen in the nursing home to the delinquent youth on the other side of the leash.''

Callie was genuinely interested, and was becoming more sold on the method with every word Rhett uttered.

''And the dogs love all that attention, of course. They're incredible to watch. They instinctively appear to know why they're there. It's a riot to watch them preen and primp at being the center of attention.

Callie laughed softly. ''Somehow, I can't see Bear primping and preening.''

''Showing off, then.''

''I must admit, it sounds fascinating.''

''It is.'' Passion lined his voice, and Callie recognized the rise of envy as what it was.

If only *she* had something to believe in so fervently. Even becoming a cop wasn't like that for her. She wasn't fulfilling the desire of her heart with her work. It was more the instinctual reaction of an animal backed into a corner with nowhere to go—fighting back because it was the only thing she could do to save herself.

"Callie?"

"Hmm?" she answered absently.

Rhett chuckled. "I asked you a question."

"Oh. I'm sorry." Her cheeks burned.

"Would you like to go out with me some-time?"

Callie drew in a quick, surprised breath.

"I mean, not *go out* go out, but come with me when I'm visiting the hospital or a nursing home with the therapy dogs."

Her heart, which had moments before been doing a victory dance in her throat, dive-bombed into her toes and sat there like cement.

She could feel the color in her face rising. Of course Rhett was talking about work. How could she possibly have interpreted it any dif-ferently?

And yet she had, for one brief, wonderful second.

She composed her features automatically. Her reply hovered on the edge of her tongue, but her voice deserted her when she needed it most.

After an awkward moment, her voice re-turned. "Yes, I'd be glad to go with you." Thankfully, her voice didn't squeak.

He smiled widely at her answer, looking as pleased as a boy with a frog in his pocket.

She laid a hand on his muscular forearm, enjoying his enthusiasm for his life and work, and, deep in her heart, hoping some of it might rub off on her. She couldn't remember the last time she'd felt so enthusiastic about something. Or some*one*.

"You know, Rhett, what you're doing here is incredible. It's like a miracle or something."

She felt like a cat choking on a fur ball, and the bitter laugh that suddenly burst from the doorway made her swallow it whole.

"Yeah, right," said Brandon as both Rhett and Callie whirled around toward the entrance.

Callie felt a pump of adrenaline, as if she'd been caught doing wrong, though of course that wasn't the case. Brandon's glare made her feel as if she had; and Rhett, too.

"That's my dad. *Incredible*."

Brandon was quivering with anger, his face a mottled red under his honey-gold hair and dark eyebrows. He looked as if he were ready to burst with rage.

And the next moment, he did, slamming his

fist into the drywall and putting a hole clean through the wall next to the door.

Callie turned to Rhett, whose jaw was dropped, either in astonishment or in prelude to speech, though no words came from his effort.

She struggled for words herself, wondering what she should say or do.

One moment later it was too late to do anything at all.

Brandon was gone.

Chapter Nine

Callie looked as if she'd suddenly become enamored of the condition of her fingernails.

Even so, he felt her subversive gaze, and knew she was watching him intently. He knew she felt, as he did, the thick, electrical tension in the air that rivaled that of a thunderstorm.

No doubt she was waiting to see if he'd fly off the handle, as he'd done in the past—at least when she was present. Funny, there was a time when he banked on his rock-solid self-control. Now he couldn't even trust himself.

But maybe that was the problem here. He wasn't in control, and it bothered him incessantly.

God was in control.

His mind acknowledged the fact, but the rest of him rebelled. Where was God in all this?

Rhett couldn't be a good father to Brandon unless the heavenly Father deemed to help him out. And right now it sure didn't feel like God was anywhere close by.

Not with him, and not with Brandon.

Rhett folded his arms, his palms flat against the reassuring solidness of his chest. His lips and brows were parallel lines on his face as he glared at the doorway through which his son had disappeared.

"I'm sorry you had to see that," he said softly, his voice raw.

Callie placed a hand on his shoulder and cleared her throat, but no words came. Her mind blanked as she fished for something encouraging to say.

Despite their bad beginning, she now considered him a friend, and she was glad to be here now to help, though she wasn't sure if her presence was welcome or not.

"I—I know you and Brandon aren't on the best of terms right now. But I wouldn't worry about it too much, if I were you. I'm guessing all parents of teenagers go through this awkward stage, in one form or another."

Rhett grunted his assent. "Do you think?"

She nodded and brushed the hair back from his temple with the tips of her fingers in a feminine gesture that was old as time itself.

"Not that I'm an expert, or anything," she added.

He slumped against the desk, palms down. "I don't know what to do with him anymore. We used to get along great, when he was a kid."

"He still is a kid," Callie reminded him gently. "Have you tried talking to him?"

He burst into a bitter laugh. "I've tried. It's like I'm not speaking English or something. And I sure don't know what language he's speaking. I just don't get it."

"Too bad colleges don't give a course in Teenageeze."

He straightened and turned to look at her, a half grin on his lips. "Maybe I ought to bottle it. I could make millions. If I could just figure it out myself, for one lousy moment."

Callie's chuckle caught in her throat. "Are you going to go after him?"

Rhett glanced at the doorway and then back at her. "Should I?"

She shrugged, feeling pinned to the spot. "I can't tell you what to do."

As soon as the words were out of her mouth, she wished them back. What had she been doing all along where Rhett and Brandon were concerned, if it wasn't telling him what *she* thought he should do?

But now she knew better. Much better.

With every passing day, she realized just how much she *didn't* know about the world, never mind about Rhett Wheeler's heartrending situation.

And Brandon—how had she ever thought she could help him? What little she knew about teenagers was from her own experience, and that of her twin brother.

She had no idea whatsoever if the male adolescent experience even remotely resembled what she'd been through, which quite frankly hadn't been that great.

Colin had been sent away before his hormones had kicked in full force. She'd felt help-less then, and she felt equally helpless now.

All she did remember from her teenage years were tears and pain. *The best years of my life? I don't* think *so.*

There was Colin, of course. But look how that turned out.

Rhett quirked one dark eyebrow, and she was glad to see a sparkle of amusement back in his green eyes. "Not even some advice?"

She barked out a laugh. "I think I've given you enough of *that* to last a lifetime."

"Yeah, well, you were probably right." He frowned, his eyes turning brown with emotion. "On all counts."

"No," she denied with a vehement shake of her head. "I was sticking my nose where it didn't belong. And I'm officially unsticking it as of now."

"Should I go after him?"

She sighed. He wasn't making this turning-a-new-leaf stuff easy on her.

"If you were me, I mean. What would you do?" His expression continued to fluctuate between a scowl and a smile that slipped from time to time, reminding her how serious the situation truly was.

She ran a hand across her chin. "He's trying to make a point," she said, thinking aloud.

"Then I should go after him."

"But he's really upset, so he's not going to listen to you right now."

"Then I should give him his space until he comes to me."

"If he's really looking for attention, which I think he is—"

"Callie!" Rhett groaned. "You're not helping me out here."

She shrugged. "I think…"

"Okay, okay. I'm going after him."

She nodded in agreement. "If you give me your keys, I'll lock up for you, and drop the keys back at your place later today."

She looked around, then frowned. "You'd better put Bear away before you leave."

He grinned, his eyes sparkling with mischief. "Not afraid of a dog, are you?" he teased.

She nodded emphatically. "Absolutely. Without a doubt, terrified out of my wits."

"Funny," he answered, scrubbing a hand across his cheek. "I didn't think you were afraid of anything."

Brandon was right where Rhett thought he'd be, sulking in his room, stretched out across his water bed with his stereo blasting holes in the ceiling.

Rhett knocked twice, then entered on his own when Brandon didn't respond.

"We need to talk." He tried not to let his anxiety show, nor raise his voice, despite the noise of the stereo.

He had to keep the upper hand. He was Brandon's father. And he had to make things right.

Brandon rolled to his back and opened a magazine, holding it up like a shield.

"I know you can hear me, so you just listen, and I'll talk."

He took a deep breath. Brandon really knew how to push his buttons, and he was pounding on them at the moment. Once again, frustration was taking the upper hand.

"No more scenes like the one today, okay?"

"Yes, *sir*. Whatever you say, *sir*," snapped Brandon caustically.

''Knock it off, buster. I should be grounding you for this. Until you're thirty, if I had my way.''

As soon as the words were out, Rhett clamped his jaw closed and mentally pounded himself in the head.

Once again, Brandon had provoked him to anger; and Rhett, in turn, had blown things completely out of proportion.

Lord, help me here! He prayed, feeling apprehensive and volatile. *I'm blowing it. Again. Make me a better father, You, who are the Father of the world. You must know what it's like to deal with children who won't listen to You.*

That thought sobered him.

''Talk to me.'' It was more of a request than a command, and he hoped his son took it that way.

Brandon didn't budge, and Rhett couldn't see his face from where he was standing, so he had no idea what his son was—or wasn't—thinking.

''Brandon, talk to me.'' He was nearly begging now, and it was making him angry. How was he supposed to help his kid if Brandon wouldn't even give him the time of day?

Taking another deep breath, he knelt by the edge of the bed. "Will you pray with me?"

That appeared to have caught his son off guard, because he put the magazine down in his lap. "You want to pray?"

"Sure."

"To confess my sins?" Brandon queried, the bitterness of his tone slicing into Rhett like a knife.

Rhett shook his head adamantly. "No, son. Not to confess *your* sins. To confess *mine*."

Chapter Ten

I didn't think you were afraid of anything.

Rhett's words echoed in her mind during the short drive from the field house back to her home. Taunted her, almost, though she knew he'd been joking.

All her life she'd kept herself aloof, except for Colin. And now Rhett. Under his inspection, her tough-cop facade was as flimsy as the thinnest veneer.

She didn't want him to discover the truth about her—that she was afraid of everything, and Rhett most of all. There were more sparks between the two of them than the skies of

Oregon on the Fourth of July, and she was completely and utterly terrified of going up in flames.

As she pulled down her street, she was surprised to find a polished hunter-green, full-size sports utility vehicle parked in her driveway. She recognized the make and model of the vehicle, but not the license plates, which she thought might be out of state.

Maybe one of her neighbors was having company stay over, though why they'd park in *her* driveway was a mystery.

Curious, she pulled up next to the curb in front of her house and stepped out of her car.

"Callie."

Her world immediately tilted and began to spin.

She grappled for something solid, and clutched at the hood of her car for support.

The man's voice was a soft, lilting tenor as he said her name. A voice she'd heard before, knew every bit as well as her own.

Even if she hadn't heard him speak in years.

Even if the last time she'd seen him they were both sixteen.

"Colin."

A single word. And a lifetime of emotion.

She looked out over the hood of her car to the house across the way, unable to turn and face her long-lost brother, afraid he might fade into the mist if she turned around: The blood that was momentarily frozen in her veins was suddenly rushing to her face.

"How's it going, sis?" How well she remembered the constant tone of lightness and laughter in his voice. It was deeper than when he was sixteen, but it was definitely Colin.

"How's it going?" She was yelling, but she neither knew, nor cared. "You disappear off the face of the planet for ten years and then you waltz in here as casual as all get-out to ask me *how it's going?* What right do you have?"

"I officially waive all my rights." His voice was right behind her ear.

Startled, she whirled around, continuing to grip the hood of her SUV.

Colin embraced her, holding her tight while she pummeled his back with her fists. He didn't offer a word of explanation, and he didn't attempt to stop her outburst of emotion, or her abuse.

"You could have called, Colin, even if you didn't want to come home." That she was talking about a time eleven years in their past was irrelevant. Hot tears streamed down her face, but she ignored them.

Just as quickly as it had appeared, the fight abruptly shattered, leaving her drained and sobbing into her brother's shoulder. "You could have called."

"I know. I should have called. But I was so angry. I felt betrayed. And then it had been so long, I was afraid." He spoke softly, hesitantly. "After a while, it was easier not to call at all."

She stepped back, brushing the tears off her cheeks with her palms. The world was still spinning, but she was beginning to be able to link one coherent thought with another.

Maybe she'd eventually be able to think this through like a rational individual. Until then, she'd have to do the best she could.

Colin was here. He'd grown into a handsome heartbreaker of a man, with broad shoulders and his silver-blond hair cut in a military style that accented his dress-white uniform.

"Dad said you'd probably gone off and joined the Marines," she said, sniffling into the handkerchief he offered. "I guess he was right."

Colin smiled, but his blue eyes were sad. Unlike Callie's silver-blue, her twin's eyes were a wide, clear sky-blue. "Half right," he replied briskly, and Callie wondered whether that was from his experience in the military, or from the subject at hand. "I joined the navy."

"The *navy?*" The more Colin talked, the less sense he made. "But I thought you hated military school!"

"Oh, I did," was his immediate reply. "More than you'll ever know."

His voice took on a hard edge, and Callie wished she hadn't been quite so forthright in quizzing him about his past.

"I may as well have been sent to a halfway house, Callie. In fact, in many ways, I would have preferred it. Being sent away from your family—from your twin sister..."

He didn't bother to finish his sentence, but forged on into new territory. "Dunworthy Academy was just as much of a prison as any jail cell could have been for me. Maybe worse, sometimes. A lot of times.''

"Then why did you go and join the navy?" He wasn't making any sense, and she ached with every part of her being to understand.

It had been so long. Too long.

Colin looked away, off toward the sunset. "I wanted to disappear. The navy offered me an easy out."

She frowned, unable to keep her hurt feelings from showing. "You obviously liked it well enough to have made it a career."

He squared his shoulders and nodded, his mouth quirking into a half smile. It was an achingly familiar gesture, and though she hadn't seen it in years, it worked on her as it had when she was a child, and she instantly forgave him, just as she had always done.

Stubborn, mule-headed Colin, running off to join the navy just to spite their father. She couldn't say that it came as a total surprise.

"You couldn't think of anything better to do?" The sentence was spoken as an accusation, and she gestured to his uniform.

His jaw tightened until she could see the

pulse beating at the corner of his freshly shaven cheek. But amusement sparkled in his eyes, so she knew he wasn't *really* angry.

"I can understand your reasons behind joining the navy," she coaxed, not giving him a chance to answer between her comments.

"I'll even admit my part in it. I should have gone to your graduation, no matter what Dad said. Nevertheless—"

He opened his mouth to speak, but she held him off with a wave of her hand. "*Nevertheless,* I fail to understand why you made the military your career if you hated it so much, *or* why you suddenly decided to show up on my doorstep after all these years."

She leveled him with a glare. "Two simple questions. Why the navy? And why come home now? Did you develop a conscience on one of the ships of yours?"

That last was spontaneous, but she wasn't sorry she said it.

"The navy has been good to me, Callie," he explained patiently.

Callie balked at his tone, sensing condescension there. "Oh, yeah. Navy's family, right?"

A pained look crossed his face, and he sighed deeply. "I guess I had that coming."

"What did you expect, Colin?" The anger of many years of holding her emotions deep inside her overcame her good sense.

She began shaking uncontrollably both inside and out. It was as if something had snapped within her heart. "Hey, brother, welcome home! Been a while."

"No. Of course I didn't think... I hoped that we... Oh, I don't know."

"Well, I do." She straightened up and glared at her twin. "You can march your fancy, spit-shined shoes and fine military uniform elsewhere. I'm not interested in renewing old *acquaintances.*"

Without another word, she lifted her chin and walked past him toward the front door of her house with as much dignity as a woman who'd just had her world turned upside down could muster.

"Acquaintances? Callie, listen to me!"

She held one hand in the air, palm outward. "I don't want to hear anything you've got to say."

"Callie!"

"Save it for someone who cares, Colin." She wasn't angry so much any more as resigned to the inevitable.

"I don't believe you're turning me away like this," Colin protested. "I came all the way from Midway Island just to talk to you. Do you know how many hours of standby plane travel that is? Don't cut me off like this without letting me explain."

Despite her best intentions, she whirled on him, her veneer cracking. "Explain? I thought you were already finished *explaining*."

She turned her back on him again, though she didn't continue the path to her front door. In a softer voice, she continued. "I'm not the one who cut our ties, Colin. I didn't run off without a word."

"I can explain that."

"Maybe I don't want you to explain."

"Callie—" he began.

She cut him short. "Do you have any idea what I went through those first few months, trying desperately to find you? I didn't have the money to hire a private investigator as a poor kid working her way through college. But believe me when I say I tried every other option I could think of.''

She blew her air out in a big huff. "I even got religious for a while. I prayed my heart out, asking God to bring you home to me. But He didn't answer, Colin. I don't even think He heard me.''

"He heard you," Colin replied, his voice cracking with emotion. "God heard you." He stepped forward and took both her hands in his. "God is why I'm here.''

"Oh, I see. Of course. Why didn't I realize that earlier? You've got God's stamp right on your forehead. Heaven's post office isn't very efficient, is it?''

She didn't care that she sounded cynical. She *was* cynical.

Colin wasn't charging back into her life because God was answering her prayers. She'd stopped praying a long time ago. "He must have gotten behind on His requests. Or maybe I'm just not real high on His list of priorities.''

"Callie, don't.''

"No, *you* don't. I don't want to hear any more.''

He scrubbed his fingers across his scalp, ruffling the short tips of his hair and ruining his impeccable military image.

"Do you remember back when we were schoolkids, and we went to that vacation Bible school where everyone dressed up like Bible times?"

"Sure," she answered, wondering where he was going with the question. It seemed an odd thing to bring up at the moment, and she definitely wasn't in the mood for games.

"Do you remember anything...*special* that happened while we were there?"

She glared at her twin, letting him know she wasn't overjoyed by his line of questioning, but nonetheless, she found herself searching the recesses of her mind for something, anything, she might say in reply.

Colin grinned.

"What?" she asked, annoyed.

"It's just so great to see you again."

She rolled her eyes.

"We accepted Jesus into our hearts."

"What?"

"At vacation Bible school. Remember?

There was this neat little book we made of construction paper. It didn't have any words in it, but it told a story.'' His voice brimmed with childlike enthusiasm.

She nodded as the memory returned, and she fought not to smile. Those were good times, when the twins were the dearest of friends. "As I recall, each page was a different color."

"Yes. Now you remember."

"Only vaguely. And I'd like to know what this has to do with you blasting into my life all of a sudden."

"Black for our sins, red for Christ's blood, white for our hearts after Jesus washed them clean," he continued as if she hadn't said a word.

A clean heart? Hardly. Enough was enough, already. "What's your point?"

"In the navy, I'm an RPS."

"What is that, the military's version of a funeral director?"

He chuckled. "Religious Programs Specialist. It's an overglorified name for a secretary."

"You're a *secretary*," Callie repeated, hardly believing her own ears. "There's justice for you."

"You haven't heard the worst of it. I handle the paperwork for the navy chaplains.

"Oh, now there's a good one." She chuckled. How many times as a child had Colin been the instigator of trouble which Callie usually took the brunt of the blame for? With one major exception—shoplifting.

For a kid who'd been carted off to military school, ending up as a preacher's secretary was truly ironic.

Maybe what came around really did go around. At least in Colin's case.

"What a riot."

"I thought the same thing—for a while. But being around men and women of faith just changes you, somehow. They have this peace about life, even when things go wrong, when there aren't explanations for the bad things that happen."

"I guess you see a lot of bad things in the navy."

He nodded. "Sometimes. Eventually, I started asking questions. I wanted to know what it was that gave their lives so much meaning."

She immediately thought of Rhett, and wondered if she saw the same thing in him as Colin saw in the chaplains. Rhett went to church every weekend, and he talked openly about his faith.

She'd wondered more than once why an otherwise competent man would rely on his faith rather than his own strength. "I think I understand."

"Do you?" Colin smiled eagerly. "It took me a while to realize it wasn't *what* they had, but *Who.*"

She frowned. "You lost me."

"Jesus. I rediscovered my relationship with Christ that I lost all those years ago."

"I'm so happy for you."

"I'm serious, Callie."

She met his gaze head-on. "So am I."

"That's why I returned."

"Jesus told you to drive to Oregon and sit on my doorstep?"

"Not in so many words. But when I recommitted myself to God, I realized I had a lot of unresolved issues."

Oh, so now she was an *unresolved issue.* This was getting better and better. "Go home, Colin.

You've done your duty before God. You're off the hook.''

"It's not like that.''

"Whatever. I don't really care.''

That wasn't the truth, of course. She cared—too much. But she wouldn't let on. What good would that do? So the new, improved Colin Brockman would feel better for abandoning his twin sister all those years ago?

She wasn't ready to go that far. Not by a long shot.

"I'm going,'' Colin said through a stiff jaw. "But not far. I'll be at the Quest Motel at Second and Main. When you're ready, give me a call.''

"Don't sit by the phone,'' she retorted, putting her key into the lock.

"You're the reason I'm here, Callie, and I'm not leaving until we've talked.''

"Whatever.'' Her temples were pounding, and she could think of nothing beyond taking a couple of aspirin and having a good cry.

She stepped through the front door and swung it closed, but even the solid oak of the door didn't keep out Colin's closing remark.

"God bless you, Callie. I'll be praying.''

Chapter Eleven

When Callie didn't return with his keys, Rhett became concerned. It wasn't that he didn't trust her—quite the opposite, in fact.

She was a woman who kept her word, which was why he became antsy when she didn't show. He wouldn't say he was *worried*, exactly.

Okay, so he *was* worried.

Especially considering the last time he'd seen her was the field house. He could think of all kinds of trouble for her to get into there.

What if one of the boys on parole decided to show up and give her a hard time? What if one of the dogs got loose and she panicked?

He wasn't worried so much about the dogs, knowing they'd sooner lick her to death than harm her, but he was concerned about Callie's reaction to having the situation out of her control.

He knew her well enough to know she was a control freak. And if she didn't appear confident around the dogs, his less-trained dogs would sense her anxiety and become agitated and unpredictable.

And if one of the big dogs got loose and Callie panicked...

That thought alone was enough to make him grab his car keys, which, thankfully, weren't attached to the field house keys, and drive down to the field house. Just to make sure everything was all right, and Callie was home safe and sound, simply forgetting she'd promised to return them this evening.

He was overreacting, he kept telling himself, but the thought of Callie in any kind of danger drove him on, despite the knowledge of how foolish he'd feel if he were wrong.

He didn't know whether to be relieved or troubled to find that Callie wasn't at the field house. He didn't have the key to get in, but the doors were locked and the safety lights were on.

Apparently, she'd done exactly what she'd said she would do, locked up and gone home.

He chuckled. He was seeing shadows behind every tree these days, and most of them of his own making. So much for the wisdom and maturity of age and faith.

Still smiling, he got on the police radio and asked the dispatcher for Callie's home address, deciding to save her a trip out later. That he was also reassuring his overactive imagination he wouldn't admit—except to himself.

He had to knock twice before she answered.

She peeked out through the one inch of space her chain lock allowed, but even so, Rhett could see that she'd been crying.

"Can I come in?" he asked gently, his concern resurfacing with a vengeance.

Without a word, she closed the door.

He thought that action was the definitive answer to his question until he heard the lock turning, at which point his heart swelled until he could hardly breathe. She reopened the door and gestured him inside.

Her small, ranch-style cottage was typical of the neighborhood. Old and run-down. But he immediately noticed just how much Callie had done with the place to make her house a home.

Frilly gingham curtains hung in the windows, and there were houseplants galore in every corner of the room.

Not only that, but there was the distinct smell of cinnamon in the air, so alluring it made Rhett's mouth water on the spot.

Arms akimbo, she stared at him for a moment, then shrugged as if in answer to an unspoken question. "I've been baking sugar cookies. Do you want one?"

"You don't have to ask me twice," Rhett agreed, following her into the kitchen. He sat on a bar stool at the end of a breakfast nook while she served him, noting with pleasure the fresh flowers in a vase at the center of the counter.

He wouldn't have pegged Callie as the home-making type. He didn't know exactly what he *had* expected, but somehow he hadn't pictured her buying flowers for herself.

She wasn't the frilly type.

Or was she?

That question was a revelation in itself, and he vowed to learn more about this mysterious entity known as Callie Brockman. It was only in viewing the inside of her house that he realized how much he *didn't* know about her.

And how much he wanted to learn.

She was a tough, independent cop, and he'd stereotyped her right down to the polyester uniform.

He shook his head. That wouldn't happen again.

"Do you have some milk, by any chance?" he asked, giving her his award-winning smile, the one that had served him well in the past.

Callie didn't appear to notice, never mind be struck down by his charm. "Skim, if that's okay," was her only reply, and that, he thought, was halfhearted.

"Perfect." His grin widened despite her lack of reaction to his previous efforts. "Ever since I was a kid, I've liked to dunk my cookies."

"Me, too." She grimaced in what Rhett guessed was supposed to be a smile, his first hint, besides the red rims of her eyes, that indicated all was not well in Callie's world.

She held up her own half-empty glass of milk, which had been sitting on the counter next to a cookie. "My twin, Colin, and I used to have cookie-dunking races. I guess old habits die hard."

Her bottom lip quivered a moment before her expression turned rigid. Rhett's internal psychologist alarm went off loud and clear. "What's wrong?"

She turned away from him, focusing on taking another batch of cookies out of the oven and placing them, one by one, on some paper towels to cool.

"Callie?"

She threw her spatula onto the counter and grasped the edge with both hands. Staring down at the cookies with a dull glaze over her eyes, she looked very much like someone whose world was spinning out of control.

"There's nothing wrong."

He stood abruptly, his chair nearly tipping underneath him. "Oh, yes there is. I'm a psychologist, remember? Let me help you."

He was surprised at the intensity of his own words. He'd never wanted to help anyone more in his life, except his son.

Perhaps it was *because* of Brandon that Rhett needed to help Callie work out her problems. At least he could help *someone* he cared for.

She remained frozen to the spot, her shoulders shaking with the effort of keeping her emotions restrained.

Years full of helplessness and frustration raged through Rhett, and he sprinted forward, grabbing her by the elbow and twirling her around to face him in a single, fluid motion.

Quickly and deliberately, he slid his hands to her shoulders and gripped her firmly, if tenderly, both amazed and fascinated by how fragile her frame felt beneath his fingers.

The whole of his being reacted to her. Mind. Soul. Body. Spirit.

He wanted to be there for her. With her. He wanted her to know of Jesus, the Rock to which she could cling, and of a mortal man who would be there for her whenever she needed him.

Starting now.

"I can't help you unless you talk to me."

She glared up at him, tears pouring down her cheeks. "You can't help me."

"You don't *know* that."

Before he even realized what he was doing, he'd bent his head, capturing her lips with his own.

He hadn't intended to kiss her, didn't know how or why it had happened; but when she wrapped her arms around his neck, digging her fingers into the hair on the base of his neck and clinging for all she was worth, he deepened the kiss, showing in the best way—the *only* way—he knew how, that she could trust him. That he did care. That he'd be there for her, no matter what.

Words were not enough. Not for the strength and intensity of her emotions. And his.

She wasn't alone.

And neither, he realized, his grip still tight around her, was he.

An audible groan crossed his lips as he wrapped his arms more tightly around her. It seemed like forever since he'd kissed Callie, and it felt good.

Better than good. Phenomenal. Perfect.

With a sudden panicked gasp, she broke off the kiss and slapped her hand over her mouth, as if horrified at what they'd done.

He dropped his arms at once. An apology hovered on his lips, but as he made to move away, she turned and stepped back into his embrace, burying her head on his shoulder and wrapping her arms tightly around his waist, as if he were her only anchor amidst a violent storm.

Sighing, he pulled her close, inhaling the soft, musky smell that was Callie. He brushed stray wisps of her silky, silver hair away from her temple with his fingertips, mumbling softly all the while, giving her everything he possessed, words of peace and strength.

As for himself, he was content with the moment.

For once in his life, the first time in more years than he cared to count, he really believed things were going to be all right. And he wanted more than anything to share that divine assurance with Callie, who was groping in the dark for a beacon, for *Light*.

To think they might have missed each other, and all because of his stubborn pride, his unwillingness to listen and his ridiculous ideas of what his future wife should be.

He now recognized his version of perfection was so far from what he *needed* that it wasn't even funny.

Or maybe funny was exactly what it was.

God knew all along. Thank God He knew.

"My twin brother came here today," she murmured, her whisper muffled by his button-down cotton shirt. "I haven't seen him in years."

Callie had mentioned she was a twin in several of their conversations together, but Rhett couldn't remember any specifics.

Even a name eluded him, which surprised him, as he was usually good at remembering names. He searched the depths of his mind, but still came up empty. "Your twin?"

"Colin."

"I take it this wasn't a planned visit."

She laughed bitterly. "It's been over 10 years. I didn't even know where to find him."

He frowned, but remained silent. She looked as if she carried the burden of the world on her slim, squared shoulders, and he wished he could carry some of the load for her, even if it were only for a moment.

"My father sent him off to military school after he got into trouble with the law. He was only sixteen—Brandon's age."

Suddenly, the whole outrageous history between them, all the times she'd spoken on Brandon's behalf, made perfect sense.

She'd already walked this road. Why hadn't he seen this earlier?

She hiccupped, and Rhett pulled a tissue from a box on the counter and handed it to her with a gentle smile. "Go on."

The least he could do now was listen. He only wished he could do more. And maybe he could, if given the right information and half a chance.

"Colin hated military school with a passion. And he hated my father for sending him there in the first place. Maybe he hated me, too, for not standing up to Dad when I should have. The whole stupid shoplifting scheme was my idea. I'm sure he thought of that often when he was put through his military paces and sculpted into something he was not."

"No," Rhett denied immediately.

No brother could hate Callie, especially a

twin. No matter what she'd thought she'd done, what role she'd played in this farce.

He wouldn't believe that of Colin, though he'd never met the man. What little Callie had spoken about her brother had been in love. Twins, in Rhett's vast experience as a counselor, shared many of the same traits.

He thought he might like to meet this Colin.

Her brother would no doubt enlighten Rhett on many facets of Callie's personality he was eager to unearth.

"My father was so bitter, he wouldn't even attend Colin's graduation. He was miserable after my mother died, and he took it out on Colin.

"I was too frightened of my own shadow to go against my father's wishes and attend Colin's graduation, and I've regretted that decision every day of my life. I should have been there. He expected it of me."

Her thoughts had turned inward, and it showed in the anger of her tone. "I betrayed him, and I've paid for it over and over again."

Rhett didn't think what happened between the twins was Callie's fault, nor did he think her twin was blaming her for half the guilt she pinned on herself.

But she wasn't ready to hear his professional opinion on the matter, so he asked a question instead.

"What happened to Colin?"

"He disappeared." She looked out the kitchen window into the darkness, the gleam of tears in her eyes making them glitter like precious metal.

"I tried to find him, but I couldn't afford a private investigator, and Colin didn't want to be found."

A lone tear slid down her cheek, and Rhett wiped it away with his fingertip.

"I've lived with that guilt ever since. It's been eleven years." She shook her head. "Eleven long, silent years with not a word from him.

"I knew he was alive, because we share a special, unexplainable bond with each other. You know—feeling each other's pain and happiness? But I couldn't find him."

Pain laced her voice, and her words explained a lot, like why she'd become a juvenile police officer, and why she was so passionate about her work.

And why she cared so much about what happened between Rhett and Brandon.

"But he showed up today." It was a statement, and she nodded.

"Where has he been all this time?"

She made a sound in her throat that was half a laugh, half a snort. "Would you believe he joined the navy?"

"I thought he hated military school."

"He did. That's what's so laughable." She didn't sound like she wanted to laugh.

"He's a career navy man?"

"Yeah. Go figure."

"Did he say why he's suddenly decided to renew family ties?"

"Oh, that's the real kicker. *God* told him to come to Oregon and find me."

"God *told* him to come?" Rhett's voice revealed the skepticism he felt.

"Well, not audibly or anything," she admitted, waving him off. "But what difference does it make? He really believes God sent him here. All I know is, God didn't mention it to me."

"Didn't He?" Rhett's heart leapt. He could feel her spiritual dilemma as if it were his own, and he remembered being in the same quandary of faith at one time.

Callie's eyebrows bunched into a V over her nose. "Give me a break. God doesn't talk to me."

"Is that a fact?"

"That's a fact," she repeated angrily. "Let's just say I'm not on God's list of good graces."

He didn't know about that.

Callie was running, and God was chasing. If he wasn't mistaken, her heels were being divinely nipped and she was panicking.

He knew the feeling well.

"Did your brother say anything specific, besides that God sent him?"

Callie shook her head. "I showed him the door. I was very upset, and not ready to deal with Colin yet. He caught me off guard."

She shook her head again, more fervently this time, and picked up her half-eaten cookie. "I bake when I need to think."

"Good thing for me," he quipped lightly, hoisting his own cookie in a salute.

"You're welcome to the whole batch of them. My hips sure don't need any encouragement."

Her hips were just perfect in Rhett's view, but he thought it expedient not to comment.

"I don't know what Colin *really* wanted, but whatever it was, he isn't through with me yet. He told me he's staying at the Quest Motel. He seemed to be under the impression I'd be contacting him soon."

"Won't you?"

She chuckled, for real this time. "I suppose. Once I get my bearings, anyway."

"Sounds to me like he might be here to ask your forgiveness."

"*My* forgiveness? I'm the one who needs to ask forgiveness. Colin didn't do anything wrong."

"Yet you're angry with him."

Callie blew out a breath. "Of course I'm angry. He could have let me know where he was. Or that he was okay, at least."

"Then you *do* need to forgive him."

"Forgive and forget," she quipped, frowning. "I don't think I'll ever forget what he put me through."

"God's not asking you to forget, Callie. But He does want you to forgive your brother."

"It hurts too much."

Rhett nodded, remembering how difficult it was to forgive Kayla after she'd left him and their marriage. There was nothing harder in the world, and he felt for Callie, being faced with what she considered her brother's betrayal.

"Forgiveness is a choice," he said slowly, softly, knowing his words wouldn't be easy for her to hear, much less come to grips with. "Not a feeling. A choice."

Her brows hit her hairline. "What's that supposed to mean?"

"It means you can forgive Colin even if you don't *feel* forgiveness in your heart."

"What? I just wave my wand around and say the magic words?"

Rhett chuckled and shook his head. "I wish it was that easy, but it isn't. Forgiving Colin— and your father—will be one of the toughest things you'll ever do."

"Leave my father out of this," she snapped.

He held up his hands, palms out. "Okay. Let's just deal with Colin right now."

Rhett didn't want to ruffle Callie's feathers. He wanted to soothe her, to take away her pain.

Yet he was compelled to continue, knowing his words weren't what Callie wanted to hear.

"Unforgiveness is like a cancer. It eats away at you, and it's every bit as terminal as any disease. The best thing you can do for *yourself* right now is to meet with your brother and initiate forgiveness. For both of you."

"So then, let me see if I've got this straight. I just have to say I forgive Colin to his face, even though I don't feel that way." To say she sounded unconvinced would have been an understatement. "And that's it?"

"No. There's more."

"Now, why am I not surprised?"

"Then," he continued, ignoring her cutting remark, "you have to act out your forgiveness. Put it all behind you and start over. Don't you want to have a relationship with your brother?"

"I don't know what I want." She popped another cookie into her mouth, chewed slowly, and swallowed. "I love my brother, but I'm too angry to even think about forgiving him right now."

"As well you should be. No one is discounting your anger."

"Not even God?"

"Especially not God. 'Be angry and sin not,' are His words, not mine."

"I'll think about it."

"Pray?" He knew he was pushing it, but his tongue got the better of him.

"Think," she assured him.

"Good enough," he conceded, knowing he'd planted a seed. She'd be thinking about her faith, even if she wouldn't call what she was doing praying.

God was doing something special here, and Rhett was blessed to be a part of it. Somehow, some way, God was going to make lemonade out of lemons.

And Rhett couldn't wait to taste the finished product.

Chapter Twelve

Callie picked up the telephone receiver again, but just as she'd done the other hundred times she'd picked it up and put it to her ear, she sighed and put it back in its cradle without dialing.

She'd never expected that seeing her brother again would be so painful, no matter how angry she was with him. No matter what was between them.

They were *twins*.

They'd been best friends as children, inseparable even as teenagers. Colin knew everything about her. They'd often thought or said the same thing at the same time, then laughed over the coincidence.

Everything was wonderful between them until Colin stole something from the five-and-dime on a dare, and had been caught in the act by the store's angry owner. It was his first offense, but the owner didn't care, and prosecuted Colin for that stupid stunt.

That one moment had changed both their lives.

She'd give anything to go back to that day, before it all happened, to beg him to stop before he started, instead of egging him on as she'd done.

In a very real sense, his crime was hers. She was the mastermind behind the plan, and she'd been the big mouth who'd made the dare Colin couldn't do anything else but accept.

The crime was hers. In every way but the way that counted. *She* hadn't been carted off to the police station. *She* hadn't been the one on the receiving end of Dad's solemn silence, so much worse than anything he said aloud. And *she* hadn't been the one sent away to military boarding school.

No, but she wished she had. *She'd* been the one left behind. And she'd regretted it with every breath since the day it happened, even if her own teenage years weren't much better than Colin's had been. How many times had she wished *she'd* been the one who was sent far away from her gruff and untouchable father?

But what was done, was done. There was no sense dredging up the past. If wishes were horses…or days…

Yet how could she ignore the past, with it staring her in the face; a living, breathing past who'd grown from a boy into a man?

And she had grown up, as well.

Should she do as Rhett suggested, and put the past to rest? Could she start new with Colin, attempt to regain the close relationship they'd once so easily shared?

But she didn't know him at all, and it frightened her. He'd been a gawky teenager the last time she'd seen him, and she'd been a painfully shy, zit-covered tenth grader.

How could they pick up where they left off? Their lives had taken such different paths. She didn't know if they had the slightest thing in common anymore, other than their birthdays and the color of their hair.

She'd spent the night tossing and turning, her mind going over Colin's abrupt arrival into her life.

Every word they'd said to each other. Every tingle of emotion she experienced.

What should she do?

She wasn't ready to face Colin. Not a morning person on the best of days, she was definitely the worse for wear from her sleepless night. She didn't think even a fully caffeinated double shot of espresso could repair the damage.

She wondered what Rhett was doing. Sleeping, if he had any sense.

He'd stayed late, casually hovering around until he was certain she'd be okay. And not for the first time, she was glad he'd been there for her. She was thankful fate—or *God,* as Rhett would say—had arranged the circumstances so he had come for his keys last night.

She should be annoyed, but she wasn't. *Grateful* was more along the lines of her feelings for Rhett right now.

Gratefulness, and something more.

She didn't know *how* to classify Rhett's kisses, or her reaction. His lips had met hers as a challenge, yet had quickly turned into something else; a different, deeper kind of challenge.

And she'd picked up the gauntlet before she had a chance to give it a rational thought.

Though he wasn't the first man she'd ever kissed, Rhett was the first man ever to affect her heart as well as her body; making her lose all sense of time and place, aware of nothing but the warmth of the ever growing ember between them.

Even *thinking* about Rhett made her weak in the knees, which was only marginally preferable to the quandary she felt when she thought of Colin.

Since it was Saturday morning and she had the day off, she pulled on an old pair of sweats, deciding she'd distract herself with a pile of rented videotapes—romantic comedies without a hint of reality in them. Not a drama or tearjerker among them.

She'd seen enough reality to last her a good long while.

* * *

Rhett mopped the perspiration off his brow with a handkerchief. Though the day was crisp and cool, he was sweating up a storm, and it wasn't from physical exertion.

Brandon was gone.

He knew something serious had been eating at his son. The fist-size hole in his office wall was proof of that. And his trouble with the law was another bright beacon in the dark night of the teenage soul.

But to run away?

Maybe he was wrong. He prayed he was mistaken. Brandon's drawers had been shuffled through and left open. Clothes had been yanked from hangers. Most telling of all, the game-winning football from his first touchdown as a running back on the Grant Union Prospectors varsity team was conspicuously missing from the center of his top bookshelf.

Rhett wanted to yell with rage and frustration. It was his fault. He'd been laboring under the misapprehension things between them were getting better, but he was obviously mistaken. He'd either genuinely misread the signs Brandon was displaying, or he was the singularly most clueless individual who'd ever roamed the planet.

At the moment, he was inclined to believe the latter.

What was going on with his son that he didn't know about? Why wasn't Brandon talking to him? Hadn't their prayer time together meant anything?

He'd been so sure, so encouraged by the progress they were making together, with God's help.

They were beginning to rebuild their relationship, the close father-son bond they'd once shared. Finally, they were moving past the problem and into solutions.

And now this.

He was leveled by the unwanted, unexpected revelation. It felt like a slap on the face.

What was he supposed to do now? What was Brandon really after? What did he want Rhett to do?

And why did he feel the need to lash out in yet another drastic, attention-getting tactic?

If that's what it was. Rhett wasn't sure of anything, anymore.

"Oh, Lord God, protect my son," he murmured, scrubbing his fingers across his scalp where a headache was forming. He breathed heavily, willing his blood to stop pounding and roaring through his head.

His heart throbbed an erratic tattoo to the beat of his guilty conscience.

All my fault. All my fault.

There wasn't anyone else here to blame. Without a woman's—a *mother's*—guidance, and with his father making only flailing attempts at parenthood, the boy was left to his own devices.

No need to mince words in his mind. If Brandon was gone, it was completely Rhett's fault.

Some dad he turned out to be.

If he felt any anxiety as an eighteen-year-old with a wife and infant son, he was under twice as much pressure now. And while there were books galore on baby care, he hadn't run across many handbooks on the care and feeding of a teenager.

He'd laugh, if he wasn't so close to tears.

When he'd arrived home after staying late at Callie's, Brandon had been sound asleep in his room, though how he could sleep with his stereo blaring loud enough to shake the walls, Rhett would never know.

Brandon didn't even twitch when Rhett brushed the hair off the boy's forehead and planted a tender, fatherly kiss on his temple.

What could have happened between last night and this morning that had set Brandon off? He hadn't heard the phone ring, nor the doorbell peal.

No matter. Either way, the boy was gone.

Rhett immediately called down to the station to request a special favor—a private investigator who'd know what to look for, where to find clues that would help them find the boy.

All this done *off* the record, of course. He knew he couldn't file a missing persons report for another day, and even then, he wasn't sure what good that would serve.

Unfortunately, it was a busy Saturday for the precinct, and every officer there was on active duty. No chance for a little off-the-record help today.

Rhett paced back and forth through his son's room, jamming his fingers through his hair.

Pounding his fist into his opposite palm. Trying to think things through when his brain felt muddled and his head was hammering with apprehension and anxiety.

Suddenly it came to him out of nowhere. Not the answer to his problem, but maybe the next best thing.

There was someone else he could call for help. He reached for Brandon's telephone.

When he found his son, things would be different. He'd pay attention to the things that Brandon was interested in, things that mattered to the boy, instead of always being so caught up in his work.

He wondered how much *more* he didn't know about his son. What else went on in Brandon's life that he didn't know about?

No wonder the kid was running.

Rhett hesitated a moment more, then set his jaw and dialed the number he'd committed to memory, though he'd never had a reason to call.

"Callie?" he bit out from between clenched jaws when she answered. "Can you come to my house?"

"Sure," she agreed amicably. "Should I bring lunch?"

"No. No lunch," he rasped.

"Rhett, what's wrong?" Worry edged her voice.

"It's nothing." *It's everything. Oh, dear Lord, Brandon is gone.* "Brandon is gone."

"What do you mean Brandon is gone? *Gone* gone?" She sounded as frantic as he felt.

"Yeah," he agreed softly. "I think so. As far as I can tell. Some of his clothes are missing, and I can't find his duffel bag." He knew he sounded like a frog with a head cold, but he didn't care.

"I'll be right over," she said hastily, just before the dial tone buzzed in his ear.

Rhett couldn't believe the relief that flooded his chest. Callie would be here soon.

Not knowing what else to do, he slumped to his knees by the side of Brandon's bed and clenched his hands together.

"Oh, God." It was in every way a prayer, though he lost his voice when he tried to go further. He bowed his head, spending an indefinite moment silently reaching for the comfort and solace of heavenly arms.

Oh, how his heart ached. God knew where Brandon was, and He was the *only* one who knew. "Please don't take Brandon away from me."

It was the prayer of a broken man.

"God wouldn't do that."

Callie's soft words made him jolt to his feet. He hadn't realized he was praying aloud, never mind that anyone other than God was listening.

Heat rushed to his face. He cleared his throat and jammed his hands into the front pockets of his jeans.

Without another word, Callie wrapped her arms around him and buried her face in his shoulder. Rhett stiffened, then bowed his head into the silky softness of her hair and clung to her like a lifeline.

After several minutes, she stepped back. Tears streamed from her eyes, wetting her cheeks with dark traces of mascara. In Rhett's estimation, she'd never looked lovelier.

"What should I do?" he asked, trying desperately to still the frantic hammering of his heart and keep his voice calm and even.

He failed miserably at both.

"Where have you searched?" Relief surged through him, acting as a buffer for all these unfamiliar, polar emotions he was experiencing.

Callie was here. She'd help him think things through in a calm, rational manner. Her mere presence made a tremendous difference.

He didn't have to face this alone.

He cleared his throat, trying to focus. "First thing after I knew he was gone, I phoned the pizza parlor, and the pool hall. He hangs out there a lot with other kids his age."

He paused and swept in a breath that stung his lungs as if it were carbon dioxide and not fresh oxygen. "I called everywhere I could think of where he might have gone."

"I even called his girlfriend," he concluded with a bitter laugh.

"That's a reasonable course of action," she assured him. "You've done the right thing, Rhett."

He wasn't sure if she referred to calling the pool hall or calling her, but it didn't make any difference.

"It doesn't feel reasonable," he snapped harshly, but Callie didn't exhibit any reaction. In fact, she didn't move a muscle.

"I *feel* like calling the precinct and putting out an all-points bulletin. But I can't even register Brandon as missing for another nineteen and a half hours."

Callie smiled sadly. "Not that you're counting."

He pursed his lips, fighting the new wave of dread washing over him. "I'm probably overreacting."

"Rhett, you're a wonderful father."

"Yeah, that's why my kid has run off."

He couldn't take it anymore. He slammed his fist into the door frame, making a small dent in the trim and a large gash on his hand. And the worst part was, it didn't hold a candle to the pain in his heart.

"You aren't going to help Brandon by hurting yourself," Callie reproved, though her voice was gentle.

She pulled a handkerchief from her purse and wrapped it around Rhett's bloody knuckles. Even through his panic, he appreciated the tender gesture.

"Are you absolutely positive he's run away? I mean, maybe he just needed a little space or something. Could he be walking around the block?''

He made a strangled sound in his throat and turned away, but Callie grabbed his elbow and turned him around.

''It's early yet,'' she said firmly, forcing his gaze to lock with hers, allowing encouragement to flow from her heart to his. ''This might not be as bad as you think.''

He shrugged. ''I guess not.''

Suddenly, she snapped her fingers and her face brightened considerably. ''Hey, I know! Did you try the church?''

He frowned. ''No. Why? Do you think he might have gone there? It's Saturday. I didn't even think about church.''

''Maybe you should have.'' Callie flashed him a confident, secretive smile. ''The church has one very important item you don't have. And I'm relatively certain he won't find that item at the pizza parlor or pool hall, either.''

''What would that be?''

''A punching bag.''

She grabbed for his hand and dragged him at a trot out of Brandon's room and down the stairs to the main entrance, excitement adding bounce to her step.

"I have a hunch, Rhett."

He had no answer to that, so he numbly followed her out to her car. It didn't even occur to him to offer to drive until they were halfway to the church, with Callie in the driver's seat.

"I was just thinking about the last time I was at the church. We were in the gym, remember?" Callie asked softly, breaking the silence.

Rhett stared forward, his jaw locked and his head throbbing.

"If I recall, we weren't on the best of terms." She reached across the seat and took his hand.

"No," he agreed quietly.

She shifted her gaze to him, then back to the road. "I'm glad we're friends, Rhett."

"Me, too, Callie," he said, interlacing their fingers and squeezing her hand gently. *Friend* didn't even begin to describe his feelings for Callie and he struggled to find words to express all she'd become to him. "I don't know what I'd do without you."

They pulled into the church parking lot and

Rhett tensed to the point of physical pain. He was afraid even to hope Callie's hunch was right, and yet...

"Well, you don't have to worry about what you'd do without me, because I'll be there whenever you need me, whether you like it or not." She squeezed his hand again.

"You're not alone. I'm here with you now, and we're going to find Brandon. Everything's going to be all right."

Callie hoped she was right.

"*God* is with Brandon," she added for good measure. "You trust God to take care of him, don't you?"

Rhett looked confused for a moment, then nodded. "God." He buried his face in his hands and his shoulders shook with the intensity of keeping his feelings under wraps.

Callie put her arm around his shoulders, encouraging him the only way she knew, as words deserted her.

If there was a God, He *had* to be listening to Rhett right now. The poor man had paid a lifetime of penance in the past half hour.

He was a good man. He didn't deserve this. He'd tried his best to raise Brandon.

Why was God punishing him this way? She directed her anger heavenward and practically dared God to send a bolt of lightning to strike her for her horrible, sacrilegious thoughts.

Better to blame God than Rhett.

She brushed aside the parallel thought that she'd once been just as judgmental about Rhett's parenting abilities as he was now being of himself.

She knew better now.

And if she knew, God knew. She had to believe that.

Rhett had to believe that. He needed a divine lifeline right about now. Callie silently prayed—*really* prayed—for the first time in years.

And then, summoning up every last bit of courage she possessed, she exited the car and waited for Rhett to do the same.

Chapter Thirteen

Rhett's first glimpse of his son was when he rushed around the corner of the door to the church gym. Brandon was giving the punching bag a series of short *one-two* bursts, sweat and what Rhett thought were tears streaming down his face.

Relief flooded through him so powerfully it almost buckled his knees. All at once, he was berating himself for overreacting, and thanking God that Brandon was safe and still in John Day.

All the bad things Rhett had imagined were swept from him by emotion so great he could barely contain it. Anger and elation warred for prominence within his heart, and he took deep, gulping breaths of air to calm himself.

Brandon's duffel bag was lying haphazardly on the floor next to him, the contents pouring out. Sweats, a T-shirt, shoulder pads, and the football that belonged in the middle of Brandon's shelf.

All present and accounted for.

Rhett felt a sharp nudge that jolted him from his stupor. He looked down and realized it was Callie's elbow jabbing into his ribs.

"Go to him," she said softly, gesturing her head in Brandon's direction.

He reached for her hand, but she pulled away. "No. This is between you and Brandon. I don't want to interfere."

He knew her words were right and true. He was a psychologist, after all, for all the good it did him. He knew the textbook theories of re-uniting families.

But even so, he needed the security of her hand in his, and dreaded facing his son alone.

What could he possibly say to make things right?

"Brandon." The word came out as a toad's croak, so he tried again. "Brandon."

"Dad!" Brandon stepped away from the punching bag and gazed wide-eyed as Rhett approached. "I didn't expect to see you here today."

"I didn't expect to see you, either," Rhett replied, feeling as if he were choking on his words. "You were gone this morning when I woke up."

"I wanted to get an early start," Brandon commented, then punched the bag *one-two*.

"An early start? At what?"

That question sent Brandon into a series of punches, and he looked as if he were fighting back tears, even through the sweat. His eyes were red rimmed and his jaw was clenched.

"I was worried about you, son."

Brandon stopped punching and wiped the sweat off his forehead with his arm. "Why?"

Rhett didn't know whether to laugh or cry. "I thought you might have run away."

It was only now that he realized *why* he'd panicked so completely when he thought Brandon had taken off on him.

Kayla.

She'd left him in the middle of the day, while he was at work. No Dear John letter. No clues explaining why she left. Just ruffled drawers, hangers all askew, and—

His stomach clenched so tightly he thought he might wretch.

The snow-globe.

She'd taken *The Phantom of the Opera* snow-globe from their mantel when she left. The expensive mask-and-rose keepsake he'd surprised her with on their first Christmas together was gone, along with his wife of eight years.

The memory drifted back, clouded and buffered by time. Kayla was a Broadway aficionado. They'd even flown to New York for a weekend one summer.

And that's how he knew for sure she was gone for good.

The snow-globe represented their marriage, in a way, though he hadn't recognized that fact until now. When he'd seen the conspicuously empty mantel, he'd broken down and cried.

And ever since that day eight years ago, he'd been paying for it with every breath he took and every beat of his heart.

They'd eventually worked out their problems, Kayla and he. And then on the verge of Kayla's return home, she'd caught meningitis and died within the week, leaving Rhett alone with an eight-year-old son to raise.

And *that* was why seeing Brandon's football missing had sent out an all-points bulletin in his mind. It was just a little too familiar for comfort.

Brandon hadn't replied to Rhett's statement, other than to continue punching the bag with renewed enthusiasm.

"Can you stop swinging for just a moment?" Rhett snapped, his fear now exhibiting as anger.

"Yeah, sure." He obeyed, but he looked sullen in complying.

"Why did you take your football with you?"

It was all he could think of to say, and he was stuttering the words through a dry throat as it was.

But he had to know.

Brandon shook his head. "I don't want to talk about it."

Without thinking, Rhett stomped forward and swung his son around by the elbow. "Well, you're *going* to talk about it, young man."

Aaauuugh. Exactly the wrong thing to say, and especially the wrong way to say it. After all this worrying, he came down hard on Brandon? Whoever said *old habits die hard* wasn't kidding.

"I'm sorry," father and son said in unison, then laughed.

"You go first." Again, they'd spoken in perfect unison.

"I came here looking for you," Rhett said, affectionately socking his son on his shoulder.

"Me? Why?"

"I think you can answer that question," he replied.

Brandon's face paled. "You thought I ran off."

Rhett could only nod, for the lump in his throat had grown to bowling ball proportions.

His son's dark eyebrows scrunched over his blue eyes. "I wouldn't do that. I'm not like—" He shut his mouth abruptly when he realized what he was going to say.

"No, you're not like your mother," Rhett assured him. "At least, not in that way." He ruffled his son's hair. "You do have her eyes."

"I'm not going anywhere, Dad," Brandon affirmed, his voice hoarse and cracking. "I swear it."

"I'm glad to hear that." Now it was Rhett's voice that was cracking, sounding every bit as awkward as his gangly teenage boy's.

"Dad?" Brandon sounded concerned.

Rhett squeezed his eyes shut for a moment and took a deep breath, regaining his control.

"Tell me," he said, pinching the top of his nose against a sudden headache, "why you took your football with you this morning."

Brandon swung a sudden left, square on. The punching bag swung wildly. "I don't want to tell you."

"Why not?"

Brandon answered with a *left-right-left*. "Because it's stupid."

Rhett reminded himself to keep it cool, composed. "Tell me anyway? When you're ready to talk, I mean."

Brandon's gaze switched to the door. "You can come in, Miss Brockman," he said, cracking his serious veneer.

Rhett's face warmed. "How did you know?"

"Are you kidding?" *Left-right-left.* "You smell like her."

"Better than I usually smell, huh?"

Brandon chuckled. "Yeah. Much better."

Callie laughed as she exposed herself from her hiding place. "I'm afraid I'm just as guilty as your father. Vanilla Musk. I never leave home without it."

"Yeah, but how come *I* smell like Vanilla Musk?" he asked, rubbing the back of his neck, kneading his pinched muscles.

The movement did, in fact, send a whiff of her delicious-smelling perfume through his senses.

"I always put a dab of perfume on my wrist in the morning," she admitted.

Now why did her wide grin remind Rhett of the Cheshire cat's craftiness?

"It must have rubbed off when you were holding my hand."

The cinders already scorching on Rhett's face turned into a bonfire and he didn't dare look at his son. What must Brandon think?

"Should I get out of here and leave the two of you alone?" This from his obviously incorrigible son's mouth, and Rhett's gaze immediately ping-ponged between Brandon and Callie.

Their expressions were identical—a conniving blend of indulgence and amusement. It looked suspiciously as if they were collaborating.

Rhett crossed his arms over his chest and huffed. The brunt of a joke, when only moments before he'd been in a heart-wrenching situation.

The two in question laughed out loud at his harebrained reaction to their teasing.

His gaze switched to Callie, and he belatedly realized what she'd done. With one smile, she had turned a tension-wrought situation *he'd* created into circumstances they could all smile and joke about.

For the first time since he'd discovered Brandon missing that morning, he smiled as well.

Thank you, Jesus!

Callie definitely deserved his thanks, as well. It was a team effort, if he'd ever seen one.

''You want to show me how to throw this thing?'' Callie asked Brandon, hefting his prize-winning football.

"He can teach you how to be a linebacker," Rhett teased. "But a quarterback he's not."

"Linebacker? That sounds daunting."

"Nah. You can do it. Go out for a pass." Brandon popped the ball from Callie's grasp and ran backward, hefting the ball with one arm. "Not a quarterback, huh, Dad?"

"The only kind of *going out* I know about involves dinner and a movie." Callie laughed and waggled her eyebrows.

"He means run that way," Rhett said, pointing to the far wall.

"Okay, if you say so." Callie took off at a jog.

"I suggest you look back from time to time," Rhett coached, "or Brandon's liable to zing you in the back of your head."

"Dad. I'm not *that* bad."

"Just warning her."

"What am I supposed to do now?" Callie called from the other side of the gym.

Rhett chuckled. "Look heavenward and pray."

Both Brandon and Callie proved him wrong in an instant, and his jaw dropped in amazement.

Not only did Brandon spiral the football right into her arms, but Callie *caught* it, and didn't even bother to make it look difficult.

Her arms in a victory *V*, she trotted back to where Rhett and Brandon were standing, wide-eyed. "Yeah! And the crowd goes wild!"

Rhett narrowed his eyes on her, his suspicion growing. "Dinner and a movie, huh?"

Callie shrugged and bent over the football. "Blue Thirty-Two," she called to her left. "Blue Thirty-Two," she called to her right. "Hut, hut."

She pulled the ball shoulder high and faked a pass. "Okay, Shrink, go long."

She didn't have to tell him twice. Rhett tossed a glance behind him and ran for the opposite end of the gym, his tennis shoes squeaking on the polished wood floor.

"Hey, Brandon, are you going to blitz her or not?" he called, but a moment later the football hit him square in the chest—a throw any dolt could catch, much less a man who was once a high school halfback.

As he returned the ball, the light, silvery peal of Callie's laughter rang in his ears.

"Where did I go wrong?" he asked, grinning like an ape with a bushel of bananas.

"You forgot I have a twin brother," she said, playfully socking him on the shoulder. "Colin didn't go for dolls, so I learned how to play football."

"Cool," Brandon said, knocking the football from his father and tossing it in the air.

"Smear, to be exact."

"*Smear?*" asked Rhett and Brandon simultaneously.

Callie flushed. "I'm showing my age here, aren't I?

"Too old for you," she said ruffling Brandon's hair. "And too young for you." She winked at Rhett.

"Hey, now," he warned. "Watch the cheap shots. What are the rules for this Smear I'm too old to play?" he teased. "It sounds promising to me."

"Trust me, you're too old," she said, her eyes sparkling. "*I'm* too old. I'm definitely not suggesting it as a family game."

Her cheeks flamed attractively, and she rushed on, covering her faux pas with more words. "Smear is a game for the *very* young—those that don't mind getting their brains bashed in."

"That's my son," Rhett said, slapping Brandon on the back. "He goes out of his way to find opportunities for him to get his brains bashed in."

"Dad," Brandon warned. And to Callie, "Can you show me how to play?"

Callie barked out a laugh. "No, I won't show you. But I'll tell you about it, if you're that interested."

"Humor us," Rhett entreated.

"Okay. Well, the guy—or girl—with the football spirals it straight into the air. Then whoever catches the ball dodges around trying to get away from everyone else."

She smiled widely. "Who are, of course, all aiming to tackle the one with the ball."

Rhett lifted his eyebrows. "That's it?"

Callie nodded emphatically. "That's it. I told you it was for young people who wanted their brains bashed in. No reasonable, mature adult would play Smear."

Brandon laughed aloud, then tossed the ball in the air and called, "Smear!"

"The really scary thing," Callie continued, ignoring the football that bounced off her shoulder, "is that Colin used to talk me into *catching* the ball when we played that game as kids. Is that lame or what?"

"Sounds pretty gutsy to me," said Rhett.

"Stupid, not gutsy," Callie corrected. "Which is, perhaps, why my present circumstances compel me to carry a gun and get my brains bashed in on a regular basis. Those young-girl brain cells that were supposed to protect me from such idiocy obviously got knocked out of me playing Smear."

She flashed both of them a feisty grin, her silver-blue eyes sparkling with mirth. "Hmm. I wonder what that says about male brain cells, since little *boys* usually…"

She let the sentence dangle.

Rhett wrapped his arms around her tiny waist and swung her around, tickling her ribs.

She screeched in protest.

"Don't go there, lady," he warned with a low, playful growl.

"So, hey," Brandon interrupted. "Are we going to play football, or what?"

Callie reached for the ball. "As long as it's not Smear, you're on."

Rhett grinned wickedly. "Boys against girls?"

Her laugh was light and silvery, as was the gleam in her eyes. "Of course," she said, tucking the football under her arm. "What else?"

Chapter Fourteen

"So anyway, since I've been forbidden to go out for football this year," explained Brandon as he swept out the gym, "I decided to see if I could form a team at church."

Callie was impressed. Football was obviously a big part of Brandon's life. He didn't make the statement with any kind of malice, but rather with a remarkable maturity that showed he could swallow the pills life offered, accepting the bitter with the good.

"And?" Rhett asked, looking up from where he was mopping the floor.

Callie's throat swelled with emotion as she

witnessed the love and compassion shining like a beacon from Rhett's eyes.

It was that look, more than the feel of his arms around her waist earlier—as nice as that had been—that made her heart soar. She wanted to throw her arms around his neck and never let go.

Fortunately for both the Wheeler men, she restrained herself admirably.

"Did the other kids leave before we got here?" Callie asked, remembering the train of conversation and Rhett's unanswered question.

"They never showed."

Brandon murmured the words under his breath, and Callie thought Rhett probably didn't hear his answer.

"No one?" she asked gently, quietly, instinctively certain Brandon didn't want his father to know.

"No one," Brandon confirmed, looking away.

"Oh, now, you can't say that," she admonished loudly, bringing Rhett into the picture without exposing Brandon's inner heart for public display. "Your old man and I play a mean game of football."

Brandon smiled, the same adorable, lopsided grin that made his father so attractive. "Yeah, I guess you're right. No big deal."

"I'm glad to hear it," Rhett said, misinterpreting the words.

Callie didn't try to enlighten him. "Are you big, sweaty fellows ready to get some chow, or am I the only one with a rumbly in my tumbly?"

Rhett laid an arm across her shoulders and guided her toward the door. He was drenched with sweat, she hadn't been kidding about that. But she wasn't about to squawk about the steamy, appealing mix of aftershave, sweat and man. He was all male, and she was enjoying every moment in his arms.

It was only now, playing football with Rhett and his son, that she realized why her heart zinged every time she saw—or even thought about—Rhett Wheeler. Smiling, she kept her newfound knowledge to herself.

"Pooh Bear, in case you were wondering about the reference," she said instead, patting her stomach.

"I knew that," Rhett insisted. "What, do

you think I had a deprived childhood or something?''

She didn't want to shrug, afraid he'd remove his arm from her shoulders, so she just cocked her head so she could smell the fresh wintergreen of his breath. ''I wouldn't say *deprived,* exactly. It's just that all that football…''

''She's got you there, Dad,'' Brandon chimed in. ''I think we ought to go out for pizza. What do you say, Callie?''

Callie exchanged glances with Rhett to see his reaction. He smiled and nodded.

''Anything but those disgusting little fishy-things,'' she agreed happily.

Rhett snapped his fingers and shook his head. ''And here Brandon and I were looking forward to our usual—double anchovies with extra fish—I mean, cheese.''

Since she and Rhett had arrived in her SUV, she handed him the keys and motioned Brandon into the back seat.

''You put so much as a scratch on this truck and you won't like what's coming to you, Wheeler,'' she teased. ''No mercy.''

He threw his hands up in protest. ''Hey. I'm an excellent driver.''

"I'll drive," Brandon offered.

"No," both adults said simultaneously.

"Sheesh, I was only asking."

"Ask with somebody else's vehicle, kiddo," Callie said, shaking her finger at him in rebuke. "Buck here is my pride and joy."

"Buck?" asked Rhett, his voice a combination of disbelief and amusement.

"Buck the Wonder Truck." She gave him her best Southern belle smile. "What, you big, handsome, muscle-bound men don't name your cars?" She swatted him with a fan made of her spread fingers. "Now, Rhett!"

He grinned. "Frankly, my dear—" he paused and flashed her his crooked grin. "Men do *not* name their vehicles."

"Well, women do." She paused and scrunched her eyebrows together. "At least, I do."

"Must be all those extra brain cells," Brandon commented from the back seat.

"Keep it up, kiddo, and you're going to get anchovies for dinner, hold the pizza." Callie shot him her best scowl.

They pulled into the pizza joint, and Brandon was out the door without a word.

"We won't see him until the pizza arrives," Rhett explained with a laugh. "He'll get busy playing arcade games with his friends and forget all about us."

He led her to a booth tucked far away from the blaring jukebox. The vinyl booths were a garish red, typical of a pizza joint, and Callie stuck to the seat as she slid toward the wall.

As a waitress approached, Rhett slid in next to her, sending Callie's heart slamming against her rib cage. Her equilibrium became even more off balance when he casually rested his right arm over the seat back.

"What can I get you to drink?" asked the waitress with a practiced smile, and Callie silently blessed her for giving her something else to think about besides Rhett's nearness.

"Cola," Rhett answered.

"That sounds good. I'll have one, too." Callie slid her glance to Rhett and smiled.

"Domestic bottles and beer on tap is two for one until six," the waitress suggested in a monotone, not looking as if she cared much one way or another. "Happy hour, you know?"

"Thank you, but no," Rhett said, friendly

and polite, sending the waitress off with their two soda orders.

"What about Brandon?" Callie asked, amazed she could think straight, never mind find her voice, in this close a proximity to Rhett.

"He'll get his own soda. Root beer from the fountain. It's his favorite."

Rhett turned his attention to the menu, giving Callie the much needed opportunity to adjust to the curves being thrown at her.

Why was he sitting next to her?

She slid her glance to Rhett, but he appeared to be studying the menu and didn't notice her perusal.

Of course he didn't sit across from you.

She carried on her internal conversation, trying to reason with her treacherous emotions.

He and Brandon couldn't share one side of a booth, and it would be awkward for Brandon to sit with a cop—especially one who'd brought him home from the station only weeks before.

That's all it was. Courtesy. Rhett was simply the nicest, kindest man she'd ever met.

But her heart refused to hear it, preferring a

tune of its own, a song where Rhett and Callie rode off into the sunset on a strong, gallant steed.

And, of course, the obligatory happily-ever-after. What fantasy would be complete without it?

All this, and she hadn't read a fairy tale in years. Maybe getting jarred playing football *had* shaken up some of her childhood brain cells.

"Pepperoni okay?" Rhett asked, breaking her away from her thoughts.

"Mmm. Yes. Extra cheese."

"And no anchovies." He signaled to the waitress and placed their order.

When she was gone, Rhett chuckled and shook his head. "You'll get a real kick out of watching Brandon when the pizza arrives."

"How's that?"

Rhett was a "hand talker," someone who couldn't speak a sentence without gesturing with his hands. And every time he gestured with his right hand, Callie very nearly jumped out of her skin, especially when his fingers brushed the sensitive area on the back of her neck.

"You just watch," Rhett continued, appearing not to notice the way the casual stroke of his fingers in her hair was affecting her. "Brandon has a pizza beacon. The moment the waitress shows up with the goods, he'll be slouching in his seat as if he'd been there all along. And stuffing pizza in his face at the speed of light."

Callie chuckled, ultra-aware of the movement of his fingers in her hair. If he kept it up, or worse, slid his arm down to her shoulder, she wasn't positive her lungs would remember to function.

As it was right now, she could barely breathe, and had to coach herself.

Breathe in. Breathe out.

She'd make a great Lamaze instructor some day, she thought wryly.

"You might want to be careful of your fingers when you go to get a slice of pizza for yourself," he suggested, brushing her shoulder blade.

Her breath caught. If anyone needed to be careful with their fingers...

"Around food, I mean. Especially pizza," he continued, stroking her hair.

"Brandon turns into an animal, starts eating everything and anything. It's not a pretty sight."

"No, I expect not." Callie unwrapped her silverware from the napkin and twirled the spoon around her fingertips.

Did Rhett feel the tension crackling in the air between them, or was it all one-sided, a figment of her overactive imagination?

"Why haven't you ever remarried?" she blurted.

It wasn't exactly small talk, but then again, Callie had never been good at keeping her mouth shut when she should.

Rhett looked stunned, and Callie prayed for a hole to open up in the floor and swallow her.

Not only was her question serious and personal, but it was none of her business, and they both knew it. Blurting such a question out of the blue gave it the impact of a nuclear weapon detonating.

Chalk up a new most embarrassing moment for Callie Brockman. But there was no sense dwelling on it. She couldn't take it back.

She sipped at her soda and plunged forward.

"Let me guess. Your Desired Attributes in a Wife list is so lofty a real woman can't possibly hope to attain that status. Impossible to fulfill. So long it makes Santa's list seem like child's play."

Rhett took his time answering, thoughtfully tapping the menu against the table, turning it at square corners with every tap.

At long last, he smiled, which Callie took as a positive sign.

"Okay. I admit I had a list."

"You did?" He couldn't have surprised her more if he'd said he was already married.

He shrugged. "I didn't write it down," he protested. "But I guess I was looking for a certain type of woman. It was more of a mental list."

"Enlighten me," she begged, keeping the teasing tone in her voice. "We women have shared our list for centuries, but you guys have been a little tight-lipped."

"Yeah? I'm interested. What's this womanly list of manhunting? I married young, so I must have missed that information."

She winked at him. "Oh, come on. You

couldn't possibly have missed it. It's been around since Adam and Eve.''

''It has?'' Absently, he brushed the hair on her neck with his fingers, making it exceedingly hard for her to concentrate.

''Why, tall, dark and handsome, of course. Don't tell me you haven't heard that before.''

Rhett laughed. ''You were beginning to have me worried. I thought maybe I really missed out.''

She gave him a blatant once-over. ''Believe me, Rhett,'' she said, her voice husky, ''you didn't miss out on one of them. Tall, dark and definitely handsome.''

He blushed. Thirty-some-odd years old, and he actually blushed! Callie was beginning to like this game.

''You're going to laugh if I tell you what I thought,'' he said, chuckling softly.

''Do tell.''

''I wanted a woman who baked homemade cookies.'' He was blushing again.

''I make homemade cookies,'' she blurted, then immediately regretted it. When was she ever going to learn to leave well enough alone and keep her *mouth shut?*

He grinned. "You certainly do. And I have to say, they were the best sugar cookies I've ever tasted."

Callie folded her hands on the table and stared through them. *Oh boy.*

They sat silently, each with their own thoughts, for several minutes, then Rhett turned to her, his free hand stroking her chin. "Truth?"

"Truth."

"I think God's got a wife already planned for me."

Normally, she would have laughed derisively at such a statement, but not with Rhett's green eyes, almost brown in the hue of his brown leather jacket, shining with his faith.

"How are you supposed to know she's the right one?" she asked, and realized she honestly wanted to know.

"I'll know," he affirmed resolutely. "Here." He thumped himself on the chest. "Faith is the substance of things hoped for, and the evidence of things not seen."

She assumed the quote was from the Bible, though she'd never heard it before. Rhett's words—or maybe more accurately, *God's* words—branded themselves in her mind.

"So she has to be a Christian," she said, as a statement rather than a question.

Rhett nodded. "God will work it out."

She reached up and ran the backs of her fingers across the rough stubble of his cheek. "I hope you find her. I really do."

Callie could hear the mental *scritch-scratch* of her name being crossed off Rhett Wheeler's list. And for some reason, that rejection hurt more than she thought it would, or should.

But she didn't blame Rhett.

His faith was important—no, *vital*—to his life. Callie couldn't share that, though she wished with all her heart she could.

"I'll know her when I see her." He sounded so sure of himself and of God, that Callie believed him. How could she not? God was real, for Rhett.

"Pizza," exclaimed Brandon, appearing just as miraculously as Rhett had said he would. Moments later, a huge, steaming pepperoni pizza with extra cheese was set on their table.

"You know, Brandon," said Rhett with a casual smile, "since we've been playing football this afternoon, it got me to thinking."

Brandon only nodded, as his mouth was already full of pepperoni pizza.

Rhett put his elbows on the table and steepled his fingers. "About football."

Callie's throat caught, as she realized where Rhett was directing the conversation. She remembered that first night they met, when she'd accused him of being a bad father.

That seemed so long ago, now. She hadn't known the tremendous integrity of the man beside her.

"Is it too late for you to go out for the Prospectors team?"

Brandon shook his head. "They're only halfway through training camp. Why?"

"So you can still walk on?"

"Sure." Brandon took another bite of pizza, nearly half a slice in one mouthful.

"Good. I'm glad to hear it. I want you to walk on. You deserve your shot at the varsity team. I'm only sorry I didn't tell you earlier, or that I ever said you couldn't go out for the game at all."

Brandon shook his head and took a long gulp of soda to wash down his pizza.

Callie raised her eyebrows at Brandon's denial. She glanced at Rhett to see how he was taking it, and saw a mirror image of her expression on his face.

"Why not?"

Brandon put his palms to his head and shoved his fingers through his hair. He looked more uncomfortable now than the night she'd brought him home from the police station.

"Talk to me, son," Rhett said, his voice low and even.

"I don't want to play football, Dad."

Rhett frowned, his dark eyebrows forming a *V* over his nose. "Come again?"

"I don't want to play football."

Rhett turned his gaze to Callie. "Do I have cotton in my ears, or did my son just say he didn't want to go out for football?"

"Sounded that way to me," she said lightly.

He turned back to Brandon. "Why don't you want to play football? You've always wanted to play football, ever since you were six years old. Of course you want to play football."

Rhett nodded and stuffed a breadstick in his mouth, saying without speaking that the subject was closed.

"You don't know what I want anymore," Brandon grumbled under his breath.

Callie had the sneaking suspicion the Wheeler men had just forgotten her existence. They glared at each other across the table, both too stubborn to speak.

Must be a family trait.

She decided to jump in, willing to risk her neck for the men in her life. "If you ask me, I think you should—"

Rhett and Brandon both jumped as if startled, then looked at her with a combination of surprise and annoyance.

She shrugged. "I just thought that…well, that you should talk."

Chapter Fifteen

❧

"We *are* talking," Rhett said through gritted teeth. Naturally, a woman would have a different idea about what it meant to talk. But he was glad she was here with him, nonetheless.

Brandon scowled.

"Um, actually, no. You're ordering, and Brandon is growling. Pretty typical dad-teenager conversation, I think."

Now wasn't that just like a woman to point out the obvious, Rhett thought irritably.

He reached his arm around her and pulled her into the crook of his shoulder, brushing back her silky hair with his hand. He felt more confident when he had his arms around her. "You know what? You're right. I am being overbearing."

Brandon grinned.

"Don't agree," Rhett warned.

Brandon shrugged. "I didn't say anything."

"You didn't have to."

"Shall we start again?" Callie asked, a little too brightly.

"You should have been Ann Landers," Rhett grumbled, pulling her closer so she knew he was kidding.

He leaned forward, wanting to convey the intensity he felt. Brandon would never know how much Rhett loved him, but he could communicate some of what he felt.

"Talk, Brandon. I'm serious. I know I haven't paid enough attention to you. But I'll make you a promise. Right here, right now, I'm listening to you."

Brandon looked away for a moment, and Rhett wondered if it was his imagination, or if he saw the sheen of tears in his son's eyes.

Either way, Rhett swallowed hard.

"I like football," the boy admitted. "But that's not what I want to do with my life."

With Callie's encouragement, Rhett nodded. "What I really want to do is be like you."

Callie reached across the table and took Brandon's hand. "You are like your father. More than you'll ever know."

The boulder in Rhett's throat grew larger, and he found it difficult to swallow.

"What I mean is, I want to work with you, Dad. I like what you do with the therapy dogs and stuff. I want to do that, too."

"My therapy dogs?" Rhett questioned, stunned. He would never have suspected his son to be interested in social work—which just went to show how little he really knew about the boy he'd been living with for the past sixteen years.

Brandon's blue eyes lit with enthusiasm. "What you do with those dogs and those kids is just awesome, Dad."

Rhett grinned so wide he thought his face might split. His son wanted to follow in his footsteps. Who would have guessed? He certainly had no clue.

"That's why you stole that shirt, isn't it, Brandon?" Callie asked softly, and the question was like a knife in the chest for Rhett. "So you could be near your father, have some of the attention he gives to the delinquent kids he works with. And the dogs."

Brandon nodded for Callie's benefit, but his gaze was locked on Rhett, who didn't know *what* to say. He did know what to do, though—kick himself in the backside a thousand times over for not realizing Brandon's desire earlier.

"I want to learn about your work. I want to help people like you do." His enthusiasm was contagious, and excitement brimmed from his eyes.

"Really?" Rhett hoped he didn't sound as choked up as he felt.

"I guess I pretty much have to participate in the therapy dog program, at this point," Brandon said, looking chagrined but pleased.

"Yeah, I guess you pretty much do," Rhett agreed. "I suppose you'll have to join ASAP."

He stopped and grinned. "How does Monday after school grab you?"

Callie reached under the table for his free hand and squeezed it hard, making his heart nearly stop. Her hand was so soft and warm, he was disappointed when she pulled it away.

"Can I go now?" Brandon asked, easily switching to an unrelated topic in typical teenage fashion.

"Get out of here," Rhett said affectionately.

When his son was out of hearing distance, he turned to Callie, who was beaming at him, her eyes full of tears.

"Did I do something wrong?" he asked, concerned.

"No," she said, sniffling. She wiped her eyes with the corner of her napkin and flashed him a wavering smile. "You did everything right."

"Well, that's a first," he quipped. "Sometimes I feel like a real lughead."

"You're not."

"Glad to hear it." He balled up his napkin and tossed it on the table.

"So…" he said casually, though what he was feeling was anything *but* casual, "What are your plans for tomorrow morning?"

"Sunday? The usual. Sleep in. Clean house. Watch TV. Why do you ask?"

"A couple of reasons."

"And they are…?"

"First," he said, making an effort to catch

her gaze and hold it, "I'd like you to attend church with Brandon and me."

Her eyes widened until she looked like a deer caught by headlights.

"If you aren't comfortable with that..."

"Oh, no. It's not that. It's just that no one has ever invited me to church before." She looked away, over his left shoulder, and her silver eyes glistened with tears.

"You've never been to church?"

"I went when I was a kid. But no, not as an adult. "Except that time with Brandon in the gym," she added with a shrug. "And I guess that doesn't really count, since I didn't actually make it to the service."

He brushed her cheek with his palm. "Then it's high time for you to go, don't you think?"

After a long pause, she spoke. "Yes. I do think." She grinned, putting him at ease. "What's number two?"

Rhett surreptitiously glanced around to make sure Brandon was out of hearing distance—not that he was overly concerned about it in a restaurant with the flashy lure of the brassy chirp and bang of video games.

"I want you to go with me to a breeder's kennel."

Her eyebrows rose in surprise. "I thought you got your dogs from the pound."

"I do." He paused and bowed his head toward her ear. "But this puppy isn't for the therapy dog program."

His heart welled in his chest and he grinned secretively. "At least, not directly."

Callie squealed and clapped her hands together. "Brandon!"

Rhett chuckled, feeling so happy he thought he might burst. "Yes, Brandon."

"What kind of dog are you getting him?"

As soon as she'd asked the question, she slapped a hand over her mouth and looked furtively around. "Oh, good. He's not around."

"If you really want to know," he said, trying to look as mysterious as possible, "I'll pick you up at 8:00 a.m. tomorrow morning."

"That's all you'll tell me?" she asked, laughing and playfully swatting him with her napkin.

"Oh, yeah. Don't you like surprises?"

"Of course. What woman doesn't?"

"Until tomorrow, then." Rhett popped another breadstick in his mouth, and the subject was closed.

For real this time.

Chapter Sixteen

Callie was pleasantly surprised to find she wasn't as uncomfortable at the church service as she'd imagined she'd be. The small community chapel was lovely, and the people were friendly, introducing themselves one after another and telling her how glad they were that she'd attended their service.

The oddest part about the service was the pastor's message. He presented a heartrending tale of God on a cross, forgiving those who crucified Him.

How could Jesus forgive the men who took his life?

She puzzled over that long after they'd gone on to the holy Eucharist and the closing hymn. This was a Jesus she hadn't met before, and she tucked the church bulletin into her purse so she could look up the passage in the Bible later, when she was alone.

Rhett was bouncing around like a kid on Christmas morning, anxious to be underway.

"God's really watching out for me," he exclaimed as he opened the car door for her and then slid behind the wheel. He let out a low whistle that sounded almost more like a cheer.

Callie grinned at his enthusiasm.

"I just happened to know about these puppies, and the timing couldn't be better. They're eight weeks old and ready for a new home."

"Am I still supposed to be in the dark as far as this puppy goes?" she teased.

He chuckled. "Okay. I guess I can let the cat—or *dog,* to be precise—out of the bag."

She slapped him playfully on his arm. "Oh, Rhett. You're teasing me again."

"I like to see you blush."

She grinned. "You better watch yourself, big guy. I like to see you blush, too."

His eyebrows disappeared under his hairline. "Do you, now?"

Callie looked away, knowing that the blush they were speaking of was spidering up her neck and onto her cheeks at that very moment.

When had it gotten so warm in here? She pulled on the collar of her blouse, wishing she'd thought to change into jeans and a T-shirt instead of the blouse and skirt she was wearing.

Panty hose weren't exactly an asset when going to look at a litter of puppies.

They pulled up to the breeder's house, an old-fashioned log-paneled A-frame, and as Callie stepped from the car, she immediately recognized that wasn't the only difference between this house nestled at the end of the block, and the others.

The backyard, a field, really, was deafeningly busy with the cheerful yip and bark of playful canines. Callie froze, her instinctive fear of dogs rising to the surface. Then she met Rhett's concerned gaze and found courage.

Rhett led her around the side of the house and through a chain-link gate to the back porch, where the breeder waited with nine roly-poly golden retriever puppies, ranging from a large, almost bronze-colored pup to a small, cream-colored fellow.

After Rhett introduced Callie to the breeder, a fifty-something lady named Tamara whose branding trait was her short, spike-tufted red hair, they were encouraged to interact with the pups—and their sire and dam, which were both on the property.

It was important to see the parents, Rhett explained, because that was a good indication of how the pups would turn out. These goldens were both of champion lineage, and had each earned titles in their own right.

Callie was amused by that fact, though she kept her thoughts to herself. While Rhett made a point of "rescuing" dogs from the pound for his therapy dog work, he wanted a certified, papered pup for his son.

Rhett reached for the bronze-colored girl, while Callie followed the cream-colored boy, who was, she decided after looking the other puppies over, the runt of the litter.

That probably explained why her heart went out to the little guy, whom she'd already mentally christened Butterboy. She had a perpetual weak spot for stragglers, especially one with the spunk and fight this little guy was showing.

Rhett pushed the bronze-colored puppy toward her, and she held the cuddly ball of fur in her arms, turning her on her back to scratch her tummy.

"What do you think of her?" Rhett asked, his face beaming with enthusiasm. "She's the biggest one of the bunch. Tamara said she was born first. And she's very laid-back. She likes to be held and cuddled."

Callie nodded and put the puppy down on the ground to see what she'd do. She whined and scratched at Callie's leg to get back into the warmth of her embrace.

"I like her," Callie admitted, "but I have to say this little guy stole my heart from the moment I saw him." She pointed toward the cream-colored pup, who was pulling at his big sister's tail and growling playfully.

"Stole your heart, huh?" Rhett chuckled and scooped up the runt. "Maybe he could teach me a lesson or two."

Callie's breath caught in her throat when he

winked at her, but she reminded herself he was only teasing her. Hadn't he told her just moments ago that he liked to see her blush?

"I don't know what it is about him, but something…I think Brandon will really like him. What do you think, Butterboy?"

Rhett raised an eyebrow. "Butterboy?"

"Well, I had to call him *something*."

"Yeah, but *Butterboy?*"

Callie laughed. "Hey, I was under pressure."

She reached out and scratched Butterboy behind the ears. He barked and wriggled, attempting to remove himself from Rhett's grasp and go back to Callie.

"Butterboy," Rhett said again, crossing his arms over his chest. "Hmm. Well, what I want to know is if you're going to come over and dog-sit when he starts barking and whining in the middle of the night? I'm pretty certain that dark puppy won't keep me up nights, but I don't know about this little guy here. He looks like a handful."

She sat down cross-legged and Butterboy immediately crawled into her lap and nipped at her fingers. She was glad he was playing—he had razor sharp teeth that hadn't been dulled by years of chewing.

Rhett crouched by her and offered his finger for dessert, laughing when Butterboy wrestled with his hand.

"You're the dog expert," she insisted. "You'd know better than I would which puppy is the best, especially to use in therapy dog work."

She chuckled when Butterboy jumped up on his hind legs and licked her chin. "Besides, it'll be Brandon's dog. You're definitely a better authority where your son is concerned."

Rhett grimaced. "I don't know about that."

She reached out and squeezed his hand, not knowing what to say, or how to talk her way out of it.

Rhett didn't react, except to scoop the puppy off her lap and turn him over in his hand, tickling his tummy. The puppy wiggled, but accepted the treatment with relative, if squirmy, equanimity.

After another minute of silent inspection, including taking a good look at Butterboy's teeth, Rhett turned to Tamara, who'd been sitting quietly on the porch, allowing them to interact with the puppies at their leisure.

"We'll take Butterball," he said, dropping the pup into Callie's lap while he fished for his wallet.

"But, Rhett—"

He cut her off, his eyes glinting with amusement. "I brought you for a reason. Picking a puppy is a heart thing. I knew you'd pick the one most suited for my son. And I was right. So don't argue."

Rhett grinned at the breeder and pointed at the cream-colored puppy again. "This one."

"But, Rhett…"

"I told you not to argue."

"I was just going to point out that Butterball is a turkey. It's Butter*boy* you're buying."

He laughed and shook his head. "Okay, but I'm warning you—Brandon is *not* going to go for that name."

She shrugged and tried to look offended. "I didn't expect him to."

After getting the papers signed and the pup in a carrier, they headed to Rhett's house to find Brandon.

"Have you talked to your brother yet?" Rhett asked, thinking of how upset she'd been when Colin had arrived in John Day.

Callie looked away. "No. I don't want to think about that today."

He chuckled. "Okay, Scarlett O'Hara."

"Hey, it worked for her," she protested. "Tomorrow *is* another day."

"Has he tried to contact you?"

She frowned and shook her head. "No. I thought he might, but he didn't."

"I think he's giving you space to come to grips with his return."

"Maybe."

Rhett knew he was treading on thin ice, but he continued anyway. "I think that shows how much he loves you."

Her eyebrows scrunched so low he could hardly see her eyes. "How's that?"

"If he didn't care so much, he would have pushed you to accept him back in your life. Or at least called you a lot."

Callie sighed. "Yeah. I guess you're right."

"So when are you going to call him?" he gently pressed.

"Talking about puppies was much nicer."

"I know. But you can't put it off forever."
He pulled his car to the curb and cut the engine.
"You have to work this out eventually."

Callie was out like a flash, opening the back
seat door so she could get Butterboy's carrier.
"I hope Brandon's home."

Rhett nodded in agreement and let the subject
drop.

Callie's situation was between her, Colin and
God. He only hoped she considered him enough
of a friend to turn to him if she needed help.

Besides, he was probably digging up old dirt
on Callie just to keep from thinking of his own
collection of problems. Brandon had said he
wanted a dog, but Rhett worried nonetheless.

At least his son was home, if the regular
pump of a bass guitar was any indication. What
was it about teenagers that made them feel the
need to turn their music high enough to break
the sound barrier?

"You'd better go in and get that kid to turn
his music off," Callie suggested. "It'll scare
poor Butterboy to death."

"Tell you what. You take B-boy out back,

and I'll bring Brandon outside to meet him.'' He took a deep breath and brushed his fingers through his hair. "I hope he'll be surprised.''

She rubbed her palm against his biceps, encouraging him even without the words that followed. "Don't worry, hon. He'll be surprised.''

"Brandon Adam,'' he called up the stairs, trying to sound as if he were angry. "Get your sorry carcass down here.''

The same words he'd used the night he met Callie. How appropriate.

"And turn off that music!''

Immediately the pounding bass ceased, much to Rhett's satisfaction. Had he ever been young?

"What's up?'' Brandon asked, taking the stairs three at a time. His expression said, *What have I done now?*

"Get out here,'' Rhett demanded, pointing to the back door. "I can't believe you, boy.''

Brandon frowned and headed out the door, Rhett moving in right behind him.

"I don't know what I di—''

He came to an abrupt halt in both word and action as his eyes lighted on the puppy.

Rhett grinned. "I thought this little fellow might come in handy in the therapy dog program."

Brandon whirled around, his whole face beaming. "It's for me?"

"*He's* for you," Callie corrected.

"Trust me. You *don't* want to know what she calls the poor fellow," Rhett added, enjoying the color that rose to Callie's cheeks.

"Brandon can name him," she insisted. "I just needed something to call him besides puppy, at least until we brought him home."

Brandon dropped to his knees and the golden retriever sprang for him. They tussled back and forth, the puppy yipping and the boy laughing.

"He's really mine," he said as if he needed to hear the words again to make them true. "To keep."

Laughing, Callie sat down on the lawn. "Come here, Butterboy," she called, slapping her thigh and making kissing noises.

"Butterboy?" Brandon protested.

"Well, his fur is the color of butter." She defended her choice of names with a dignified sniff.

"I told you that name wouldn't fly," Rhett teased. "It sounds like he's supposed to be for Thanksgiving dinner."

"Butterboy," Brandon said again. "Butterboy. Butter...*B*... Hey! How about Bullet? Here, Bullet, boy!"

The dog apparently liked his new name, for he made a beeline to Brandon.

Callie stood and stretched. "I like it. It fits his personality." She reached as if to pet the puppy, then ruffled Brandon's hair instead.

"Congratulations, kiddo," she said, affection lining her voice.

Rhett could only watch her, as he was both speechless and breathless.

What a difference a woman could make in this bachelor dad's life, never mind his son's. Callie was some special woman. He was beginning to think he might have to keep her.

Chapter Seventeen

Rhett felt foolish standing on Callie's doorstep and holding his breath like a teenager on his first date. He'd missed all this in high school, since he'd already been dating Kayla. Dating was an entirely new experience for him, and he wasn't sure he liked it. "Will you go to the homecoming dance with me?"

Understandably, her eyebrows disappeared under her hairline, but she recovered quickly. "Come again?"

Rhett cleared his throat and tried again. "I…er…wanted to know if you'd come with me to—"

"The homecoming dance. Yes, I heard that part."

"That's all I said."

Callie laughed. "I'm not sure I get it."

"What's to get?" Rhett parried, relaxing. As was typical whenever Callie was around, he felt at ease and completely, vibrantly alive and wonderful. "You, me, the dance…"

"Is this invitation in some official capacity? You need an extra cop on the premises to keep things under control?"

"In a small town?" He chuckled. "No, actually I—" he shifted from one foot to the other "—need a date. That is, if you're not busy."

She laid a hand on his arm. "I'd love to."

Grinning, he blew out the breath he hadn't realized he'd still been holding.

"When is the dance?"

He shrugged apologetically. "Tonight."

"Tonight?" she screeched.

"I know it's late notice…"

"Rhett, a *week* is late notice. This borders on *insanely* late. What time?"

"Er…now."

She nodded and pursed her lips. "Now, why am I not surprised?"

He dug into the pocket of his bomber jacket. "I bought you a corsage," he said, thrusting the orchid at her.

She took the flower graciously but didn't comment, which was a rare enough occurrence for Rhett to ask, "I haven't stunned you speechless, have I?"

A smile hovered on her lips, and as she raised her gaze, amusement brimmed from her sparkling eyes. "It's just that it's been a—ahem— a *while* since anyone's asked me to homecoming."

"Then you'll go?" He gave her his best wide-eyed puppy-dog look. "For me?"

"Well…" she hedged. "I'll miss the reruns of my favorite sitcom…."

"Please?"

"When you put it that way, how can I refuse?"

Her smile was contagious, and it left an imprint on Rhett's heart long after she'd run down the hall to change.

When she emerged from the hallway, the result was every bit as effective as if she'd waltzed down a grand spiral staircase. Rhett was the one stunned speechless. The short, sleek white dress subtly set off every womanly curve.

Rhett swallowed hard, and didn't stop gawking until she'd slid her arm through his.

"You're staring."

He cleared his throat. "Sorry."

"Is my dress not appropriate? Should I change into something different? I didn't have much notice to prepare," she slid an accusatory glance at him, "so I grabbed the first dress I found."

"It's perfect," Rhett choked out.

"I feel self-conscious," she continued. "I don't wear a dress very often. Will I embarrass you?"

If it had been any other woman, Rhett would assume she was fishing for a compliment; but with Callie, she appeared genuinely distressed, and he scrambled to put her at ease.

"Embarrassed? I'm going to be the envy of every man there."

"Speaking of which, why exactly are we going to this dance? I'm assuming most of the *men* there will be a little young for me."

Rhett chuckled. ''I forgot I'd promised to chaperon until Brandon came downstairs in a suit.''

It took only minutes to drive to the school. Callie held back when they made their entrance, but Rhett urged her on. He hadn't been lying to suggest he was proud to have her on his arm.

Brandon spotted them nearly the moment they walked in, and shyly introduced his pretty, vivaciously giggly girlfriend Kim to Callie. Brandon neglected to mention Callie was his parole officer, Rhett noticed; rather, she was introduced as Rhett's friend.

He was pleased to know that was true. As much as he treasured their working relationship, he much preferred the evenings at home they'd been spending together, sometimes talking late into the night, and sometimes splurging with popcorn and videos.

Giggling, Kim whispered something in Brandon's ear that made him grin, and the two teens slipped away. Rhett hardly noticed. In fact, very little caught his attention besides every gesture and nuance of Callie Brockman. Some moments he felt he could barely breathe, and other times he was light-headed, as if he'd taken in too much air.

Callie fidgeted, uncomfortable in her hose and heels, and even more disturbed by the odd way Rhett looked at her. She was wishing back the familiarity of true-blue polyester; anything to ward off this belated attack of adolescent awkwardness. She turned her thoughts to the music, but the pounding pulse of the bass coming from the speakers was enough to make her deaf for a week.

She breathed a sigh of relief when the DJ announced a slow set. But it was only a momentary blessing, for the DJ's next words shattered that moment of peace.

"I have a young man here who'd like to dedicate this song to his dad and his...parole officer?"

Callie's heart stopped dead as the DJ hooted with glee. "Now there's a combination for you. Dad and Cop, you know who you are."

The DJ put on a tango, at least Callie thought it was a tango, or maybe a mambo, well, something with a Latin beat, anyway.

Rhett dragged her halfway to the dance floor

before she realized his intentions. "I can't dance," she whispered, pulling back with all her weight.

Rhett chuckled. "Well, I can. I'll lead."

It was *much* more complicated than that. Callie had the proverbial two left feet, and dance lessons as a young single hadn't helped her a bit.

"You didn't say I had to dance," she whispered frantically.

Rhett continued to look unfazed, and shrugged casually. "Well, they do call it a *dance* for a reason, you know. Besides, we'll hurt Brandon's feelings if we don't dance."

"Oh, well, I..." She was suddenly wishing for the loud, fast music she'd moments before been wishing away. Reluctantly, she allowed Rhett to lead her to the dance floor. "Don't say I didn't warn you," she muttered under her breath.

As he took her in his arms, his soft, clean scent enveloped her. She felt dizzy, and she wasn't sure whether it was nerves or Rhett's nearness.

"Hold on, sweetheart, 'cause we're gonna

rumba,'' he whispered as he whisked her around.

She stumbled through the first few steps, but then the strong, syncopated music began to work its magic and she forgot about her feet, forgot about breathing. Her senses magnified until she could hear the beat of her own heart. As if in a dream, she forgot about everything except being in the arms of the man she loved.

Loved.

When the music ended and Rhett twirled her to a dip, her world turned upside down in more ways than one.

Chapter Eighteen

"Keep turning Bullet in a square," Rhett instructed, watching his son with the gangly puppy that, in a mere month, had learned how to sit, stay and heel to the boy's command.

"When can I start working with him off lead?" Brandon asked, keeping up with his exercise despite his obvious enthusiasm. "I think Bullet is ready."

"He may be, but you're not," Rhett said, laughing. "Learning to train dogs doesn't happen overnight."

Brandon commanded Bullet to sit, then let him off lead to run off his energy in the field house.

"Have you finished the book I gave you?"

"Yeah. But I'm going back through it, highlighting the areas I'll want to go back and study later."

"You're really serious about this, aren't you?" Rhett asked, pride welling in his chest. He'd never have thought his son would follow in his footsteps, yet Brandon had shown an amazing affinity, not only for dog training, but for working with people, as well. He didn't know how he'd missed his son's natural talent.

The boy didn't protest when Rhett insisted he clean kennels as an initiation into the business of social work and therapy dogs.

He spent his evenings reading dog-training books, saying he'd save his social work studies for college. And he'd been pestering Rhett for a week to take him on a *real* therapy dog visit.

"Tomorrow," he said aloud.

"Tomorrow, what?" asked Brandon, checking the food and water level of the dogs in the first two kennels.

"Tomorrow we'll go to Portland."

Brandon perked up. "For a therapy dog session?"

Rhett nodded, chuckling. "You have some community service to work off, remember?"

The boy had the good grace to look chagrined. "Yeah. Don't remind me."

"I'm going to invite Lance to come along, as well. He's almost finished his service, thanks to working with Bear."

Brandon caught his dad's gaze and held it, his look serious but his blue eyes gleaming with amusement. "Are you going to invite Callie?"

"Maybe. Why?"

"Because she's in love with you."

Rhett perked up as his heart took an emotional roller-coaster ride, but he tried to keep his expression in check. "What makes you say that?"

"Oh, come on, Dad. Everyone knows it."

"Define *everyone*."

"At church. At the station. Everyone at school who saw you two dancing. Even Bobby the dispatcher thinks you guys should be married."

Rhett tried not to look *too* pleased. "He does, does he?"

Brandon nodded emphatically.

"Well, I guess the only important opinion in this situation is Callie's," he commented, wishing he felt as sure as his son looked.

"She's a goner, Dad, trust me on this. She's over here every day anyway. She might as well move in and save herself the trip. And you—"

"We weren't discussing me," he inserted hastily. "Do you think I should call her?"

Brandon rolled his eyes. "Dad!"

He looked as if he thought his father had lost all his marbles. Maybe he had, Rhett thought, reaching for the phone.

In any case, he'd lost his heart long ago to a silver-blond lady cop who annoyed him almost as much as she exhilarated him.

"Callie," he said when she answered.

Brandon waggled his eyebrows. Rhett narrowed his eyes on his son, then turned around and cupped the receiver for what little privacy that afforded.

"It's Rhett."

"Yes, I know," she said in a teasing tone.

"Was it something I said?" he quipped, and her laughter reverberated through the phone line.

"Brandon and I are going to Portland tomorrow for a therapy dog session at the hospital." He lowered his voice, though he knew Brandon was directly behind him, and was no doubt straining to hear his father make an idiot of himself over a woman. "I thought you might like to join us."

"I'd love to," she exclaimed, then fell into a sudden silence.

"Callie?"

"I can't go," she answered, sounding as if the words were forced from her throat. "I have…something else I have to do."

Rhett waved Brandon away and sat down at his desk, gripping the phone with both hands. "Does this something have to do with your brother?"

He could almost see Callie cringe at the question.

After another extended silence, she answered. "Yes."

"You're going to confront him."

"*Confront* isn't the word I'd use, but it's been a month and it looks like that stubborn, mule-headed brother of mine is taking up permanent residence at the Quest Motel."

"He still hasn't tried to contact you?" he asked, surprised.

He would have thought by now Colin would have either hunted her down and forced the issue, or given up on restoring the relationship and moved on to other things.

"No," she answered, sounding equally as surprised. "Not after that first time."

Rhett frowned, stroking the rough stubble on his chin with the curve of his pointer finger. He wanted to help, but how?

"Tell you what," he said at length. "How about I take you out for breakfast tomorrow morning. Then we can go see your brother, and still have plenty of time to get to Portland with the dogs."

"You'd do that for me?" She sounded choked up, but relief was evident in her voice.

"Of course," he agreed immediately, grinning despite the fact she couldn't see him. "Why should you have to face this alone?"

And that wasn't all. He had the sneaking suspicion this confrontation, or encounter, or whatever Callie wanted to call it, would make or break the relationship, not only with her brother, but with him as well.

It was time for his love for her to stand the test of family—sometimes the toughest test in a relationship.

He was still unclear about Callie's faith commitment, but she'd been attending church regularly, and had even mentioned one day that she'd been reading the Bible he bought her.

So they stood a chance. Maybe.

And it was that big *if* that loomed before them, feeling every bit as large as the Grand Canyon. They were being tested through fire—and Rhett wasn't positive he'd come out unscathed.

But he had to risk it. He just had to.

Callie turned up the radio, hoping the familiar tune would erase the fear and uncertainty from her mind.

She'd been avoiding the unavoidable, prolonging the inevitable. And yet...

This last month had seen a change in her. Spending time with Rhett and Brandon became the highlight of her day, and even when she wasn't with them, they were never far from her mind.

They almost felt like a *family*.

But she'd blown it with her own, so how could she hope to make it with Rhett and Brandon, who'd already been through so much?

The closer she became to the Wheeler men, the more she knew she needed to finish what Colin had started—to make right that which once was wrong. To 'fess up to her part in Colin's painful past, and try to make a new go of it, brother and sister—and even her father, though God would have to work that part out, since her father had died several years ago in a freak car accident.

She knew in her heart the time had come to make things right.

And the oddest part was, she felt ready, and it was in part due to Colin's words on the day he'd returned.

She'd been thinking over that vacation Bible school experience, remembering the sanctity of the moment when she gave her heart to Jesus.

Was that just a childhood thing, or did it really mean something eternal?

Until she answered that question, she couldn't commit to Rhett, and she knew the relationship between the two of them was deepening to the point where commitment—*permanent* commitment—was more than a possibility. More like a probability.

She loved Rhett and Brandon with her whole heart, but they were both committed to the Lord. That stood between them like a chasm, and neither she nor Rhett could bridge that gap.

It had to be God.

Somehow, some way, the God whom she'd once denied even existed had to bring her over to His side of the playing field. And how He would do that, Callie couldn't say. She only knew she had to see Colin again, and take what came afterward one baby step at a time.

So when Rhett picked her up for breakfast, she was shaking with nerves, feeling as if her whole existence pivoted on this one point in time.

"Nervous?" Rhett asked in the car on the way to the Quest Motel.

She tittered through a scratchy throat. "Do I look it?"

He glanced at her and grinned. "Yeah."

"It figures. Where's the cop persona when I need it?"

"I don't think you need it, sweetheart," he said softly. "Just be yourself. And don't be shocked if Colin surprises you."

Five minutes later, she was standing before the door to Colin's room, trying to force air into her lungs when they refused to work on their own. She was feeling a little woozy, and wanted to sit down.

"You're hyperventilating," Rhett commented as he placed a reassuring hand on her back.

"I don't suppose you have a paper bag handy," she joked, though in truth she was quivering with apprehension.

"Don't take deep breaths, just slow ones," he counseled, pulling her to him for a hug. "And don't forget I'm right by your side."

"How could I forget?" She laughed shakily. "You're all that's holding me up."

"Are you going to be okay?"

She nodded. "I'm sure I'm making more out of this than it really is. Colin is my twin, after all."

She reached her hand up to knock and jumped back when the door flew open before she could lay a hand on it.

"Callie!" Colin exclaimed as surprise turned to pleasure.

He enveloped Callie in a bear hug, which by necessity included Rhett, also, since his arm was still firmly around her waist.

"Colin Brockman," he said, stepping back and thrusting out his right hand. "Callie's twin."

"Rhett Wheeler," he said without hesitating. "Callie's told me a lot about you."

Colin's glance went from Rhett to Callie, and then back to Rhett again. "Good stuff, I hope."

"What else?" inserted Callie, wanting to keep control of the conversation. "Rhett is with social services, so we work together," she said by way of explanation.

Colin gestured them both inside. "Any friend of Callie's is a friend of mine," he said, the humorous sparkle in his sky-blue eyes, remarkably like Callie's, indicating he suspected the relationship between his sister and the social worker was more than just friendship.

"Were you going out?" Callie asked, parking herself on one of the two double beds. "We can come back later."

Rhett's gaze flashed to hers, telling her without speaking that they were going to take care of this now, one way or the other.

"I was just going for a walk in the park. I've had a lot of time alone to think."

Callie looked down at her shoes. "I'm sorry about that," she said through a dry throat. "I should have come earlier."

Colin held up his hands. "No. I realized after I'd already contacted you that barreling into your life wasn't exactly the most brilliant way of reestablishing our relationship."

"It's my fault, too, Colin. I won't let you take all the blame."

"Let's call it even, then," he suggested with a wide smile.

"Now," he said, sitting on the bed across from Callie and rubbing his palms together, "did you bring a social worker to counsel us through this?"

Rhett chuckled and waved them away. "I'm only here for moral support."

"And physical support. I was so nervous before I came in here I nearly lost my footing."

"I'm glad someone is looking out for my sis," Colin said, flashing Rhett a grateful smile.

"Oh, believe me, she's the one looking out for me," Rhett said. "I'd be happy to pay her back just a little for all she's done for my son and me."

"He's exaggerating," Callie said, chuckling.

Still, her heart beat double-time, seeing the way her twin and the man she loved sized each other up. There'd been a time when Colin was ready to take off the head of any guy stupid enough to ask his sister out on a date.

But that had been a long time ago. They weren't kids anymore. And what she felt for Rhett wasn't a teenage crush.

Colin's eyes shone with mirth as he watched his sister's expression. "This sounds like a story I'd like to hear sometime."

His smile faded, and he reached across the beds and took both Callie's hands in his. "But first, I'd like to know why you've come."

Callie's heart swelled up with so much love she wasn't sure she could contain it. She wanted to laugh and cry all at once.

The speech she'd planned—the one where she explained how God had touched her life, and how she now understood why Colin had come—went whistling out of her brain, leaving a big blank spot and a mountain of emotion in its place.

"I love you," she blurted, hurling herself into her twin's arms. She *was* laughing and crying at the same time.

Then she found herself wrapped in two very strong sets of arms, one man on either side of her. "I love you," she said again, this time including Rhett in her proclamation. "And I'm making a royal fool of myself."

She sat back down on the bed and wiped her eyes while the men looked on. "I should have come to your graduation," she said to Colin. "And you'll never know how sorry I am that I didn't."

"I don't blame you for that, Callie. I know how Dad was. You didn't have a choice."

He paused and looked out the window. "I just wish we could talk to Dad now. Unresolved issues, and all that."

He was obviously trying for a light tone, but Callie could hear the pain in his voice.

"We can't change what's past," she said, wondering where this wisdom was coming from, "but we can forge on from here."

"Philippians," Colin said, hugging Callie one more time.

Yes, that was where she'd heard it before. "Listen to me, spouting Scripture. Go figure."

Both men beamed at her.

"God had this all planned out," Colin said, his assurance evident in his tone. "I would have had to leave tomorrow, whether you'd come to see me or not."

"Leave?" Callie repeated, aghast. "But we've only just started mending our relationship."

Rhett sat down next to her, and the comfort of his arm around her waist gave her the encouragement and strength she needed to deal with the new curve thrown at her.

"I'd love to stay, Callie, but I'm starting school on Monday."

"School? I thought you were in the navy."

Rhett ran his hand up and down her spine, and she focused on the movement instead of her flighty emotions.

"I am. I've managed to acquire my bachelor's degree there. But now—" he paused and licked his lips "—I'm going into the seminary, Callie. I'm going to be a navy chaplain."

"Oh, how wonderful!" Callie exclaimed, and realized only afterward that it was true. She *was* happy for her brother.

"I wish you the best," Rhett said, reaching out to shake Colin's hand.

"I'll be coming up here on breaks, so we can get to know each other again. And we can spend the Christmas holiday together."

He glanced from Callie to Rhett, then grinned. "Maybe we'll have something else to celebrate?"

Callie's face felt as if she'd been baked in the sunshine, but Rhett only smiled.

"Maybe," he agreed, tightening his grip on Callie.

Now what, thought Callie, was *that* supposed to mean?

She could only hope.

Chapter Nineteen

Rhett checked the leashes on all the dogs, tightened the bright-red sashes that proclaimed them therapy dogs, then pronounced everyone ready to enter the hospital.

He'd decided not to bring a dog for himself so he could concentrate on the others, especially since he was bringing in three rookie people and one rookie dog.

Not that he anticipated trouble. He didn't. In fact, he couldn't think of more pleasant company than his son, the woman he loved and a kid who'd gone from belligerent to buoyant. He surveyed his team with a smile.

Brandon and Bullet both looked antsy and wired. Callie, brimming with excitement, had her hands full with her black lab Merlin, who was at that gangly teenage-dog phase where everything he did looked awkward, and who was picking up on Callie's mood, which only made things worse for her. Lance stood nervously to the side, stroking Bear's head. Bear, of course, was just as laid-back as ever, ready and eager to party.

"They're waiting for us in the pediatric cancer ward, but just in case anyone else stops us and inquires about the dogs, let me do the talking," he instructed. "Usually, the therapy dog sashes are all we need to get through without a problem, but occasionally there's an overzealous janitor or something who thinks our dogs have germs."

His "crew" laughed nervously, and followed closely as he led the way into the hospital. No one stopped them, and they made their way to the children's cancer ward without incident.

Just before they entered, he pulled Callie aside, sliding his arm around her waist and pulling her close under his arm, just because he liked the feel of her there.

"I wanted to prepare you for what you'll see in there," he whispered for her ears only. "These kids look really sick sometimes, and many of them have lost their hair."

He smiled and squeezed her waist. "But they're God's children, and most of them are the toughest fighters you'll ever see in your life."

Callie set her jaw. "I'm ready. I won't make a scene."

Rhett chuckled. "I didn't think you would. But I know you have a heart of gold underneath that *tough cop* exterior, and I'd like to keep it that way."

He chucked her under the chin and gestured to the door, ready for his crew to do their work.

Callie—and Brandon and Lance, too, for that matter—looked like old pros at this job. Each of them moved between the beds, taking time to speak to each of the children personally, and allowing the dogs to do their good work, as well.

Even Lance, who Rhett admitted only to himself he'd been worried about, looked enthralled with the children, and happy to be helping out.

An hour passed in the blink of an eye, and the head nurse signaled casually for their departure from the ward. Rhett, in turn, waved his crew out, and led the way down the hall.

It wasn't until they'd hit the elevator that Callie broke down and cried silently, tears pouring down her cheeks, though she kept her thoughts to herself.

Rhett was so deep in thought, and Callie was crying so softly, he probably wouldn't have noticed, except that Brandon none too lightly nudged him in the ribs with his elbow and flipped his chin in Callie's direction.

Rhett reached for her and pulled her aside. "God gives meaning even to the shortest life," he said gently, but that only served to make things worse.

"I know," she said, pulling a tissue from her purse. "They were just so dear—and so brave. Their faith in God is astounding! I just feel blessed to have that small moment in time with them."

Rhett had been afraid of Callie's heart being broken. It was only now that he realized it was his own heart in the most jeopardy, seeing how the children in the cancer ward had affected his beloved Callie.

"I'm sorry," he said softly, wondering if he'd made a mistake to bring her here.

She looked up to him, misty-eyed. "When can we go back?"

Rhett's heart did a double whammy. Now why hadn't he expected that of her? She didn't pretend to be something she wasn't.

Callie Brockman was a strong, capable woman who was able to see the bad in a situation yet work for the good with all her might.

How had he ever gotten by without her in his life?

Brandon nudged him again. "I think you guys should talk," he whispered.

Who was the adult here? Rhett wanted to snap, but Brandon only grinned and reached to take Merlin from Callie.

"You guys ought to visit the maternity ward before you go," his precocious son announced. "I'm sure Callie will feel better after she's seen a few babies."

"Brandon!" Rhett muttered, low and threatening.

Callie blew her nose. "You know, I think he's right. I would like to visit the nursery. There's always hope, isn't there? Even in the midst of death, there is life."

Rhett nodded to Callie, not knowing what to say to her profound philosophical revelation.

Instead, he turned back to his son, whom he did have words for. "You're getting away with it this time," he warned, "but don't think you're off the hook for good."

"Take your time," was Brandon's response. "Lance and I will handle the dogs just fine."

"Yeah," Rhett answered dryly. "I'm sure you will."

The elevator stopped on the first floor and the two boys, Brandon with his two puppies and Lance with Bear, exited ahead of Rhett and Callie, who had to go back up to the third floor if they were to visit the nursery in the maternity ward.

Rhett caught the door before it closed and kept it open with his palm. "Hey, Lance?"

Lance turned around, quite a feat in his baggy jeans, Rhett thought, and flipped his hair out of his eyes with a toss of his chin.

"Fine job today, son."

"Thanks, Mr. Wheeler," Lance answered, shuffling his feet and looking away. He was clearly not used to receiving praise from anyone, most especially adults.

"I want you to have Bear," he said, though he didn't know where the thought had come from. Now that he'd said it, though, he realized the strength of that idea, just how right it was.

"Me?" Lance sounded astounded.

"If your mom won't let you keep him at home, you're welcome to use the kennel at the field house for as long as you need it. But he's all yours, buddy."

"Why?"

It wasn't a belligerent question, but rather an astonished one. Lance looked as if he'd misheard, as if it couldn't be true. Excitement and apprehension boiled just under the surface, Rhett thought, watching the myriad of emotions cross the boy's face.

He reached out his free arm and clasped the boy's shoulder. "You've proven yourself responsible," he answered unreservedly. "And what's more, Bear has kind of gotten used to you. I don't think he'd like it much if another kid came along and tried to take your place.''

Lance dashed his arm across the corners of his eyes and turned away, but Rhett could still hear what he said. ''Thanks, Mr. Wheeler. I'll take good care of him. I swear I will.''

Rhett, feeling kind of choked up himself, didn't know how to answer, so he let the elevator door close and punched the button for the third floor.

He felt as big and gangly as a teenager, with all this emotion floating around. He'd never been that affected by it before—social work had given him a hard heart, in some ways.

He wasn't sure whether or not this was a good time to regain what he'd lost, though. How would he ever get through these last few minutes with Callie?

He shifted his glance in her direction as nonchalantly as possible. She was crying again, and this time, she didn't bother to wipe the tears away.

Callie was wondering what she could possibly say to a man who'd just made a juvenile delinquent into a good citizen.

But words didn't seem enough to convey what she felt, so she remained silent.

She was more than a little embarrassed at Brandon's obvious attempts at matchmaking, but she couldn't see a way to gracefully bow out without hurting anyone's feelings, so she followed Rhett onto the third floor.

Unlike the cancer ward, the nurses here looked relaxed and smiling. This was a happy place to be.

One expectant mother trotted by her at a near jog, then stopped to grasp the handle attached to the wall when a contraction hit.

Callie's eyes widened, whether from the innate fear of childbirth, or from the lady's odd combination of actions, she couldn't say.

But the pregnant woman in question appeared to notice Callie's expression amidst all the puffing and blowing, and when her contraction was done, she high-stepped it back to where Callie and Rhett stood.

"Oh, you two must be checking out the ward. This is an excellent hospital. They have twelve birthing rooms, each with a theme. If you get here when it's not too busy, they even let you pick out the wallpaper.'' She stopped to pant and laugh. ''When is your baby due?''

Callie blanched and Rhett cleared his throat.

''I'm not...that is... Why are you jogging down the hallway?'' she asked instead.

Her diversionary tactic appeared to work, at least for the moment, and Callie breathed a sigh of relief.

''Helping the contractions along,'' the woman replied cheerfully. ''My name is Janet, by the way.''

She patted Rhett on the shoulder. ''You two will learn all about labor and delivery in your Lamaze class.''

She swept her hand toward Callie. ''Enjoy it, honey. It's one of the few times in a woman's life where she gets her feet rubbed without begging for it. Mmm. Mmm. Mmm.''

Callie wondered what rubbing a woman's feet had to do with having a baby, but she wasn't about to ask.

''We'll learn about it in Lamaze,'' Rhett echoed, sounding as stymied as Callie felt.

''Oh, yes. And all the panting and puffing, too. You get to be the coach, Daddy,'' she added, addressing Rhett.

"Okay," he answered hesitantly. "If you say so."

Callie wondered if Rhett had been present at Brandon's birth, but from the look on his face, she didn't think so.

That thought brought a smile to her lips, and the pregnant woman smiled back, though her forehead was glossy with a sheen of sweat.

"You don't get a ref's whistle or anything," Janet teased Rhett. "But you can wear a baseball cap if you want to."

He snapped his fingers. "And I had my catcher's mitt all ready to go."

The lady laughed, then groaned when another contraction hit.

Rhett moved to her side, supporting her by the arm that wasn't clamped white-knuckled to the handle on the wall. "Should I call a nurse?"

The woman held up a finger for him to wait, then panted her way through the contraction. "I don't need a nurse, honey, but I'd best be getting back to my room."

She took a deep breath and wiped off a drop of sweat that was threatening to drip off the tip of her nose. "This run-walk stuff appears to be working. That was only three minutes between contractions."

Callie thought she looked both excited and nervous, but then, who could blame her for either emotion, given the circumstances?

"My husband better get back up here pronto," Janet continued. "He went out for a burger. Wouldn't it just figure if he missed Jimmy's birth?"

"Jimmy?" asked Rhett, sounding confused.

"This is our third. We know it's a boy. He's been Jimmy since our five-month ultrasound."

"I didn't know you could do that," Callie exclaimed in wonder. "Know the sex of your baby, I mean."

"It's not an exact science, by any means— at least not with an ultrasound. But sometimes they can tell." Janet chuckled pleasantly.

"I think I'd rather be surprised," said Rhett, and Callie immediately turned her gaze on him, wondering if he was teasing.

He'd never looked more serious in his life.

He insisted on walking Janet back to her room, which Callie thought was terribly gallant, then obtained directions to the newborn nursery from Janet's husband, who had just arrived, and whose chin was smeared with mustard.

Callie restrained a laugh. The man really must have hurried with his meal.

Callie had been in a hospital once in her life—the day she was born. It made her nervous, and she wondered if she was taking on nervous energy from the maternity floor itself.

Labor and delivery. A baby of her own.

It wasn't something she'd given much thought to in the past. Until Rhett came along, she hadn't given *any* relationship much thought.

But now, staring at a row full of newborns behind warped Plexiglas, her opinions on relationships and babies did a sharp one-eighty.

"I'd like to have a baby of my own someday," she murmured, watching a newborn baby girl trying unsuccessfully to put her thumb in her mouth.

Unfortunately for the newborn, her fist kept getting in the way, and Callie laughed.

Rhett wrapped his arms around her waist and nestled his lips into the soft space at the back of her neck, sending shivers up her spine.

She froze, wanting to etch this moment in her memory. Right this instant, she was perfectly happy, perfectly content, and all was well with God and the world.

"You can have my baby," Rhett said, his voice low and husky.

She whirled on him, the spell broken. "I can't believe you said that!" she whispered harshly, not wanting to make a scene.

"What?" he responded, looking thoroughly flabbergasted. And annoyingly innocent. "What did I say?"

"You said… You said…"

She couldn't make herself say the words.

Rhett burst into laughter, gaining himself a stern look from the head nurse across the way. Callie tried to wiggle from his grasp as he reached his arms around her, but there was no stopping him from what he wanted, and it appeared, at the moment, that he wanted to hang on to Callie.

There was no doubt he could overbear her physically, so she simply froze in his arms and hoped her icy gaze would be enough to deter any *other* wandering thoughts that might be running through that mind of his.

He ignored her scowl and cocked his head until his forehead was touching hers and his warm breath caressed her cheek. "I wasn't coming on to you, Callie," he said with a chuckle, in that honey-rich voice that always made her knees turn to jelly.

Until *now*.

"I don't think this is anything to laugh about," she retorted. "And yes, you *were* coming on to me. I know a line when I hear it."

Again, he chuckled. "What I was trying to say—and what, I'm sure, Brandon is pacing around the car *hoping* I'll say, given his tactless hints—is, would you be my wife?"

Callie had been waiting her whole life for those words, but when she heard them, she couldn't believe they were true. "But you said…"

"That I'd like to have a baby with you." He grinned like the Cheshire cat. "And that's the God's honest truth. I want us to get married as soon as possible."

"As soon as possible?" she repeated numbly, waiting for her heart to start beating again.

"Tomorrow would be good."

"Tomorrow?" She screeched in full this time, and the head nurse sent another warning glare their direction.

"So Colin can be there. I'd hate for him to miss giving you away, and I surely can't wait for Christmas vacation to make you my wife."

"Your wife," she repeated, beginning to feel like a parrot, unable to come up with a thought or a word of her own, as every joyful emotion in the world washed over her in waves.

Callie couldn't think of a thing to say, but Rhett didn't seem to notice.

Apparently, he was lost in his own thoughts.

"My wife," he agreed enthusiastically.

He flashed her that heart-stopping, lopsided smile that made the laugh lines fan attractively around his warm green eyes, which were twinkling with merriment.

"And now," he said, kissing her between each word for emphasis, "maybe we can talk about those babies I mentioned...."

Epilogue

The young man set his jaw, his throat corded with strain. Surprisingly dark eyebrows scrunched grimly over wide blue eyes, a shady contrast to his closely cropped golden-blond hair. Long, muscular arms with hands tightly fisted crossed over a chest just beginning to show a hint of breadth.

He looked scared, completely out of his wits.

Callie smiled weakly and flashed a glance to the boy's erstwhile father. "Will you please explain to our son that babies have been coming for ages? He looks like he's about to have a nervous breakdown."

Rhett chuckled. He looked every bit as ruffled as Brandon: haggard from lack of sleep, his hair in adorable disarray. The Wheeler men. *Her* men.

"Callie did the hard part," he said, his voice gruff with emotion.

Callie waved him away. "Not that anyone can tell, what with you strutting around like a peacock," she teased affectionately.

Turning her attention back to her stepson, she asked, "Would you like to hold her?"

Brandon's gaze sprang to hers. "Me? Well, yeah. If you think I won't hurt her or anything."

"Piece of cake, kiddo," she assured him. "Your new sister is as excited to meet you as you are to see her." Callie carefully unwrapped the small bundle at her side. "Just support her neck to keep her head from bobbing."

Brandon didn't look too confident, and Rhett cavalierly moved to his side. "Hello, little pumpkinhead," Rhett crooned over the baby in a high, singsong voice.

"Please tell me you aren't going to call her that," Callie groaned.

"What's wrong with pumpkinhead?" He protested, looking offended.

"Her name is Abigail."

"Oh, but it's okay for you to name your truck Buck, and Brandon's dog—"

"Butterboy—I mean, *Bullet*—isn't the issue here," she interjected.

Abby squealed her agreement, and the three of them laughed.

Brandon held out a finger and laughed when the baby gripped it in her fist. The sight of her two favorite men with the precious gift of their new baby was almost too much happiness for Callie to bear. Her heart swelled until she thought it might burst. She silently thanked God for answering her prayers, even when she hadn't known she was praying.

Who knew that there could ever be such Love in the world?

* * * * *

Dear Reader,

Spending time in John Day, Oregon, with my characters in this novel, Rhett and Callie, was a special experience for me. Many of my extended relatives live in the John Day Valley, so it was a joy to bring to life a place where I spent many happy hours during my childhood.

But even more remarkable was the spiritual journey I experienced with these characters, from bitterness and resentment into joy and forgiveness.

As Callie Brockman learned, forgiveness is a choice, not an emotion. There's no mistaking that it's a tough choice to make, but usually the one we hurt most by clinging to the root of bitterness is us.

Jesus Christ forgave our sins when we were yet enemies of the cross. Can we in good faith do any less for those who've hurt or betrayed us?

I hope you'll take this moment to thank God for His wonderful gift of forgiveness, and to shed whatever burdens you may be carrying, as well; for His yoke is easy and His burden is light.

Your continued servant in Christ,

Deb Kastner

A DADDY AT HEART

A PADDY AT HEART

In this you greatly rejoice, though now for a little while, if need be, you have been grieved by various trials, that the genuineness of your faith, being much more precious than gold that perishes, though it is tested by fire, may be found to praise, honor and glory at the revelation of Jesus Christ.
—*I Peter* 1:6-7

To the Lord, for sustaining me through the valleys as well as the mountaintops. Without the strength, guidance and peace I've found in my Lord Jesus Christ, there would be no light in my days and no life in my steps.

To Joseph C., always. Without you, my books would never see life. Bless you for coming home from work and making dinner when I'm caught up in my work, and for understanding that I'm not *really* a space cadet—I'm just working on my book!

And to Annie, Kimmie and Katie.

Mommy loves you very much!

Chapter One

Ethan Wheeler shot a cocky grin at the woman across from him and leaned forward, resting his left forearm lightly on the cold steel of Glory Weston's desk.

Desk being a loose term, he thought as it shifted under the weight of his arm. The beat-up steel entity looked as if it had seen better days.

Lots and lots of better days, and some worse.

He pursed his lips against a smile. Most everything else in this office looked well used, from the beat-up file cabinets to the frayed white wicker trash can.

The pictures lining the walls gave the office both a professional appearance and a feminine touch, but he recognized them as prints, the type you found at a discount store. Nothing at all like the original—and very expensive— paintings he had hanging in his office.

Quite a contrast. But Ethan thrived on contrast. His confident grin widened at the thought.

The only exception to the organized chaos was shelter director Glory Weston herself. She looked as fresh as the first morning dew, her large green eyes joyfully flickering behind her glasses, and her short auburn curls bouncing with every toss of her head.

Ethan inhaled deeply of her light floral scent that had his head spinning for a moment. Nothing like the whiff of a sweet-smelling woman to start his day right, and Glory was making his day grand.

He turned his wandering attention to the stacks of paperwork lining her desk, and wondered if all the work was hers.

He thought it might be.

"Ms. Weston," he began, the first words of a well-rehearsed speech.

''Glory,'' she corrected, waving the file folder containing the proposal he'd given her.

The folder, he noticed with a frown, hadn't yet been opened. His gaze swept from the file to her face, and her own gaze snared him completely.

Her eyes, even from behind aqua-colored tortoiseshell-rimmed glasses, were extraordinarily clear, making him feel as if he could read the depths of her heart, except that it was like reading a foreign language. He knew the letters but the words didn't make any sense.

What he *had* seen was a subtle shift in her emotions, a faint wariness overshadowing her politeness. He was certain his own gaze hadn't changed, so why the sudden shift in hers?

He was determined to find out. He was good at ferreting out answers to tricky questions, especially with regard to people.

''Glory.'' Always start with a name, especially a first name. It put things on a personal level, which was where he wanted *this* particular conversation to be. A lot rested on this discussion, but he couldn't completely put aside that he was dealing with an especially pretty woman.

The pretty woman in question pasted a smile on her face that Ethan thought was as fake as his grandmother's front teeth. She pushed her glasses up on her face with a world-weary sigh.

Civil, but just short of friendly. Fire and ice. Even the unreliable Seattle weather didn't change that quickly.

Again, he shifted mental gears. "Look," he said, inhaling sharply. "I'm not just some guy off the street."

Glory chuckled. "Obviously."

Her gaze roved over his navy Armani suit and settled on the Serengeti sunglasses he'd half slipped into the front pocket of his crisp white cotton shirt.

Ethan fought the urge to squirm like a schoolboy. Instead, he straightened his shoulders and narrowed his gaze on her.

He didn't like the way his burgundy necktie felt suddenly, as if it were intent on strangling him, and he cleared his throat against the sensation.

"Maybe I should have sent my secretary."

She cocked a dark eyebrow over her questioning, slightly hostile eyes. "And why would that be? Not," she amended, "that I haven't dealt with my fair share of secretaries as shelter director."

Ethan shrugged, the answer suddenly eluding him. "I don't know."

He knocked a crisp beat on her desk with his knuckles and gave her his best grin. It was the best he could do at the moment.

One thing was for sure—his secretary, Mrs. Brewster, wouldn't be so flustered and tongue-tied by Glory Weston. How was he supposed to know a knockout like Glory would be running a shelter? He'd have pulled his lawyer facade a little closer had he known, and avoided the troubles of jabbering too much or coming up blank with nothing to say.

"What's your point?"

Ow! A knockout. Literally and figuratively. The woman was nothing if not direct.

"I only meant that I thought you might be more comfortable dealing with a…woman," he ended lamely.

"Why is that?"

"The, er—subject at hand. I, uh—guess."

It was amazing how a pair of green eyes

could make a lawyer who'd won national debate tournaments in college turn into a blithering idiot. He watched any semblance of maturity fly away.

"Look, Mr. Wheeler, I appreciate your concern, but I can assure you that you're no threat to me."

And I won't let you threaten my ladies, either. She didn't have to say it. He could read it in her eyes.

He wasn't a threat. She had to know. "I just thought…"

"I know," she interrupted. "And honestly, your thoughtfulness is much appreciated. However, it's quite unwarranted in this case."

She blew a wisp of hair from her forehead, and again, Ethan thought he detected a hint of weariness in her tone.

"I see."

"Do you, Mr. Wheeler?"

Ethan blinked, her candidness once again catching him off guard. "I see a perfectly capable woman who looks like she could use a vacation."

Ethan snapped his jaw closed so quickly his

teeth clicked. Where had that statement come from?

"I just want to help," he muttered, furiously backpedaling.

Glory sighed and pushed up her glasses, the hint of a smile playing at the corner of her mouth. "I know you do."

She steepled her fingers and tried to examine the man before her in an impartial manner. If, indeed, the ability for her to be impartial even existed.

Even seated, Ethan Wheeler looked tall enough to balance out his broad shoulders. He was a good-looking man by anyone's standards, hers most of all.

And his smile was unquestionably contagious. When he smiled, she wanted to smile, too.

It wasn't the first time she'd been approached by a large corporation wanting to make a donation to Angel's Wings Women's Shelter, which she administrated under the authority of a local board of directors. But it was definitely the first time she'd had the CEO of such a corporation make a personal call to her downtown office where she met with clients, under this, or any other circumstances.

The *Wheeler* in Wheeler and Associates, a most respected law firm. She took a deep breath, and another good, long look. Ethan Wheeler fit the bill, but not the description.

Lawyers didn't smile, did they?

She didn't particularly care for corporate write-offs as a means of funding, since she personally thought it was more a way to knock down corporate taxes than to make a real difference to the women who sought Angel's Wings for refuge.

But beggars couldn't be choosers, no matter what her personal feelings dictated. So she'd accept the money Mr. Wheeler offered just as she'd done with many before him. Then she'd send him on his merry way, and use each dollar he gave her to the best of her ability to help the maximum number of needy women and children in her care.

She'd even gone so far as to solicit such funding, which was why, she assumed, Ethan was here.

And yet....

She met his intense, brilliant-blue-eyed gaze head-on, and he smiled crookedly in return, displaying dazzling whites she couldn't help but admire. Along with everything else about him.

The man was flawless in every feature—every hair in place, every intricate detail of his clothing attended to, from his polished leather shoes to the crisply folded burgundy paisley handkerchief peeking out of his coat pocket.

His striking gaze, and a laughing, honey-coated tenor. No doubt about it—Ethan Wheeler was one of God's finer creations. She couldn't help but admire him.

"I want to help," he said simply, reaching for the inside pocket of his suit jacket and pulling out his checkbook.

For a reason unclear to Glory, she believed him. She didn't even cringe when the leather of his checkbook cover slapped onto the desktop.

"Thank you." She cleared her throat. "I believe I can speak for the Angel's Wings' board of directors when I tell you your money is both needed and appreciated."

His smile dipped and wavered for a moment. Pain flashed in his eyes before he dropped his gaze, suddenly intent on selecting a pen from the variety of writing utensils in the glass pickle jar on her desk.

Glory wondered at what she saw, trying to discern a personal element in this meeting, a reason beyond a simple tax write-off. Her heart suggested he cared, and she speculated on the numerous possibilities that impression aroused.

He'd grown up in an abusive home? He'd had personal contact with a battered woman? His secretary, maybe? A friend?

Then again, it might be something as dispassionate and impersonal as having seen an investigative report on a prime time television news show. Or, as she'd first suspected, a donation to offset his Learjet and his summer home on the Hawaiian Islands, only with a Do Good for Humanity tag on it.

In any case, he looked distinctly uncomfortable.

Ethan cleared his throat and tapped his checkbook on the desktop, turning it one-quarter turn for each tap. ''I didn't come here to donate money.''

He straightened suddenly, crossing his arms

across his broad chest. He looked up and met her gaze, which only served to confuse her more.

"At least, I don't want to contribute *just* money." Abruptly, he slapped the checkbook to the table.

She couldn't tell if he looked more annoyed or frustrated. On examination, she decided he looked both.

"Go on," she urged.

"I can give you some money, too, if you need it. But will you look at my proposal? Please?"

Her eyes widened, and she nodded. For a man who didn't want to donate money, his checkbook was certainly prominent, yet there *was* something else...something important to him. Curious, she flipped open the file and began reading.

The blue-backed papers inside looked like a business contract, and as she read the title, she discovered that it was, in fact, a legal document.

Legalese with who-knew-what meaning. Latin and politics hadn't been her forte in college. She looked at Ethan and cocked a brow.

"I'm a lawyer," he admitted wryly, pursing his lips in a way that was just short of a smirk. "Contracts are my language."

She chuckled. "Well, they aren't mine. Do you care to interpret for me?"

Ethan blinked and cleared his throat. "I want to buy computers for your shelter, have them installed on a network, and get some extra phone lines put in so the women in your shelter will have access to the Internet," he said in one breath.

"I see," she said, though she didn't.

He stood so suddenly his chair spun on its casters. Leaning forward across the desk, he rested his knuckles on the file folder and caught her gaze with his.

"Anyone can give you money," he said, his voice low and fervent. "But money often gets routed into needless or unnecessary administrative details. No fault of yours, of course," he amended with a nod and chuckle in her direction.

"Of course," she answered wryly.

"I'm not doing this very well. The point I'm trying to make is that I want to do more for you." He paused. "For Angel's Wings."

"In the form of buying computers."

"Buying and *maintaining* computers. Head to toe. Extra phone lines and everything." He grinned persuasively. "I'm ready to write you a check today to cover setup expenses."

Now that he was standing, he was nearly dancing around her desk, both in an effort to convince her and as a way to release excess energy. The man exuded energy.

"I'll be back regularly to make sure everything is carried out as planned. I won't miss a single detail, I promise." He chuckled. "Easy as pie, punch and all those other *P* words. All you have to do today is sign on the dotted line."

"Said the spider to the fly," she said, teasing the self-assured man.

Color rushed to his face, a trait Glory found endearing in a man who looked as if he'd already taken on the world and won.

An idea hovered at the edge of her mind, and Glory mentally scrambled for it. It wasn't the first time she'd experienced the still, small twinge of heart that marked time with God doing His work, whispering His will in her ears.

But what did He want her to do?

Like a spring butterfly, the answer slipped past her grasp, flaunting itself and then eluding her just as it was about to land.

Ethan crossed his arms and stood silent, watching her reaction to his plans. His gaze went from amused to worried and back a hundred times, but he didn't say a word.

The feeling of God's peace grew as she watched the man. God had plans for Ethan Wheeler, plans that included her in some way.

But what? Glory prayed in silent petition to her Maker. *What do I have to do with Ethan Wheeler? Why is he really here?*

"I can see you need time to think it over," he said, his voice toned down a notch from where it had been before, his excitement dampened like a spring thunderstorm.

"No, it's not that," she assured, though he didn't react to her words.

"You'll want the opportunity to run it by the board of directors, of course. You can't make a decision of this magnitude on your own, right this very minute."

She opened her mouth to reply, but he appeared to have worked it out himself within his monologue.

He gave her a short smile. ''I run a business. And I know how nonprofits work.'' He shook his head. ''Sorry. Temporary brain lapse.''

She nodded, stunned. God was pulling, Ethan was pushing, and she was most definitely trapped in the middle. Strained to the point of snapping, she thought wryly.

Not that it was anything new to be in the middle of a spiritual tug-of-war. God tended to spring things on her suddenly, something that went against her grain. She was stable. Organized. Self-controlled.

Maybe that was it. Maybe God was throwing Ethan Wheeler into her life to keep her off balance, to keep her reaching for the Lord and not depend on herself for everything. Reaching.

She was reaching now. She stood and came around to the front of the desk.

''When will I see you again?'' she rasped, embarrassed that her voice sounded hoarse. She straightened her shoulders and regained her dignity.

He pressed a business card into her palm.

"Please give me a call when you've made your decision. You can leave a message with my secretary at my office, or please feel free to call my cell phone. Oh, and I've written my home telephone number on the back."

He gave a guttural chuckle. "I know you can see I'm anxious to get started."

With crisp movements, he flipped his checkbook open and scrawled numbers and a quick signature. "Here's a thousand bucks."

"A thousand bucks?" she echoed, her voice having gone from hoarse to shrill. Hurriedly, she shifted her gaze to the file still in her hand.

His smile was wide and firm and never wavered for a second, though she couldn't say the same for his gaze, which moved from his checkbook to her and back again.

"Use the money however you want. Give it to your board for administration and paperwork and all that good stuff." He winked and grinned. "We can talk computers later, at your convenience."

His words were soft, but everything he said hit her with the force of a bullet. And every other phrase in his vocabulary was presented in a teasing tone.

After an exaggerated look at his wristwatch, he shrugged and continued.

''Mmm. Look at the time. My Meggie is waiting at home for me.'' He paused and winked. ''You know how women can be. So I'll leave you to it. Have a great evening and don't work too hard.''

The first thought to hit Glory was that he intended to leave. Of course he did. He'd pocketed his checkbook, turned around and was hiking toward the door with crisp, even steps. He didn't pause or look back.

Her second thought was of Meggie.

He was going home to a woman named Meggie. It certainly didn't surprise her that Ethan wasn't available. He was no doubt happily married with 3.2 kids and a dog.

What *did* surprise her was that she'd noticed Ethan at all—as a man. She certainly didn't notice *every* man who walked in her door. And in her experience, the old adage that all the good men were taken held true.

Of course a man like Ethan would have a woman in his life. He wasn't wearing a wedding ring, but that didn't signify anything these days.

She quickly gathered her wayward thoughts as Ethan reached the door. She couldn't let him walk away from her without giving him an answer.

And much more than that, without giving *God* an answer.

If only it were that simple.

Minor problems and quibbles aside, she didn't know the question, much less the answer she was to give.

And then, suddenly, she did know, and she wanted to laugh at how simple it really was. She refrained from laughing, but her smile was wide and steady.

"Mr. Wheeler, do you believe in God?"

Chapter Two

She hadn't realized she'd voiced her thought aloud until he'd turned an about-face on his toes, and she recognized the expression of sheer astonishment that he wore.

She looked away as a wave of dizziness made her stomach roil. One second she was in perfect peace. The next moment she was mortified, absolutely and completely mortified.

The spiritual lives of the CEOs making charitable tax deductions to Angel's Wings was less than none of her business. And to blurt out such a personal question was rude under any circumstances, most especially when speaking to a complete stranger, as she had with Ethan Wheeler.

But he'd been walking away. What else was there to do? And it had been right. Somehow, she knew it had been right.

He'd frozen in place for a moment, then slowly walked toward her, his lips pressed together in a firm, straight line. He narrowed his gaze on her, and Glory experienced an alarming feeling that he might yell at her.

She cringed inwardly that her fear instinct could still be raised so easily. Outside, she remained composed, ready for whatever passed.

He wouldn't be the first man to raise his voice, and she'd known many; both as the director of the women's shelter, and in her own life as a child with an abusive father.

For a moment, Ethan merely stood silent and watched her. She wondered if he could see the jarring emotional ride she was taking.

When he did speak, his voice was anything but loud, and Glory let out a sigh of relief. His warm tenor was soft and calm, perhaps even amused, if she didn't miss her guess. "Why do you ask?"

Now that was the question of the hour. Why *had* she asked? She wished she knew.

She glanced down at the check she still held in her hand, trying to recall what her sudden burst of genius had been all about.

She licked her dry lips and plunged in. "This check is from your personal account."

Ethan shrugged. "You don't take donations from individuals?"

"Oh, no. I mean—yes. Not usually for such high dollar amounts, but—"

"You thought I was another stone-hearted businessman looking for a tax break."

Heat rushed to her cheeks, and she harbored no hope that he'd miss her red-faced embarrassment.

To Glory, Ethan appeared to be the type of man who didn't miss much. She pushed her glasses up, then hastily dropped her arms when she realized she was calling additional attention to her flushed face.

"I really didn't think that, Ethan," she said.

It was the truth. Granted, she'd suspected his motives when he'd first walked in, sparkling like a new penny.

But now…what *did* she think?

Frowning at Glory, Ethan stroked his jaw with his thumb and forefinger. He needed a shave already, having inherited his tendency toward a five-o'clock shadow from his father.

He wished he could have had some time to think everything over, which had been his reason for attempting a hasty exit. He had a bad habit of acting and speaking first and regretting it later.

He wasn't sure why he'd come here tonight, except that he'd considered his plans and couldn't wait to get them in motion. He couldn't wait to sweep some of the guilt from his back.

On the bright side, meeting Glory had certainly been an unexpected pleasure, even if it threw him off balance. Being around pretty women always did.

This was different, though. Glory Weston wasn't like other women of his acquaintance. She'd stand out in any crowd with that red hair of hers, but there was much more to Glory than that.

He'd known plenty of women who would,

given the opportunity and the motive, knock a man down and tread all over him. Who only wanted the best for themselves, and were oblivious to everything and everyone else around them.

A man could only handle a woman like that for so long before he had to make a break for it. Ethan grinned at the thought, and Glory smiled back at him, subtly shifting from one foot to the other, her only concession to the impatience he guessed she felt.

Glory wasn't like those other women. She appeared more like one of those quiet and efficient women, the ones who could run the world without raising her voice.

She wasn't that, either, though.

Glory was the better part of both kinds of women, with a little sugar mixed in for good measure.

He was woolgathering, and Glory was waiting.

But how to answer her question?

Did he believe in God?

Was this a yes or no question?

"I guess I fall into the category of slight to moderate," he said after a pause.

Honesty, however, would definitely be the best policy here. Was there some sort of spiritual requirement to donate to a Christian charity such as Angel's Wings?

He was uncomfortable revealing *any* personal information. He couldn't think of an easy way out, but didn't want to weave a web of lies.

His private life was private, though, and for good reason. He frowned.

"Sitting on a fence?" Her tone was carefully light and nonjudgmental, but curious. Ethan guessed that was for her benefit as much as his, considering the pleasant blush across her cheeks.

"Yes, I suppose I am a fence-sitter. I believe in the God of the Bible. But I have to admit I'm a sporadic churchgoer." He cringed inwardly. "I have some…*sticky wickets* I need to work out." He broke his gaze away from hers and stared unseeingly at one of the prints on her wall.

Glory nodded. "I understand."

Ethan swung his gaze back to her. "Yeah?"

She made a choking sound in her throat. "Let's just say, 'Been there, done that.'"

Again, a pat answer, but he could see by the serious look in her eyes she was telling the truth.

"Why do you ask about my faith?" Might as well be as up-front as she was trying to be. "Is there some kind of spiritual requirements for donators or something? Do I need to sign a statement of faith?"

"No, Ethan." She waved the check like a flag of surrender. "No requirements. Listen, I'm going to hang on to this check until I've spoken to the board. Our next scheduled meeting is a week from Friday, so I should know soon."

"Great!"

"Definitely. Unless I miss my guess, the board will be unanimously ecstatic about your proposal." She smiled widely at him, but she was back to her business presentation. "And about your generous support."

He shrugged and looked away, oddly disappointed that she'd closed up as quickly as she'd flowered. "It's nothing."

Glory wanted to deny his statement, to make him see how much his generosity would help these desperate women and children who had no place else to go, no one else to turn to. He had no way of knowing the joy even a small gesture could do.

And this was grand. But she'd seen his expression on other faces at other times, and knew her words would fall on deaf ears. They would mean nothing to the man before her.

He didn't see the magnitude of his own good works. As good-natured and pleasant as he was, he was burdened, and burdened heavily.

But God changed hearts. He changed lives. And He removed burdens, taking them upon Himself.

She'd been the same way not so long ago— the expression she recognized on Ethan was reminiscent of the one she saw when she had looked in the mirror.

Still, she couldn't finish the conversation she'd started, couldn't discuss her faith. Ethan's faith.

Maybe in time….

He wouldn't believe her words, but she knew something he would believe. ''I've got some ideas of my own to run by the board, and…other inquiries to make,'' she said evasively.

A background check on Ethan was at the top of her list, but she couldn't tell him that—not yet, anyway. Ethan was a lawyer. Surely he knew he'd be investigated—an absolute imperative where a battered women's shelter was concerned, even for donators.

It was a frightening and sobering job, running a battered women's shelter. More than once, she'd discovered a donator to be an enraged husband attempting to get his wife back.

Ethan didn't fall into that category. She was sure of it. Still…policies had to be enforced, and procedures followed.

Ethan grinned, and she smiled back. ''I'll speak with the board tomorrow morning, and then I'll be in touch.''

''In touch,'' Ethan repeated softly, his warm voice sending a tremor of delight through Glory's veins.

And then he smiled, and her world tilted. ''I'll be looking forward to that.''

Chapter Three

As Glory suspected, the board voted unanimously in favor of implementing Ethan's program, including her added suggestions about the man in question.

So it was a mere two weeks later that she found herself calling Ethan's office, her heart beating erratically as she waited for his secretary to transfer the call to his office. As elevator music played in her ears, she rehearsed what she might say to him.

Nothing sounded right to her. She couldn't think of a single rational, intelligent thing to say, beyond hello.

Where was her professional polish? Where was the facade that kept her calm, cool and collected in the varied and sometimes dangerous situations she found herself in?

She'd obviously left her refinement at home, for anxiety overrode any sense of coherent thought. She hadn't been this nervous talking to a man in years, maybe since high school.

At length, Ethan finally answered.

It was now or never, with *now* definitely pulling into the lead. She took a deep breath, ran her tongue across her dry lips and plunged in.

"Ethan, it's Glory Weston with Angel's Wings."

So far, so good.

"Glad to hear from you."

She clutched the phone closer at the pleasant sound of his rich tenor. "I hope you'll be equally glad to hear the board unanimously approved your proposal. I'd—" she cleared her throat "—*we'd* like you to come down to the shelter at your earliest convenience to tour our facilities.

"You'll also be able to examine our electrical situation and make up a preliminary list of

changes we'll need to make in order to imple-
ment your program.'' It was only as she swept
in a breath that she realized she'd been rambling.

It wasn't like her to babble. Her sister Ginger
was the talkative one of the family. Glory was
the quiet one. *Usually.*

Glad he couldn't see her blush, she closed
her mouth and allowed the phone line to crackle
quietly.

''How does this evening sound?''

Her heart bolted to life. You'd have thought
he'd asked her out or something. Too bad it was
a simple business arrangement.

''Tonight would be perfect.''

Trembling with eagerness, she gave him directions to the shelter. They agreed on a time,
and the line went static again.

''Oh—and Ethan?''

''Hmm?''

She swallowed hard and forced the words
through her lips. ''Feel free to bring Meggie
with you this evening.''

''Really? I'm glad you offered. I like to take
her with me everywhere, and I think she'd love

to come along. I'll just bet you two will become fast friends.''

She pressed her lips together. ''I'm certain we will be.''

It wasn't difficult to hear the affection and enthusiasm in Ethan's voice for the wonderful lady in his life. She wondered if Meggie knew just how blessed she was. She hoped so, for Ethan's sake.

Ethan arrived at the shelter ten minutes early, and though he'd turned off the ignition to his convertible, he made no move to enter the building.

''Guess this is it, huh, Meggie girl?''

Meggie didn't answer, but then, he hadn't expected her to. She was busily looking out the window, and obviously enraptured by what she saw.

It was a pretty view. To his surprise, the shelter was a large, well-kept blue-with-white-trim Victorian house set back in a patch of blue spruce. A white picket porch surrounded the entire house, and there was a large garden with a gazebo in the middle.

The property was marked by a white picket fence, but that was the extent of protection, as far as Ethan could see. He was no doubt missing the true security, a service perhaps, or guard dogs.

It bothered him that he could pull all the way up to the house and no one even stopped him. What if a batterer came looking for his wife?

He decided he'd have to bring the subject up with Glory. He was sure she'd have an explanation.

He tapped his palms against the steering wheel, then sat back and jammed his fingers through his hair. "I don't know why I'm nervous. I couldn't have asked for things to turn out better than they did."

That wasn't entirely true; part of his nervousness was that he was attracted to the shelter's pretty director.

And that was nothing to say about the importance of this project. He *needed* to succeed.

When he couldn't delay any longer, he made his way to the front door, glad Meggie's hand was tucked firmly in his. She gave him a sense of strength, peacefulness and composure that he wouldn't otherwise have had, just by her very presence here.

Glory met him at the door with a smile and a welcome. Immediately her gaze switched to the sweetheart on his arm, and she pushed up her glasses and exclaimed her delighted surprise.

"So this is Meggie? Come in! Come in! I can't say how pleased I am to meet you, Meggie."

Ethan glanced down at his adorable blond, curly-haired adopted daughter and smiled, his chest swelling with a father's love and pride. "Meggie, meet Miss Weston."

Meggie gave her best curtsy, and Ethan chuckled. "I think she's pleased to meet you, too."

Glory laughed as she recovered her composure. Her heart soared. Meggie was a toddler! She stooped to the child's level.

"You can call me Miss Glory. All the other children here do."

Meggie nodded, her eyes wide. "Miss Glory. You smell good."

Ethan and Glory shared their laughter as

Meggie took a big whiff of Miss Glory's floral perfume. "Smell her, Papa Ethan."

Ethan's eyes lit with friendly fire. "I may just have to do that, sweetheart."

Glory didn't know whether to take his statement as a threat or a promise. His eyes suggested both. And always, there was mirth.

"Would you like to make some new friends?" she asked hastily, trying to divert attention from her perfume. "We have a lot of children just your age living here, and I'm sure they'd like to play with you. If Papa Ethan doesn't mind, you can play in our dayroom."

Meggie nodded, then held her arms up to Ethan. "Up, Papa Ethan. Up."

Papa Ethan scooped the child up with one quick, efficient movement, and a broad grin to match. "Show us the way, Miss Glory."

As good as Ethan looked in Armani, he looked that much better in faded blue jeans and a tight white T-shirt. She definitely preferred the casual look, though he wore both styles with equal ease.

Mentally stilling her racing heart, she showed her two guests inside and began their quick tour. Their first stop was one of the two large dayrooms filled with couches, beanbags for the children, blaring televisions and a hodgepodge of long, mismatched scuffed coffee tables.

Equally mismatching square end tables in every corner were topped with brightly colored floral bouquets that gave life to the room. Even the wallpaper had flowers on it, a recent addition she was especially pleased with, considering she'd pasted the wall herself and picked out the pattern. She loved the look and smell of flowers of every variety.

Leading her visitors down the hall, she briefly passed by a few small, sparsely fitted sitting rooms with large, square windows which needed to be cleaned.

Shelter ladies used these rooms often as a haven to which they could retire when they needed to be alone.

It wasn't much, but she knew how much the women treasured their quiet time.

With a grand gesture, she introduced her favorite room in the shelter, the chapel. The room was outfitted with a crude altar, a wooden cross on the wall with a beautiful, sheer white scarf laced through it, and a couple of rough benches with kneelers for prayer.

She'd hung stained-glass pictures on the walls, one of the Good Shepherd with His sheep, and another of the Holy Spirit racing straight to heaven on the wings of a dove.

Every time she stepped into the chapel, she forgot her troubles for a moment in the solitude of peace, and experienced a renewal of strength for the great fight she fought in Jesus' name. She closed her eyes and inhaled deeply.

"Beautiful," Ethan complimented in a whisper.

Funny, how everyone always whispered in the chapel.

"Nice pictures."

Glory was jolted back to the present with his words. She smoothed her jeans with her palms. "Thanks. This room is my favorite."

"I can see why," he said, his voice low and scratchy.

He sounded uncomfortable, so she moved on without further comment. She'd already been over that territory on their first visit.

She wanted to remind him of the joy of faith

in Christ and a personal relationship with God, but first she needed to prove his trust in her was warranted. She didn't know the burdens he carried, only that he suffered, despite his naturally joyful and exuberant personality.

Reluctantly, she showed him to a large, concrete-walled dining room filled with long, foldable tables that reminded Glory of a high school cafeteria, especially with the way the echo of voices blared when the room was full.

It was a far cry from relaxing and homey, in her opinion, which was the atmosphere she constantly strove for for the ladies and children here at Angel's Wings.

With the dining room, she didn't even know where to start. Flowers, even bouquets in vases, were difficult in a room that saw so many people through it in a day, with tables folding up and down and being pushed around at the same rate.

She rushed on through, gesturing to the kitchen before moving on. At Ethan's insistence, they skipped the women's living quarters in respect to those housed there.

He was quite resolute not to cause any harm,

even unintentionally, to Angel's Wings' inhabitants, explaining quietly that he knew for these women, men were only batterers and bums.

Instead, they wandered back to the larger of the two dayrooms, where they'd mutually agreed the computers should go.

"Might any of the ladies wander in here this evening?" he queried lightly. "I wouldn't want to take anyone by surprise."

Respect for Ethan swelled in Glory's heart, usurped only by her racing thoughts. He'd hit the nail right on the head without even knowing a jot about her intentions.

That's where you come in, Ethan Wheeler.

"They all know you're going to be here," she answered, waving him off. "Most of them are okay with men, as long as it's a comfortable, nonrestrictive environment."

Ethan nodded. "Great. I'd like to meet some of them. I mean, if they know I'm here, and want to come out and say hi."

God also knew Ethan was going to be here tonight, Glory thought with a grin. And He had even bigger plans for Ethan than she did.

Speaking of plans, she hadn't yet figured out

how to tactfully introduce him to the ideas she had thought up. Maybe, for now, it was better simply to keep her mouth shut and let the cards fall where they would.

God was at work here, even if Ethan was unaware of His divine intervention. He'd figure it out on his own, given time. As she well knew, God could be very persistent when He was knocking on the door of somebody's heart.

She prayed it would be Ethan's heart. He needed the peace only God could give.

"What are you smiling about?" he asked softly, so close she felt the warmth of his breath on her face.

The sound of his voice and the slight, brisk scent of his cologne did funny things to her equilibrium, and she stepped backward in response. "What?"

"Just now. You got a distant look in your eyes, and then you smiled."

"Hmm," she said, waving off any significance her expression might have held with a toss of her hand. "Who knows? Just woolgathering, I assure you."

"I don't expect you have much time for that

here.'' He sounded so sincere it neared zealousness.

"No." Her voice was husky, and she cleared her throat. "No, I don't. Now, if you'd like to take Meggie in with the other children...."

He shook his head and handed Meggie off to Glory, who was surprised how light, if wiggly, the toddler felt in her arms.

"You take her to see the other kids, and I'll just—" he brushed his fingers through his hair and looked around the room with a meticulous eye "—have a look at these outlets."

She nodded, glad someone was being sensible, for she certainly wasn't being anything of the sort. Her rational mind had abandoned her in favor of her senses, and they were screaming in favor of Ethan, everything about him—his sight, smell, sound, touch and....

Glory Weston, you idiot! she thought to herself, giving her head a mental smack. Get a grip on yourself this instant!

Fortunately, she had an errand to run. Away from Ethan.

It took her only minutes to deposit Meggie in the children's playroom and make her way back to the dayroom, but Ethan had disappeared. The room felt empty without him, which was ridiculous, since until this evening, he'd never set foot in the room.

There was a moment of panic when she considered that he might be after one of the women, but she knew that wasn't possible. She'd had him thoroughly investigated before accepting his offer. To say nothing of that notion of rightness God continued to nudge her with.

And last but certainly not least, Ethan had been nothing but quiet and respectful around her, and when speaking of Angel's Wings. She couldn't be wrong about him.

But where was he?

She made a thorough pass around the dayroom, then walked outside and around the shelter, calling his name to no avail.

Finally, she looked in the dining room, even stooping to look under tables, thinking Ethan might be studying the electrical system of the building.

It was the sound of water that finally alerted her to Ethan's whereabouts, although her conclusion left her quite stymied; because light peeked from beneath the kitchen door, and the sound of water running was definitely coming from there.

As she approached the kitchen door, Glory realized she heard the cheerful sound of whistling. Eyebrows raised, she burst through the door.

"Ethan, what on earth are you doing in the—"

She swallowed the rest of her sentence whole at the sight of Ethan, up to his biceps in dishwater and wearing an exceptionally frilly white apron to cover his cotton T-shirt.

The oddest thing about the picture was Glory's reaction. Where most men would have looked ridiculous, Ethan's masculinity was heightened for donning the frills.

It was the perfect paradox, and one she wanted to study in detail, she thought with a smile.

That he was perfectly comfortable, not only in the apron, but in the dishwater, came as quite another shock for Glory. "I— What are you doing?"

Ethan grinned. "What does it look like I'm doing? Dishes."

"Yes, but—"

"They have to be done, right?"

"Yes, but—"

"And I've got two arms to scrub with, right?"

Two arms and a willing heart. "Yes, but—"

"It's settled, then."

Glory shook her head, bemused. She was not at all sure she and Ethan were having the same conversation. "Er...what have we settled?"

He made a big production of shaking his wet hands off and reaching for a towel. Moments later, he launched that very same towel at her head. It pegged her squarely on the jaw, and she laughed as she unwrapped it from around her neck.

"We've settled," he explained with mock patience and a catty grin, "that you're going to dry."

Chapter Four

There was one tense moment as Glory paused, and Ethan had reason to wonder if he'd made a mistake in his effort to loosen things up a little bit.

But only for a moment.

Then she pegged him back with the towel and they both laughed. "You don't leave me much choice, now, do you?"

"You're welcome to wash," he offered, gesturing to the soapy sink full of dishes.

"No, really. Please continue."

She slipped the towel from around his neck and picked up a clean dish to dry. That small movement was enough to send the light, sweet floral scent of her perfume into his nostrils and spinning through his senses.

Grinning, he began to whistle. How long had it been since he'd done dishes?

He thought it could have been since he'd been a teenager. His older brother Erik had become stricter than his father when their mother passed away.

Not that he could strictly blame Erik. Their father had become a virtual recluse, sleeping out on the range more often than home at the ranch. Baby brother Rhett had still been a little guy, so Ethan caught the brunt of Erik's attempts to maintain civility.

Ethan had done enough dishes and housework to last a lifetime, and had sworn he'd never do such menial work again.

And he hadn't, until today, when he'd walked into the kitchen and seen the mess.

He still didn't know why he'd filled the sink with soap and tackled the disarray of plates, cups and saucers, but something inside his chest urged him on persistently.

He slid a glance to Glory, who was nibbling

on her thick bottom lip, looking as if she were concentrating furiously on the glass in her hand she was shining. She looked like an overzealous bartender.

Ethan's grin froze.

She looked like an angel.

He turned his gaze to the soap in the sink, then back at the solemn-looking shelter director, who'd just picked up another glass.

He wouldn't.

One corner of his lip curled up in a smile.

He couldn't.

The other corner joined the first.

He shouldn't.

Oh, but he was going to!

Making a circle with his hands, Ethan picked up a handful of the frothy, bubbly dish soap and deposited it lightly on the top of her head.

She screeched, waving him away wildly with her hands.

"What did you do that for?" She sounded surprised, but thankfully, not angry.

He shrugged and tried to look innocent. "You know, you look like an angel when you dry dishes, and I just thought you should have a halo."

"A halo, is it?" Her green eyes sparkled with mischief. "Well, if I'm an angel—" she paused, reaching for her own handful of dish soap "—that would make you..."

She left her sentence dangling as she made two neat little soapsuds horns on Ethan's head. She had to reach on tiptoe to do it, which brought her scent and warmth dangerously near.

Ethan reached for the counter to keep from reaching for her.

"You know you're in dangerous territory now," he threatened, cocking one eyebrow.

She only smiled. "Is that so?" In two steps she was at a rinsing hose, and it only took a couple of seconds more before Ethan was the target of a long spray of cold water.

He hollered and twirled around to keep from being soaked, though all the dancing in the world wouldn't have kept him out of the cold water. But no one had ever accused him of running away from a fight.

"All's fair..." he warned with a chuckle, reaching for a glass and filling it with hot, soapy water.

She shrieked as he advanced. "At least

mine's warm," he accused. He took his time, stalking her slowly, intent on his prey.

She squeaked like a mouse and tried to duck down, but he still managed to douse her shoulder. "So it's war, is it?"

"Glory, are you okay? Glory? I heard yelling and I…"

Ethan and Glory both whirled at the sound of the voice, but Glory regained her composure first.

"Lena. I'm sorry we disturbed you." She dabbed ineffectively at her wet shoulder with the towel. "I—we—"

Ethan looked from woman to woman, wondering who looked more surprised.

Lena, whom he gathered to be a current tenant of Angel's Wings, looked mildly stunned, though he thought he saw a sparkle of understanding in her eyes.

Glory looked downright traumatized, as if they'd been caught in a misdeed.

He didn't think a water fight was too terrible an offense, and he was pretty sure Lena didn't think so, either. Still, he stepped forward cautiously, using his fingers as a comb on his dripping hair as he cleared his throat. "My name is Ethan Wheeler."

He met Lena's gaze with what he hoped was calm reassurance, though his heart continued to beat double time.

Glancing at Glory, he continued. "I'll be installing computers here at the shelter."

Lena's large brown eyes widened noticeably.

"I know," he said with a shrug. "I look like the janitor."

That brought a chuckle from both women, and his smile widened. Maybe this wouldn't be as hard as he thought.

"Glory was just showing me around."

"You're installing our computers in the kitchen?" Lena queried with a wavering smile.

It was Ethan's turn to laugh. "I'm afraid I can't take the blame here. Glory made the mistake of leaving me alone, and I got into mischief."

He slid a glance at Glory, who hadn't spoken since Lena had first entered the room. She was chewing her bottom lip again, looking as if she were trying to remember the answer to something important.

''It really is all her fault,'' he said, winking at both women.

''It is not!''

Glory found her voice with difficulty. She'd been mortified when Lena had found her clowning around with Ethan in the kitchen. It felt terribly, horribly wrong, having fun when the women and children just down the hall were suffering through some of the worst times of their lives.

She knew what her sister Ginger would say: Lighten up, Glory.

But she couldn't do that. It never worked for her. She was an all-or-nothing woman, and she'd just compromised her principles.

''I apologize for what it looked like,'' she said, firming her resolve with every word. It had been a mistake bringing Ethan here. What must poor Lena think? If she told the other women....

''It didn't look like anything.'' Lena turned her gaze to Glory. ''How did you get a handsome guy like this to wash dishes for you? Wherever you got him from, you need to share the wealth.''

A wave of sadness washed over Lena's expression, but her smile quickly returned.

Glory didn't know whether to be shocked or relieved. Glancing between Lena and Ethan, it looked like they were sharing a private joke. She seemed to be the only one making a big deal over the situation.

"Are you going to be teaching the computer classes, too, Ethan? Or is your only specialty dishes?" Lena winked at Ethan and leaned against a counter, folding her arms around her.

Ethan laughed loudly, slapped a dry towel across one shoulder, and returned to the sink.

Glory watched Lena closely, feeling she'd done Ethan a disservice. She'd given a lot of thought before introducing him to Angel's Wings, not to mention feeling it was what God wanted her to do, yet she'd completely panicked at the first real test.

Ethan *would* be good for the women at Angel's Wings. He'd easily adapted to a situation that would have sent most men fleeing for their lives.

He'd not only responded well to a withdrawn woman with a bad history where men were concerned, but he now had her comfortably conversing with him. He was certainly gifted with people.

And he was utterly charming.

"Unfortunately," he was saying, "I'm neither an expert at computers *nor* dishes."

"Which is really too bad, don't you think, Lena?" Glory teased, inching her way back into the conversation. "And to think he could have majored in soapsuds."

"A real shame," Lena agreed.

"I guess I was also laboring under the false perception that you were going to teach the computer stuff, Ethan," Glory said, bewildered. "I mean, we never really discussed it, but I just thought...."

Her sentence trailed off, but when Ethan raised his eyebrows at her, she felt it was necessary to defend herself.

"It *was* your idea."

Ethan shrugged. "It's my *money*. I'm afraid I'm not much good past the green. However, I'm certain I can locate someone appropriate for you with a little research."

"That won't be necessary," Lena said quietly. Glory and Ethan both turned to her.

"It won't?" Glory tried not to sound as befuddled as she felt.

"Of course not." She was speaking to Glory, but she never took her eyes off Ethan. "Glory's sister Ginger works in the computer industry. She'd be perfect for the job."

"Does she live in Seattle?" Ethan queried, sounding relieved to be let off the hook.

"Bothell," Glory answered quickly. "Across the lake. But I'm really not sure she's the woman for the job."

"She hangs around here enough." Lena smoothed down her hair with her palm. "She's such a friendly soul. I can't imagine that she'd mind sharing a little bit of her wisdom with us."

"Probably not," Glory admitted.

Quite the opposite, in fact, she thought, trying to bottle up her resentfulness. Ginger would no doubt steal the show, and be glad to do it.

The truth was that her sister would use this computer thing as an excuse to be around the shelter even more often than she already was. And that meant, among other things, the inevitable lectures on how big sister Glory ought to get a life.

She had a life, thank you very much, though Ginger refused to concede to the point. Still, she supposed it wasn't such a bad idea to ask her sister to help. She did know computers.

"I'll ask her," she said at last, clearing her throat against the grainy sound her voice made.

She turned to Ethan. "Does that mean you won't be here for the installation, either? I had rather thought you'd want to be here."

She didn't want to think about the reason her gut clenched at the mere thought of Ethan walking out the door tonight and never coming back.

He chuckled loudly. "You couldn't scare me away with enough bears to fill a circus," he promised. "In fact, if your sister is any good, I may just show up for the computer classes."

He winked at both of them. "That all right with you, Lena?" he asked, before turning to wash a plate, whistling softly.

"Oh, it's just *fine* with me."

Lena's gaze met Glory's as she answered, her sometimes frightened brown eyes now sparkling with mirth, and Glory felt her face warm even before the next words were uttered.

"I'm sure *Glory* would *love* to have you."

Chapter Five

Ethan leaned over the side of the white Jenny Lind crib, softly stroking Meggie's golden hair away from her forehead. She slept the sleep of the innocent, her little chest moving up and down in a slow, regular rhythm that comforted him.

Poor Meggie. She'd never know her real mother, or *any* mother, in all likelihood.

He frowned at the direction of his thoughts. He had enough to worry about without reliving events he couldn't change and pondering a future he couldn't see.

Tonight, when he'd met Lena's gaze, he'd

felt such a resurgence of helplessness—of hopelessness—that he'd barely been able to contain his rage.

How could a man batter a woman—harm her so terribly that she needed to run away from home to escape him? Especially a husband who'd promised before God and witnesses to love and cherish his wife? Who would be there to protect her if the man she loved turned against her?

It was completely beyond his comprehension.

He'd asked himself that same question over and over again in the two years since his cousin Sabrina died at the hands of her husband.

He still didn't understand. He still couldn't comprehend such madness, such vice.

Frustration and rage poured through him. He tempered it only by scooping the tiny form of his still-sleeping little girl into his arms and sitting down in the rocking chair in the corner.

Each day, more and more, she reminded him of Sabrina. Her soft, golden hair, her sweet, innocent blue eyes. She'd be a knockout when she was older.

Just like Sabrina.

How could God allow such things to happen?

He could still see Sabrina's face as she confided her plans for escape, to get herself and Meggie far away from her husband, Jason.

She'd been terrified, and it was no wonder. Jason had threatened more than once to kill her. Sabrina had said she'd rather he hit her, because at least then she knew he wasn't going to hit Meggie.

And later, always later, Jason would brush off his threats and his abuse as no more than his Irish temper. He'd be soft and persuasive, but Sabrina had learned the hard way that it meant nothing.

Ethan still remembered the expression on her face as she sat across the booth from him in the secluded coffeehouse across from the college campus where they'd both taken prelaw, her eyes were full of determination and purpose.

Her six-month-old baby Meggie would never suffer hurt from her father, not as long as Sabrina was around to protect her.

Ethan squeezed his eyes shut against the tears forming. Sometimes he could think about Sabrina and remember the good times, smile at the happy memories, but on this cold, dark night, what he remembered was the pain.

He kissed Meggie's forehead, just where a stray curl had fallen, and for the hundredth time since he'd walked into Glory Weston's office, he wondered if he was making a mistake getting involved.

For one thing, he feared for Meggie's safety at Angel's Wings.

Meggie's father was behind bars, for the time being, anyway, but he knew the women at the shelter were hiding from men who *weren't* behind bars. And he still hadn't seen any security measures at the house.

The last thing Ethan wanted to do was let Meggie get hurt—the very reason he kept her beside him twenty-four hours a day, even to the point of opening a daycare center right next door to his law office.

He wouldn't leave Meggie behind with a baby-sitter. But could he abandon Glory—his project at Angel's Wings?

He *could,* of course.

The money had passed hands. The computers would be installed within a week. And Glory's sister Ginger would give the women the knowledge they needed to access the Internet and change their lives for the better.

What more was there left for him to do? That was the way he'd meant it to be, funding a project for the shelter and walking away.

He'd never meant·to get involved.

But he *was* involved. Glory had seen to that. She'd trusted him enough to bring him to the shelter.

He knew deep in his heart he couldn't let Glory down. He couldn't let Meggie down. Maybe this time around, he wouldn't let *himself* down.

After one last snuggle, he stood and placed Meggie back in her crib. He loved the smell of her—most of the time, anyway, he thought with a chuckle.

Admittedly, it would be hard for him to spend time at the shelter, to face his demons head-on. But it hadn't been as hard as he'd supposed it would be. He'd enjoyed talking to Lena, after he relaxed, and she realized he wouldn't break any unspoken boundaries between them.

Might he not be able to do the same for other women at the shelter? Be an honorable male role model for the kids, and a man these women could trust?

He frowned and shook his head at the thought. He wasn't up for sainthood. He'd already let one woman down. But at least he could wash dishes and mop floors and do any other chores that needed doing.

He brushed Meggie's curly hair back from her forehead. She brought a soft smile to his lips. Meggie was the one good thing to come from an otherwise tragic situation.

His younger brother Rhett would say God was in control, and for the first time in many years, Ethan thought he might be right.

Maybe, just maybe, God *was* in control.

In a little over a week, the new computers were delivered and installed, and the following Saturday marked the first day of computer class. Whatever Ethan had done to hasten the process had certainly worked without a glitch.

Glory, however, had to tussle with the phone company when it came to putting in extra lines, but it was worth the trouble to see the enthu-siasm in the ladies', not to mention the chil-dren's, faces.

Ethan had been right about the computers. And Lena had been right about Ginger. It had taken less than five minutes to get her younger sister to commit to an indefinite and ongoing number of weeks training the shelter women on Internet tactics for education, relocation, and eventually, employment.

She frowned down at her beat-up, legal-size brown clipboard, which she held snug to her waist with her left hand, and thoughtfully tapped a pencil against with her right.

Ostensibly, she was making notes on the first day's work in progress, but something else was bothering her far more than the overwhelming success she knew this day would be.

Ethan had promised he'd be here for the in-augural class, but there was no sign of him and Meggie. With only ten minutes to go, she was beginning to think he wouldn't show at all.

"What are you frowning about?" Ginger tapped against the back of Glory's clipboard with her fingers, sending it out of her grasp and flapping awkwardly to the ground, papers everywhere.

"Ginger," Glory protested, the note of warning in her voice so clear even her tenaciously thickheaded sister couldn't mistake it for anything else.

"You don't need that old clipboard anyway. You're too pretty to hide behind papers."

"Ginger." The protest in her eyes became a silent plea. "We're not teenagers anymore. I don't have to dress up or look pretty to run this shelter right. After all, I'm not going out on a date."

"Maybe that's just what you need," she suggested audaciously.

"What does Glory need?"

Glory whirled at the honey-rich male voice speaking just over her shoulder, and found Ethan grinning down on her, Meggie riding on his shoulders with a happy smile of her own.

"Ethan. I wasn't sure you were going to show."

Ethan raised his brows. "What? And miss the grand opening? I wouldn't think of it."

"Hello, Ethan," Ginger said, her voice annoyingly sultry as she raised her hand to shake his. "I don't think we've met."

Glory stopped just short of rolling her eyes, but she had to bite her bottom lip to keep from laughing. Her sister was terminally incorrigible in every area of her life, most especially in regard to men.

Ethan shook Ginger's hand, but his mischievous gaze was on Glory. "This must be the sister you were talking about."

"Oh, so she's mentioned me to you," Ginger gushed. "She certainly kept *you* a secret." She slid a glance at Glory, who sighed loudly.

Ethan chuckled, and Glory reached for the clipboard on the floor to hide her flushed cheeks. Fortunately for Ginger, she was in good humor, now that Ethan was here.

Her sister was doing it again. In younger years, Glory would have clocked her for such behavior.

"Are you sure you weren't switched at birth with some kid under a cabbage leaf? We can't possibly be related by blood," she commented wryly, pulling the clipboard under her chin. Naturally outgoing and flamboyant, Ginger was the near opposite of dedicated and determined Glory.

Staid and stodgy, Ginger would say.

For the first time, Glory worried that her sister might be right. She was mortified at the jealousy sparking through her when Ethan shook Ginger's hand, and found herself almost wishing she *did* know how to flirt with a man.

This was new ground for her. She didn't like feeling out of control, and she'd never felt so helpless as she was at that moment.

And then Ethan turned his toothy grin on her, and she completely forgot to be jealous. In fact, she forgot to breathe. It was a good thing her heart beat on its own, or she'd be in real trouble.

He swept Meggie down with a whoop, then whirled her around until she squealed with laughter. "I come bearing gifts," he said straightening, yet still holding the toddler by the hand.

"Don't you think you've done enough?" Glory asked, only now beginning to regain her equilibrium.

"I've barely started."

She wondered if that was a threat or a promise, and hoped Ginger wouldn't ask, which of course she would.

"How so?" Glory asked unwillingly.

"I've brought two of the seven deadly sins to share with everybody." He paused dramatically and waggled his eyebrows. "Caffeine and chocolate. They're in the trunk of my car. If you can watch Meggie for a moment, I'll bring them in."

It was only a minute before Ethan returned, laden with a case of soda cans and several boxes of brownies.

He set them before her with a flourish. "I'd say I baked them myself, but you'd know I was lying. Besides, I'd rather be spending quality time at my local women's shelter."

"Is that what it's called now?" quipped Ginger, with a sly glance at her sister. "Quality time."

Ethan looked offended. "I'll have you know I'm a man of the millennium, P.C. in every way." He pursed his lips and grinned. "Perfectly Clever."

"Oh, you're that," Ginger said, laughing. "That and a *lot* more."

Glory shot her sister another warning look, wondering if her face was going to freeze that way from overuse.

"Looks like we're going to have some trouble," Ethan commented, gesturing at the neat lines of computers.

Glory spun around and ran her gaze over the area. "How's that?"

Ginger laughed. "I think he means the kids." She sashayed over to Glory and bent toward her ear. "Lighten up, sis. This is going to be fun."

Fun.

Now there was a word not in Glory Weston's dictionary. When was the last time she'd had fun?

But life wasn't about fun. It wasn't about flirting and laughing and playing, as much as Ginger might think it was.

Real life was about fighting. It was about trying to survive.

Meggie squealed as Ethan swung her to the ground. "Can you show me where the kids' dayroom is?" Ethan shrugged, making his sea-blue sweater tighten over his shoulders in a very eye-catching way.

Ginger immediately stepped forward and offered her hand to the toddler. "I'm not on for another ten minutes yet. I'd be happy to take her, and you two can talk. About whatever."

Glory opened her mouth to protest and then snapped it closed again. There was no use arguing with her sister over anything. It would just call attention to her words, and embarrass Glory further.

Ginger was hopelessly flighty, just as Glory was hopelessly grounded. God had certainly created polar opposites in her family.

Ethan reached for her hand and led her around the room, moving from computer to computer and speaking to each young occupant in turn. He made the funny video game sounds boys made and twisted and twirled his way down the aisle.

During all this, he never once let go of her hand. He'd twist it around his waist, and one time even twirled her around. She didn't know whether she felt uncomfortable because she was, in effect, dancing with the man in the middle of a crowded room with no music playing, or if it was the very touch of his hand, the crook of his mouth or the smile in his eyes that made her feel flushed.

"That's a pretty cool video game," he said to one eight-year-old boy, and ruffled his thick black hair when the boy laughed.

"This is Stephen," Glory said quietly. "He's Lena's boy."

She didn't miss the shade of pain that passed over Ethan's eyes as he took her arm and led her a short distance away. But then, with a quirk of his lips, the pain was gone, replaced by his usual good cheer.

"How long have they been here?" he asked quietly. "Lena and Stephen, I mean."

"They've been here four months. Stephen is amazingly well-adjusted to this place." She looked away. "Not every child, or woman, for that matter, does so well as the Bostwick family has done. Stephen has lived through enough anguish to last a lifetime."

Without warning, Ethan cupped her chin in his hand, gently stroking her cheek with his thumb as he turned her face to his. His breath was warm, the brisk scent of his aftershave comforting.

Glory could neither breathe nor speak, so she simply stared up at him, noting the sadness that crossed his eyes, and wishing her words hadn't put it there.

Her world was a world of pain and sorrow, and she suddenly wished she hadn't inflicted it upon smiling, good-natured Ethan. But it was too late to urge him and his child to leave and not return.

"Don't be sad, sweet Glory," he whispered softly, then dropped his hand and turned away.

She didn't want him to leave. She'd known it before, but as she'd gazed up into his shining blue eyes, feeling the tender, gentle roughness of his hand on her cheek, she thought her heart might not withstand the impact of his leaving should he go away.

Chapter Six

Ethan watched the swirl of women around him, most of them tired and ragged, some giving sly, interested glances in the direction of the computers; but only a couple of them actually sat down behind a computer screen.

He could fix this problem. All he needed was...a chair and a...drum.

But a brownie pan would do.

He stood on the chair and banged the aluminum pan with his fist. It wasn't pretty, but it got the job done.

"Let's get this show on the road," he announced, making the sentence sound like a song. "C'mon, Ginger, we've got some ladies here who are rea-dy."

That got him a chuckle or two. He grinned at Glory, briefly wishing he could get her to smile more. She had such a beautiful smile.

"And let's start our lesson with a hearty round of applause for the lady that made all this possible, our fantastic director, Glory Weston!"

He hopped down as the women cheered and hooted along with him. The more noise the better, as far as Ethan was concerned.

"Ethan," Glory whispered, her voice low and scratchy. "All this is your doing, not mine."

Ethan just grinned. "You just don't give yourself enough credit." He cocked an eyebrow. "Therein lies the problem, my dear," he said, hoping he sounded like an antiquated doctor.

"I'm glad you told her that," Ginger interjected. "She won't listen to me."

He hoped she'd listened to him, but like Ginger, he doubted it.

It wasn't so much that Glory had a bad self-image, as much that she was so wrapped up in what she was doing here at the center, she forgot herself completely. He'd bank on the idea of Glory having missed meals and sleep. He'd bet a dollar she spent late nights with paperwork and shelter issues, a candy bar her only meal.

Glory switched into her shelter director mode, squaring her shoulders and stepping forward.

"All of you ladies already know my sister Ginger, but I'm proud to introduce her as the new instructor for our computer and Internet classes."

After slight applause, the women settled down to work behind their computers. Some still looked stiff and uncomfortable, to Ethan's way of thinking, but he'd done the best he could, short of starting a conga line.

Not such a bad idea at that, except Glory would throw him out on his can. And for some reason, he didn't want to be thrown out, at least not yet. Not until he'd been able to corner the irascible shelter director someplace private.

It was half his reason for coming. He'd made a promise to Meggie, and he was going to keep it. With a secretive smile, he winked at Ginger and swept through the aisle, helping out whenever he could, if the lady in question was open to help from a man.

Some weren't, and that was okay. He made a mental note of their names and faces and gave them the room they needed, knowing they wouldn't appreciate his antics, and knowing they had every right to feel that way.

He only hoped he could let them know, in whatever way possible, that not all men were lying, cheating, abusive nozzles.

That some men were honest, respectful and most of all, trustworthy.

Glory was doing her own mulling as she perused the room, worried not so much about the ladies' reaction to Ethan as their reaction to the computers. Most of them hadn't finished high school, much less become acquainted with a computer. She was certain some of these women were climbing mountains just to be sitting before an electronic device.

But she knew they'd do anything, no matter how difficult, that would help them pull themselves up, find new lives to live. Beat down by

life as they were, they were some of the stron-
gest women she'd ever met.

Glory liked to hope they'd find excitement in
what was ahead, once they became familiar
with the Internet and the freedom it offered
them.

They could get a degree, find a house, get a
job. A new relationship was the last thing they
wanted now, of course, but Glory hoped it for
them, someday.

Her glance rose to Ethan. He planned to fi-
nancially sponsor any woman who wanted to
pursue their degree, whether a high school di-
ploma or beyond.

The man was nothing short of amazing. He
drove her crazy with his silly antics, but he did
things for others Glory could only begin to con-
ceive of. And he did it all with that sly pucker
on his face that labeled him an irascible urchin.

"Just push the backward arrow there, Susan," she said, leaning over one of the women.
"You pushed the forward arrow one too many
times."

"This mouse is kind of tricky," Susan commented, wiggling the item in question.

Glory chuckled. "That it is. I wonder why it's called a mouse?"

"The tail," said a male voice from behind her. Ethan leaned over her and picked up the mouse, demonstrating.

By this time he had everyone's attention, of course, and Glory thought he probably knew it. He was a natural extrovert.

He pulled a black marker from his back jeans pocket. Glory watched in astonishment as he drew eyes, a nose, and whiskers on the item. A mouse!

Then, with a grin, he wiggled it again, allowing the cord to flop around.

"See? A mouse."

"It really does look like an animal, once you put life into it, Ethan," Susan said, laughing heartily. "But now, how am I going to work this ridiculous computer?"

She paused for effect. "I'm absolutely terrified of rodents."

Glory burst out laughing. "A hedgehog, maybe? How about a Chihuahua?" she suggested mildly.

"Nah," Ethan disagreed with a grunt.

''Who'd want to drag around a Chihuahua all day?''

Taking the pen in hand again, he drew two pointed ears. ''Kitten. A nice, soft, sweet, cuddly kitten.'' He placed the mouse back down on the mouse pad and lifted his pen. ''Anyone else?''

Nearly every woman wanted Ethan to change her mouse into a kitten, or at least an animated mouse, and he was happy to oblige.

With his mouth in that cute little smirk it made, he moved from computer to computer, making every woman feel like the only person in the room.

Ethan had a way about him. He could do more for these women in a minute than she could do with weeks of work. She sent up a silent, thankful prayer that God had brought Ethan into her life, and ignored the plunge of the poisonous dagger of jealousy.

She did what she could…but she could *not* do what Ethan did.

''How far are we going today?'' she asked Ginger, who was regarding her with decided interest. She ignored the look, though her hackles rose.

"I just wanted to show them how to get online, and then let them play a little bit. Next week I'll start getting into specifics on education, housing and employment." She paused and pushed a bushy wave of blond hair out of her eyes. "Was there anything else you wanted me to cover today?"

Glory shook her head. "You're definitely the expert in this field."

"Not expert enough," Ginger replied, sliding a glance at Ethan.

"What's that supposed to mean?"

"Nothing. I just think maybe you need to get out once in a while."

"Ginger, we've been over this ground before. God has given me this work to do, and I don't have time to date."

She just smiled. "But you want to marry."

"God is able to provide," Glory stated, wishing she didn't sound defensive but knowing that she was.

"Oh, He's able to provide, all right," Ginger said with a wry laugh. "If Glory won't move to the man, God will have to move the man to Glory."

She swatted Ginger affectionately on the sleeve. "You are, always have been, and always will be, incorrigible. Give or take a few minutes at birth, when you were just cute."

The sisters laughed comfortably. They might be opposites in every way, but there was only love between them. Their difficult background had allowed—no, forced—them to cling together more than other sisters, and in a cockeyed kind of way, Glory was glad.

Ginger had been looking off in the distance—probably thinking the same things Glory was. But suddenly she turned her head back, and the happy light was back in her eyes.

"I've got to have some duct tape," she announced, as if this were an everyday request.

"Duct tape?"

"Yeah. Uh—duct tape. From the uh—supply room. I'm sure I saw some up there on the shelves. You wouldn't mind getting it for me, would you, sis?"

"And you need duct tape for…?"

Ginger glanced around furtively. "Uh…."

It was beginning to be Ginger's favorite phrase, and Glory smelled a trap.

Suddenly Ginger smiled and turned her around by the shoulders with a short push off toward the supply room.

"Duct tape. To tape down all the computer wires so the kids don't trip on them. I need it right away. But I can't leave. Please?"

That sounded reasonable, though Glory did wonder why Ginger—and Ethan, and the computer techs who'd originally set up the systems—had failed to have taped the wires down in the first place.

Glory shook her head and headed for the supply room. Perhaps it was just an oversight. This had all happened so fast.

It was a big job, and she was glad Ginger had noticed the cords. There was so much that could go wrong, and they'd been blessed to have been so free of problems.

She was certain the teenagers here at the shelter would be all over the computers every chance they got, and since teens—especially boys—didn't move at a speed less than Mach 3, taping down the lines wasn't just a good idea, it was a necessity.

She was just reaching for the tape on an upper shelf, hoping she wouldn't tip the entire steel-beamed shelving unit over on top of her, when the lights went out. Not even a flicker of warning, and she was in pitch black.

For a moment she couldn't see at all, until her eyes recovered from the unexpected surprise. The darkness didn't bother her, since she'd left the door propped slightly open when she'd come in.

She was, however, standing motionless in the half-dark thinking about what an electrical shortage might have done to the computers. She prayed they were still working. If, after all the work everyone had done, they lost the computers to a power failure, she didn't know what she'd do.

A moment later the door slammed with a resounding crack, leaving her in total darkness. Her heart pumped wildly against her throat with the sudden noise, but it wasn't until she moved to open the thick wood door and found it locked, did she really panic.

She pounded as hard as she could and yelled for all she was worth.

"Ethan! Ginger! Anybody! *H-e-l-p!*"

Chapter Seven

A match ticked against a box, and the small, steady glow of a miniature candle, the kind she'd put on a birthday cake, flickered against the darkness.

"No need to shout," came a tenor voice from behind the flicker. "Help is on its way."

"Ethan!" She didn't know whether she was more irritated or relieved.

He stepped forward, so she could see his high, crooked grin against the glow of the candle, which she could now see was placed in the middle of a Twinkie.

"You'd better blow it out before wax drips on the creamy middle. It's my favorite part."

She lifted an eyebrow, but doubted Ethan could see it. Still, she didn't speak.

Neither did he, for a moment, so she did the unimaginable. The unconceivable. At least for Glory Weston, it was.

She blew out the candle.

The top lights flicked on as quickly as they had gone out, temporarily blinding Glory. She held a hand up to her eyes.

"Happy, happy, happy, happy, happy anniversary," Ethan sang, twirling around her with his Twinkie.

With a flourish, he took a big dip of cream on his forefinger and brushed it across her lips.

"Happy *what?*" she asked around her mouthful of cream.

"Anniversary. Happy *anniversary*. I'm wounded you didn't remember."

"I'm sorry. I didn't mean to—" She stopped herself flat, suspicion arising as fast as her gaze was narrowing.

"*Whose* anniversary are we celebrating?" she asked, her voice an octave higher and a good deal more screechy than she would have liked.

"Ours, of course."

Now who would have known?

She should have, in a way, at least. He looked like a little boy. A bright, happy little boy ready to celebrate in earnest. "I wanted to make it a cupcake, but your vending machine only had Twinkies."

Cupcakes. Twinkies. Anniversaries. Glory was stunned and bewildered, and she knew it showed on her face. She hadn't had this much variety in her life since her teen years, and maybe not even then.

Ethan felt like a military jet against her motorless glider.

"Today," he said, leaning close to her face, "is the one-month anniversary of the day we met."

Glory tried not to notice the cream on the corner of his mouth, tried to look in any direction but at Ethan, which was a challenge with him so near, invading her space.

"That's nice," she said at last, feeling as if he were waiting for her to speak.

"Nice? You haven't *had* nice, yet. Meggie and I have some special plans for next weekend, and you're invited."

It wasn't exactly a question, so Glory, as usual, didn't know how to respond.

Actually, she did; she just was afraid to say the words.

"Ethan, I can't be away from the shelter on the weekend. It's my busiest time, as you can see from today. The women need me."

Ethan reached for her hands, and just stood quietly before her for a moment, looking down at her with his warm, twinkling gaze, and softly brushing her palms with his thumbs.

"They'll get along without you for one Saturday."

"Ethan, I—"

"Ginger said you'd give me grief on this. Don't you want to prove your sister wrong?"

"What's Ginger got to do with this?"

"*Ginger's* going to cover for you," he said softly, persuasively.

He dropped her hands and cupped her chin, tipping her head up to meet his eyes. "She'll be here anyway, teaching computer lessons. She knows what to do, Glory. And she can handle it."

"I know, but—"

"I talked to a few of the women in the shelter. They're okay with this. More than okay. They're rooting for you.

"Glory, you need to get outside. Enjoy the scenery. See God's grandeur. Live it up a little bit."

He slid his hands down her neck to her shoulders, and she stopped breathing. "Come with me to Puget Sound. Smell the sea, embrace the air."

"Ethan, God's called me to—"

"God didn't call you to live apart from the world, Glory. *In* the world, but not out of it."

He pulled her closer, pleading as much with the gentle caresses of his hands as he was with the tone of his voice, more serious than she'd ever heard him.

"Glory, please. Come with us."

The silent air between them thickened and Glory swallowed hard.

What could she say?

What was the right answer to Ethan's simple question?

What would God want her to do?

She'd never been faced with such a situation,

and it floored her physically, emotionally and spiritually.

For a moment, she wished him away. Without Ethan in the picture, her way was clear and uncluttered.

Yet Ethan brought so much warmth and light with him wherever he went. He encouraged the work of God, with his money, but much more with his presence.

And yet....

Abruptly Ethan turned and stepped away. "Well...."

He said the word as a goodbye. Glory pinched her eyes closed against the tide of emotions running through her.

"Well...." she repeated.

Ethan looked back for a brief moment, then puckered his lips in that way he had, and walked out of the storage room. Cocky, confident and whistling softly under his breath.

The man defied incorrigible. He was irritating, annoying, sometimes obnoxious and absolutely endearing. How would she ever get by?

Whistling a bouncy polka, Ethan adjusted his tie and gazed at the figure he made in his full-length mirror. Dark denim jeans, a crisp white linen shirt, and a paisley tie that felt a little too tight.

Meggie tottered into the room, and he immediately crouched down to her level. She reached for his tie and gave it a strong tug.

"Lose the tie, huh?" he asked, chuckling when she answered him in baby talk. "I thought so, too."

He pulled at the knot and let the tie fall free to the floor. "Do you think I should roll up my sleeves, or would that be too casual?"

He stretched to his full height.

Casual.

Nothing he ever did with Glory was casual. He'd always been good with people, especially women.

Glory Weston was definitely the exception to the rule. She was the most straightforward woman Ethan had ever known.

And yet with him, her yes was no, and her no, yes.

Which was why, he guessed, she'd called him up three days after she'd turned him down and told him she'd take him up on his offer.

He wouldn't look a gift horse in the mouth. Whether it was as a result of Ginger's prodding or a decision Glory had come to on her own, he was going to take advantage of the situation.

He'd promised to show her a good time, and with Meggie at his side, he most certainly would. He'd treat both his ladies like the princesses they were.

Of course, Glory, A-type personality that she was, would be mortified to discover he really didn't have any *precise* plans where the day was concerned.

She would want to plan every millisecond, know exactly where she was going, and when she would get there.

But he wasn't going to tell her of his plans, or lack thereof. He hadn't figured much past going to Puget Sound. What Glory needed was the fresh sting of saltwater, a dab of sunshine and a few flowers thrown in for effect.

He had a general plan. They'd catch an outgoing ferry to whatever island it was headed for, and let the rest of the day take care of itself.

It always did, in his experience.

The important thing was that, planned or unplanned, he'd be with Glory. He'd have the whole, complete, wonderful day with her all to himself. He hadn't looked forward to anything like this since he was a kid going to Disneyland. Come to think of it, Glory was even better.

He grinned at Meggie and swept her into his arms. "What do you think, kiddo? Your old man ready to get serious about a lady?"

"I can't believe you talked me into this," Glory complained, glaring at her sister's reflection in the vanity mirror. She winced as her sister pulled a section of her hair tight against her scalp.

"You're the one who decided to go out with Ethan, and you know it. I just had to nudge you a little to make the right decision."

"Do the words *invasion of privacy* mean anything to you?" she teased.

Ginger burst into melodious laughter, one of many traits Glory envied in her. "Oh, yeah, right. That's why you called me as soon as you got home that night. So you could protect your *privacy.*"

"Point well taken."

Biting her lower lip, Ginger pulled up another strand of Glory's hair and then bent to survey her reflection in the mirror.

"Ouch! Watch it with the hair." Glory made a face at her sister's reflection. "If you pull any harder you're going to pull all my hair out."

"*You* were the one who wanted a French braid. If you'd gone wash-and-wear, you wouldn't be making weird faces at me."

"Ethan has seen me wash-and-wear. I wanted something a little different for this… um…outing."

"Date. It's called a *date,* Glory."

"This isn't a date." Glory shifted in her seat, afraid to give in to the moment, especially with her sister here.

Hope welled in her nonetheless. *Oh, heavenly Father,* she prayed silently. *Do I really dare to hope Ethan might be the one?*

The one. The very thought took her breath away.

She did her best to hide the flush that rose to her cheeks, but with little expectation of success. Ginger noticed everything.

Everything.

"He asked you out in a supply closet, for pity's sake. Give it up, sis. I'm on to you."

Glory wanted to laugh. Ginger had continued their conversation without missing a beat, while she herself was having major personal revelations that felt like fireworks blasting.

Or maybe that was why Ginger chattered on, not that chattering was an extraordinary characteristic for Ginger.

Suddenly and spontaneously, Glory stood and turned, embracing her sister for all she was worth, and trying hard not to cry on her shoulder. She wouldn't want to ruin the great makeup job Ginger had done in her sudden rush of happiness.

She just wanted to share what she felt, but couldn't say it out loud.

She expected Ginger to pull away after a moment, but instead, she found herself in an embrace every bit as tight and fervent as her own. And to her very great surprise, the tears being shed were a surprisingly mute Ginger's.

Chapter Eight

❧

"Honk!" The animated toddler flapped her arms and legs in excitement. "Honk, Papa Ethan. Honk!"

Ethan slipped Glory an amused glance and then smiled patronizingly at Meggie. His convertible was right in the middle of bumper-to-bumper traffic four cars across and at least ten deep.

"We have to wait for the boat, sweetie."

Meggie pointed at the dock. "Boat."

Clearly, she thought Papa Ethan was missing the obvious, and Ethan's smile widened as Glory chuckled under her breath.

"Blind, dumb or both?" he quipped.

"Ethan, that little girl obviously expects you to work miracles, as if you do it on a daily basis."

"Jesus is the only Miracle Worker, if my gray-haired Sunday school teacher has anything to say about it."

Glory nearly sat up straight in her seat. Ethan had said Jesus *is* the Miracle Worker.

Is. Maybe Ethan Wheeler's heart wasn't as hard as he thought.

She looked out over the broad dock and into Puget Sound. The sun was glimmering off the water in a way that made Glory's heart dance.

"When do we get in line for the boat?" she asked, adding quickly as an afterthought, "Not that I'm in a hurry or anything."

Ethan's gale of laughter was backed securely by the glow of amusement in his eyes. "We *are* in line."

Glory raised a brow.

"How so?" she asked, thinking the sailors on the dock might call them by rows of automobiles. Or maybe Ethan had a ticket.

She longed to get some fresh air while they

were waiting to load. The convertible was nice, but kind of cramped to be sitting for so long. She wanted to experience nature, not man-made steel.

"Don't they have a waiting area outside? The weather is so lovely today. I hate to miss it."

Ethan chuckled again. "We'll be off in a moment." Suddenly he turned to her, his expression serious. "Glory, how long have you lived in Seattle?"

"Three years. Why?"

"And how many times in those three years have you been to see the ocean?"

She'd been wondering at his line of thought, and suddenly it was clear. He was going to get on her case just like Ginger did.

She felt her heart, which had moments before been rejoicing in the day, fill with discouragement.

"Glory?" He reached across the seat and softly brushed her hair away from her face.

"All right, already," she snapped, crossing her arms over her chest and desperately wishing she'd never agreed to come. "I've never been to the ocean. Is that such a crime? I don't like seafood. I didn't see the point of going.''

She hated that she'd put in those last words. It sounded as if she were trying to justify herself, which she wasn't.

Not that it mattered. Ethan was otherwise engaged. He'd started the ignition and was slowly following the car in front of him down to the edge of the dock.

''The whole car goes onto the ferry?'' she asked in astonishment, knowing she sounded a little like a kid with a new discovery.

The cars were going line by line into the bowels of the ship, which, she discovered, were more than large enough to handle them.

Which brought Glory to another discovery, this one not so fine. ''Ethan, I'm claustrophobic.''

He chuckled loudly. ''We're in a convertible, remember?''

His hand still rested against her cheek, and he reached behind her, lightly tickling the back of her neck with his fingers. ''Don't worry, gorgeous, we don't have to stay in the car.''

''You'll never know how glad I am to hear you say that.''

Impetuously, she reached back behind her and laid her hand over his, giving his fingers a light squeeze.

He, in turn, immediately pulled both their hands over her head and down between them on the car seat, where he gently laced their fingers.

Glory swept in a surprised breath, resisting the automatic urge to pull away.

It had been a long time since she'd held hands with a man. Her urge to pull away was fight or flight, she supposed. But she wondered if holding hands with Ethan meant the same thing that holding hands with a boy did when she was younger.

She certainly hoped so.

At Ethan's direction, the three of them exited his car and made their way up the stairs to the top of the ferry, where Ethan promised she could look out over the bow and breathe in the tangy salt air. After a tour of the boat and a snack, the three of them found a place to stand next to the railing.

Glory didn't think the ferry was moving very quickly, but nevertheless, the salt spray hit her face as she leaned out over the edge of the railing. She took a deep breath of the air and gasped in delight.

Ethan, bouncing Meggie on his arm to keep her occupied, watched Glory enjoy her first taste of the sea. He smiled, a smile that came from the very depths of his heart and soul.

What was it about Glory that made him want to wrestle the world into submission and hand it to her on a platter?

Glory whirled, her arms open as if for an embrace. Her green eyes were sparkling, her short, wispy red hair framing her head like a halo. "Oh, Ethan, it was just as you said it would be."

He chuckled. "I'm glad you like it. And remember, the day is only beginning!"

"Not to inflate your ego, hon," she said, winking at him in a way that made him want to do back flips, "but you must know you've created a fairy tale here. I can't wait to see what you've got planned next."

He cleared his throat. "Planned…yes, well…."

He was saved by the sound of horns bellowing that they would soon be approaching the dock.

"Belowdecks, me swabbies," he barked, tickling Meggie's tummy as she wiggled and giggled in his arms. "We're about to dock and deploy. Let the fairy tale commence."

By the time they'd reached Ethan's car, the troops were, in fact, disembarking for fairer shores. Ethan had been secretive and close-mouthed about what they'd be doing on the island, which he refused to tell her the name of, even.

He told her he wanted to keep a bit of mystery in the day, which only served to make Glory more curious, and to increase her anticipation. Which, she supposed, was the point.

The island was green, as was all of the Seattle area, but the little island gave her a sense of being all alone in the world. Well, almost all alone, and thank God for that. She wouldn't want to discount Ethan and Meggie for the world.

"My goodness," she commented as they moved away from where they'd parked.

It was one thing to hear Ethan say they could walk around the island without the use of a vehicle, but it was quite another thing to see it was so.

"That's all you're going to say?" Ethan quipped back. "My goodness?"

He shook his head and laughed. "Should I duck and run for cover?"

She punched him playfully on the arm, and he howled accordingly.

"Cut it out, silly. I was just thinking about how the seclusion of an island kind of gives you the feeling of being able to shirk off all your worries, all your stress, you know?"

He swung his arm around her shoulders so tight that he could bend his elbow, then pulled her forehead to his.

For a moment, he didn't speak, though his mouth made that cute little pucker that was half a smile and half an indication he was thinking of speaking.

"I'm glad," he murmured at last, and then the next instant he was rushing ahead of her, swinging Meggie around and calling for Glory to hurry up and follow him up a rather steep hill.

"Things to do, places to go, people to meet. Hurry up, and don't be late!"

She knew he was teasing her, but for some funny reason, his words made her feel better than she had in years.

Maybe ever.

To Ethan's very great surprise, the fact that he didn't have a plan didn't appear to bother Glory. A new, spontaneous woman was born as they walked, talked and laughed.

Or maybe her spontaneity wasn't new at all. Maybe she'd just suppressed it.

Now he was sounding like a psychiatrist or something. Next he'd be analyzing what she ate for breakfast.

But he was sorry to see the day end.

He leaned over the railing of the ferry and took a deep breath, enjoying the cool spray. Though the Seattle area in general stayed moderately comfortable year-round, the humidity still had him sweating, especially with all the walking they'd done.

Glory—and Meggie, in her own little way—wanted to see everything, walk every inch of the island, and most especially, to check out every little shop. Glory had swept Meggie away several times to inspect the toy aisles.

He, apparently, had been brought along to carry packages, he thought, unable to keep the grin from his face.

Women!

He moved to where Glory and Meggie were sharing a double-chocolate ice-cream cone. As he sat down beside Glory and dropped a casual arm around her, he wondered which of his sweet ladies was enjoying the treat more.

"So which part did you like best?"

He could feel the shuddering motion of Glory's shoulders as she chuckled softly. "If you're asking Meggie, I think she would have to say this yummy ice-cream cone."

He leaned close to her neck, inhaling the soft, floral scent that was Glory Weston.

"I was asking *you,*" he whispered, able to feel his own breath off her skin. How close his lips were to the delicate skin beneath them. How sensitive each nerve felt as he considered the taste and feel of her skin beneath his lips.

With all his might, he pinched his lips together and pulled back, removing his arm from her and leaning hard on his elbows, clasping his hands in his lap.

Glory didn't move for a moment, then became intensely animated, bouncing Meggie on her knee and scrunching her face to look as if she were seriously contemplating his question about the day.

He knew, in fact, that she wasn't—at least, if their closeness affected her as much as it had affected him.

"I can't decide whether it was the kite flying or—" she paused to look contemplative "—the clam chowder. Yes, definitely the clam chowder."

Ethan barked out a laugh. "Yeah, Miss I-hate-fish-so-why-should-I-see-the-ocean Weston. **Have** you ever actually *had* fish before today?"

She shoved her chin in the air and looked offended. "Your father," she told the little girl on her lap, "is incorrigible. Completely incorrigible."

Ethan shook his head. "We've established that. And you're avoiding the issue."

Glory leaned in close, looking him right in

the eye. He could smell her perfume again, and wondered why he'd never noticed or been affected by a woman's scent before, as he did Glory's.

"I *hate* fish. I have *tasted* fish, and I absolutely, positively, beyond a shadow of a doubt *hate* fish."

He grinned. "Okay, then. It sounds as if maybe I've hit a soft spot with you?"

"I'm sorry, Ethan," she immediately apologized, looking genuinely contrite and pulling away from their duel of gazes.

"Hey, I was only kidding."

She made a sound that was half a laugh and half a groan. "I know you were."

He could take offense to that comment, especially the way she said it, but he wouldn't. Not when there was something bothering Glory.

"I promise I won't take you to a seafood restaurant."

Glory's gaze flashed back to Ethan. His statement could have been a joke, and probably was, however mistimed. But she didn't think so. For once, Ethan Wheeler was being completely serious.

Which left her to explain *her* outburst.

"People are allowed to dislike certain foods, but for some reason when I indicate my preferences, people always assume I've never tried fish. I guess maybe fish is one of those things like asparagus and broccoli that most kids hate, but eventually learn to like when they've grown up."

"So what you're telling me is that you haven't grown up."

Laughter burst from her before she could stop it.

"Yeah, right. That's it." She shook her head. "I've been accused of a lot of things, but never not growing up."

When the boat horn suddenly sounded, she jumped and exclaimed in surprise.

"Time to go home," she said, wondering if she sounded as disappointed as she felt. It truly had been an exceptional day. One she'd treasure always.

Ethan swept Meggie to his shoulder, helped Glory to her feet, and laced his fingers with hers. "Don't worry, sweet Glory," he whispered for her ears only as he led them down the stairs to his car. "The fairy tale is just beginning."

She thought about his comment all the way back to the shelter, where she insisted he drop her off, knowing her sister would give her a ride home. She had a mile-high stack of paper-work to do and....

A fairy tale.

She smiled softly. Why did she suddenly believe dreams just might come true?

Ethan shut down his convertible before the shelter and insisted on walking her to the door.

"Will Meggie be okay by herself?"

"She'll be fine for a minute," Ethan said next to her ear. "I've rolled her window half down, and I'm not going very far."

He grinned widely as they stopped before the door. He reached for both her hands. "Thanks for worrying about Meggie. I'm glad you care."

"Of course, I care. She's such a sweet, wonderful little girl."

He stepped closer. "Is Meggie the only one you care for?"

Glory felt herself turning every shade of red, but he wouldn't let her turn away, pulling her closer, his eyes sparkling to match his ever present grin.

"Who else?" he whispered, leaning in close.

"Okay," she admitted in a squeak, trying to look anywhere but at Ethan's face. "You."

She leaned back against the door, realizing too late she couldn't move away. Then again, maybe subconsciously she didn't want to move away.

"Just a little bit?"

One arm snaked over her, creating a shady shelter—or a steel beam against her moving to the right. She voted for the latter when he leaned even closer.

"A...lot." She wasn't sure her voice was audible, for the raging sound of her blood in her ears.

"Well," he said, hovering just over her lips, "I happen to care about you...a lot...too."

Glory closed her eyes. This was the moment she'd been dreading, and much more the moment she'd been waiting for maybe for her whole life. She could feel his breath on her cheek, and stopped breathing herself.

"Open your eyes."

Her eyes snapped open. "What?"

He grinned. "I want you to see the man you're kissing."

"Oh." She didn't know what else to say. This time, when he leaned into her, she was ready. She even leaned forward, into the space his lips would soon occupy.

Their lips.

But just as his lips brushed hers and the world began to spin, the door behind them opened.

With his arms wrapped tightly around her, they fell into the front room of the shelter, Ethan carefully twisting them so that he'd take the brunt of the fall.

A dozen pairs of eyes were looking down on them. She would have shriveled in embarrassment, were it not that every gaze, even Ginger's, was deadly serious.

It was only a split second from spinning and falling that she caught the group's emotions.

She scrambled to her feet and whirled around to face her sister. "What? What happened? What's wrong? Ginger, tell me."

Ginger grimaced. "Glory, I hate to cut your day off short on account of us, but we have a...problem."

Chapter Nine

Ethan stood, brushed off his jeans, and put a firm, comforting arm around Glory before facing the crowd. "What's up?"

Lena stepped forward. Her eyes looked like a deer caught in headlights, but her expression was cool and determined. "Mark was here."

"What?" Glory jumped out of Ethan's arms. "What do you mean Mark was *here?* At the shelter?"

Ethan was out the door as fast as he'd fallen in, returning moments later with a sleeping Meggie tucked safely in his arms.

He kissed Meggie's forehead tenderly, then

turned to the other women. "Tell me everything. From the beginning. Every single detail that might be important later on."

Ginger chuckled dryly. "You sound like a cop."

Glory lowered her gaze on Ginger, who shrugged. "A good cop," she amended.

Ethan paced back and forth as he listened to the sisters tease each other, and attempted to think through the dilemma. "A cop," he said softly, and then louder, "Hey, that's not a bad idea. Did someone call the police?"

"They won't do anything," Glory stated.

He wondered how she could be so sure of herself when she didn't know all the facts, but he didn't voice the question aloud. She'd already taken charge of the situation, and she was really very good at it.

He couldn't help but admire her strength and calm, and how her attitude radiated among the group of obviously shaken, if not terrified, women.

"Exactly," said a young blond woman toting a baby on her hip. "There's a restraining order on Mark, so they could technically come and haul him off if he was making a scene here, but Mark's too smart for that.''

"What happened?" Ethan asked again. He was surprised when it was Lena who answered.

"Mark played the oldest trick in the book. I mean, it's been on television a million times. He came dressed as a computer specialist. Said he was here to fix one of our computers." She shivered.

Ethan felt like shivering, too. "How'd he know about the computers?"

"It's hard to say," Glory answered. "He's obviously keeping a pretty close watch on us, but we don't know how he does it."

"Did you let him in?"

Ginger snorted. "I may be blond, but I'm not stupid. I sent him packing in a second."

"Didn't that make him angry?"

"He's always angry." Lena made a choking sound. "He's also smooth as butter. Good-looking, mild-mannered. The kind of guy you'd let in the front door if you didn't know better."

Ethan opened his arms to Lena. He wasn't sure she'd be wanting any contact with a man so soon after this incident, but she also looked frazzled and alone.

To his surprise, though, she accepted his proffered hug, and he offered her what comfort he could.

He wanted to do so much for her—for all the women here at Angel's Wings. And right now, he wanted to knock Mark's lights out.

These women were all putting on a brave face, but a casual observer could tell they were scared to death. And rightly so, Ethan thought, clenching his fist despite his best efforts to the contrary.

These were *his* women.

Glory was writing frantically on a clipboard, and Ginger was dancing distractedly from foot to foot.

"I'm really sorry, sis," she said quietly, for Glory's ears only. Ethan looked away, not letting on that he'd heard.

Glory shook her head and frowned. "It's not your fault. Mark made the advance, not you. You couldn't have known."

She hugged her sister tight. "I shouldn't have left the shelter. I knew better. It was my mistake."

Ethan felt his heart drop like lead into his

stomach. They'd encountered a very serious situation, and he'd do everything within his power to make sure it didn't happen again.

But he hurt like he'd never hurt before when Glory had so quickly brushed off their day together. A stabbing pain emanated from his chest, in the general vicinity of his heart.

She'd called it a mistake.

Their fairy-tale day. A mistake.

But there was no doubt Glory meant what she said. She quickly hustled the shelter women away, getting them busy at this task or that, or simply and quietly suggesting they return to their rooms.

When only he, Glory and Ginger remained, Glory ushered them into the office, where she did most of her paperwork. Sitting behind her desk, she steepled her fingers and shifted her gaze from Ethan to Ginger and back.

Ethan smiled, but Glory's expression was cold and unreadable.

He swallowed hard. She looked at him— through him—as if he were simply an employee, a casual acquaintance.

Or maybe a complete stranger.

The woman he saw staring back at him didn't believe in fairy tales.

His throat pinched tighter.

"Well?" Ginger finally asked, after a prolonged silence. "I'm assuming we're supposed to be coming up with solutions to our current crisis."

Ethan silently thanked Ginger for taking the initiative.

Glory laid her hands flat on the table and leaned forward. "Do you have any solutions?"

The room faded into uncomfortable silence. They all looked at one another, but no words were said.

After an extended moment, Ethan cleared his throat. "I, um...do."

Both women stared at him in surprise.

"Why are you surprised? You think I don't know anything about what's happening?"

Glory lifted one eyebrow.

"Okay, well, maybe not. But I have a question, at least."

"Shoot," said both sisters simultaneously, a sisterly inclination which made him want to smile deep down.

"Couldn't we beef up the level of security around here?"

Before they could answer, he continued. "Actually, my question is really, what *is* the current level of security around here? I haven't seen any. Security, that is."

He felt as if Glory were glaring at him, although, considering the turn of events, he might be wrong. Still....

"I'm not criticizing what you've done here, Glory. I'm just trying to figure out how to fix the current problem."

Ginger barked a laugh, breaking into the tension in the room. "Isn't that just like a man? Everything that's been going on around him, and he wants to *fix the problem.*"

Ethan raised both eyebrows and set his arms akimbo. "You want to talk about our feelings?"

Even Glory laughed at that one, but only for a moment.

"Sit down, Ethan," she said, sweeping an encouraging hand at a folded chair leaning against the wall. "You, too, sis. We may be here awhile."

Obligingly, Ethan unfolded a chair for Ginger, then took one for himself and turned it backward before sitting down, so he could lean his arms against the chair back.

"Our security," Glory began, "must, by necessity, remain loose."

"I don't understand," he said softly.

Glory smiled, almost indulgently. "If we put up tall fences and barbed wire around the place, it'd be a dead giveaway that this isn't just any normal, if somewhat wealthy, home set apart from the bustle of the city. Bells and whistles."

"Yeah," agreed Ginger. "Besides, barbed wire or some such might make the ladies feel like they were in prison, you know?"

Ethan chuckled, though he didn't really feel the mirth. "You ladies are making fun of me."

"Of course," said Ginger.

"Not really, Ethan," said Glory at the same time.

He shrugged. "Which is it?"

"I was exaggerating with the barbed wire, but I had a point."

"Machine guns aside, couldn't you at least hire security guards to patrol the surrounding area? Even unarmed guards would help, I think, though I'd recommend the armed variety.''

''Perhaps,'' Glory agreed with a nod. ''But then again, those same guards, who'd no doubt make some women feel safe, would also remind others just how much they've fallen from a normal, sane lifestyle.''

''Yes, but they're hiding from potentially violent husbands,'' he contended, gripping the chair back with his fists.

''Most of these guys won't ever *actually* pursue their wives or girlfriends to a shelter,'' Ginger explained quietly. ''After the initial, critical few days, most guys give up and go on to seek greener pastures.

''But the women here have to go on, and hopefully not into another abusive relationship. That's where Angel's Wings can really help. Especially thanks to your new computers.''

''They're your computers,'' he answered automatically. ''So most guys give up, but there are a few Marks out there who can't give it up.''

''Unfortunately, he's not the first man to make an issue out of his wife and children being here. There are shelters more conducive to those who know they're being pursued.''

She shook her head sadly. ''It looks like we may have to move Lena and Stephen and Mary to another shelter.''

Ethan nodded. ''I'll help. But I don't understand why they weren't moved before. Everyone seemed to know who Mark was, and to look out for him, which means this wasn't the first assault, was it?''

Glory sighed. Ethan was so zealous and fervent about every little thing. And she was tired. Very, very tired.

''I've been trying to get them to move, ever since he started sending letters and threatening notes to the shelter address.

''Unfortunately, Lena's a stubborn woman, and she doesn't want to leave. She says she's tired of feeling like a fox on the hunt, running from borough to borough every time she hears the bay of the hunter's dogs, and the bugle of the hunter's horn.''

''I can see her point.''

He would see her point, of course. She glanced tiredly at her sister, and then back to

Ethan. "Hopefully, she'll change her mind now that he's actually come to the shelter."

"More people than just Lena could get hurt in all this," Ginger pointed out grimly, before kissing Glory on the cheek and saying her goodbyes to both of them, having a prior engagement to teach at a university. "You know I'm talking truth here, Glory.

"You've got to do something. But I'll leave you two to figure it out. I have the highest confidence in you both." She chuckled tiredly, then was gone.

Glory leaned back in her chair. Even the familiar nip and squeak of the springs didn't comfort her. Not the familiar smell of fresh-cut flowers. Not even the smooth, slick feel of her old desk under her palms.

The weight of responsibility shifted heavily on her shoulders, and she called out silently to God.

How could she possibly protect all these women? How could one woman....

Ethan leaned over her desk and picked up her creased, brown leather Bible. He ran a hand across the cover, then rifled through the pages.

"You can't protect them all, Glory," he said so softly she wondered for a moment if she'd heard him right.

The next instant she wondered, mortified, if she'd spoken her private prayer aloud.

Had Ethan heard her?

Wanting to avoid his gaze, she looked up and met his kind blue eyes instead. The usual bright amusement was missing, but in its place was a deep, burning intensity that both alarmed her and reassured her, a true paradox indeed.

"I can tell what you're thinking," he explained, and relief that she hadn't spoken her prayer aloud burst out of her lungs in a rush of air.

"I have to try," was her only response. So few words, yet the very core and soul of her being met behind them. This was what she was here for, her reason for living.

"*We* have to try," he corrected gently. "And that's not what I meant. I'll be walking beside you every step of the way with this Mark guy. You won't ever be alone.

"But I think...I think the battle is greater than just Mark, or Pete or any other jerk who batters his wife."

402   *A Daddy at Heart*

She waited wordlessly for him to continue, guessing—no, *hoping*—to hear the words of comfort she so needed right now.

"God is on your side, Glory."

He placed the Bible gently on the table and once again ran his hand across the cover, brushing his fingers over the gold inscription.

"*Holy Bible.* I wish I remembered the verses I learned as a child."

He closed his eyes and bowed his head. "I *know* God wants to protect us. And Lena. I just don't know where to find the verses that say so."

Glory stood and crossed around the table so she could put her arm around Ethan. She brushed her fingers through his soft, fine blond hair, taking comfort in his presence and his words.

"Do you remember the story of the Good Shepherd, Ethan?" she asked softly.

He nodded, and the smile that lit her day returned to his face.

"The Bible talks a lot about Jesus being our Shepherd. My favorite verse is from the prophet Isaiah:

He shall lead His flock like a Shepherd,
He shall gather the lambs in His arms,
And carry them in His bosom,
And gently lead those who are with young.

When I'm afraid or overwhelmed, I simply
picture the sweet women and children in Angel's Wings as the lambs in His arms, the little
ones tucked right on up next to His heart.''

"What about you?'' Ethan whispered, reaching for her hand. "Do you see yourself as a
lamb in the Master's arms?''

The question nearly knocked Glory off her
feet, and blew the air right out of her lungs.

She was a Christian, of course. But there
were so many souls so much needier than her
own, that she rarely considered herself in the
equation.

"You are, you know,'' Ethan said, standing.
He placed a soft kiss on her forehead, then
wrapped his arms tight around her as if he
would never let go. "My sweet Glory. Jesus's
little lamb.''

Chapter Ten

Glory had just curled up on her blue gingham sofa with a cup of hot cinnamon tea. She was glad to be home. It had been a long day, and for once, she was seeking refuge in a place away from the shelter.

She hadn't turned on the television, though the radio was playing soft Celtic hymns in the background.

She was too busy thinking about the past week at the shelter to truly relax. This day alone had been one of the roughest she'd had in her time as the shelter's director.

Of course she'd had to deal with overbearing,

angry husbands a few times in the past few years, but she had never felt the sense of imminent danger to the shelter and its occupants the way she did now.

Lena sure wasn't making it easy for her.

She'd thought Mark showing up would have her begging to be transferred to another shelter; if not for herself, for her son Stephen and little daughter Mary.

But Lena was more adamant than ever. She'd put her back up and wouldn't budge an inch.

She wasn't going to leave. She was finished running scared.

While Glory admired her strength and spirit in the face of adversity, she wondered if Lena had thought her decision completely through. Did she understand that she and her children weren't the only ones at risk if Mark became enraged?

She should have pointed it out to Lena. And she would have, but she didn't want to play on the woman's fear. Though Lena would never openly admit it, she really *was* afraid.

And with good reason, Glory thought with a shudder.

Oh, to be as strong, both in spirit and in faith, as Lena daily demonstrated. Glory's own faith- fulness and commitment paled before hers. She'd never experienced anything remotely as terrifying as what Lena had gone through with Mark.

In the end, she'd knelt with Lena in prayer for rest, peace and safety for her and her chil- dren, and prayed that Mark would give up his quest to seek vengeance on Lena and leave her alone.

The thought of Mark returning left Glory thoroughly chilled. She brought her still- steaming mug of tea to her lips and took a ten- tative sip.

Just then, someone knocked loudly on her door. Glory nearly jumped out of her skin. Tea splashed onto her lap, and she yelped in pain. Sweatpants did precious little to shield her skin from the scalding liquid, she thought, as she quickly wiped the drops away with her fingers.

Placing her mug on a coaster on her oak end table, she put her palm to her chest to still her erratically racing heart. Then she shook her head and laughed quietly at her quaky nerves.

It wasn't too smart, thinking about danger, her own vulnerability, and the present menace of Lena's husband this late at night and while she was alone, even if she was far from the shelter.

Still, the knock surprised Glory. She hadn't ordered food delivered, and relatively few people knew where she lived, leastwise many acquaintances in the Kirkland area, the location of her personal town house, which she used primarily on weekends and when she'd spent the whole day at the corporate office in Seattle.

Generally, she preferred to sleep at the shelter, so she could work as late as she wanted without having to worry about driving anywhere. The paperwork involved in running a shelter was phenomenal, and she never really felt caught up.

Maybe it was Ginger, though she rarely visited without calling first. Besides, unlike Glory, Ginger had an active nightlife, and it *was* Friday night. Her sister would be out on a date.

She cautiously opened the door partway without releasing the chain lock. "Hello?"

"Surprise!" Ethan stuck his nose in the gap, and Glory jumped back, laughing.

"Ethan. What are you doing here?"

After she'd spoken, she realized how rude she sounded, and because she hadn't meant it that way, she immediately and falteringly amended her statement. "I'm really glad to see you. It's just that you're an unexpected surprise. A nice, unexpected surprise."

Ethan chuckled and flashed her a toothy grin. "I'm glad to hear you say so. I like giving you surprises, but I like being one even more."

He was relieved she wasn't angry. He hadn't known if she'd want to see him, especially since his visit was completely unannounced and it was fairly late.

He was severely breaching the embodiment of his childhood country manners to make a house call after nine o'clock in the evening. His older brother Erik, who'd raised him, would be ashamed of his rude conduct.

But Ethan was bouncing with enthusiasm, and he just couldn't wait until tomorrow.

"Are you going to let me in? I come bearing gifts. Well, I have one gift, anyway."

Glory slammed the door—almost what he would consider in his face, he noted, but she hastily removed the chain lock, so he forgave her.

"Ethan, you don't have to bring a gift every time you see me."

"Don't worry, gorgeous, the gift is for the shelter." He stepped into the door, a pajama-clad, sleeping Meggie in his arms.

"Is it chocolate?"

He grinned and shook his head. "Not this time. Do you have a blanket or something I could lay on the floor for Meggie?"

"The *floor?*"

Glory sounded absolutely appalled, and Ethan cringed, wondering what he'd said wrong now.

"Ethan Wheeler, I'm not going to put that precious child on the *floor.*"

He shrugged uncomfortably. He put Meggie on the floor all the time, with blankets underneath her, of course. And he always snuggled her up tight.

But he sure didn't want to admit to it, in case it really was the wrong thing to do. He didn't exactly have a handbook for parenting toddlers. How was he supposed to know what to do?

He'd thought he was doing all right, but....

"Will she fall off my bed, do you think?" Glory asked, pacing from one end of the room to the other, worrying her bottom lip with her teeth as she walked. "I don't have a crib, and I don't know anyone I can borrow one from. But I don't know if she'll be safe on my bed or not."

Ethan pursed his lips, then grinned widely. "That's why I put her on the floor."

To his surprise, Glory laughed. "Okay. I'll get some blankets."

In moments, they had Meggie comfortably ensconced on the floor by the sofa. Ethan gently placed Meggie's blankie over her small body and brushed her hair back from her face.

"My bright little starburst," he said softly.

No matter how much time he spent with Meggie, his heart still welled whenever he watched her peacefully sleeping. What a blessing he'd been given.

Glory rubbed a hand across his back. He looked up, smiling, to see her looking at Meggie with much the same expression as he imagined he had, only he thought it looked much better on the beautiful redhead with sparkling green eyes and a heart-soaring smile.

That is, when he could get her to smile, which wasn't often enough for his liking. Not *nearly* often enough.

She was smiling now. "Do you want to tell me about her?" she whispered, her voice soft and silky smooth.

Suddenly he very much wanted to tell her.

"How did you know there was a story?"

"A single man raising a baby girl not his own? There's a story." She smiled tenderly. "Is she your niece?"

Ethan laughed, and realized how bitter it sounded. "No. Nothing as simple as that, though we're related by blood."

Glory only leaned back onto the couch in answer, tucking her legs beneath her.

"My cousin Sabrina and I met quite by accident in law school. My immediate family is just me and my two brothers. I didn't know we even had cousins. And then Sabrina and I met, and became good friends."

He wasn't sure he'd be able to get through this, but he gritted his teeth and continued.

"She was married to a batterer. She kept hoping Jason would change, but then she had Meggie, and the stakes changed."

Glory reached out and laced her fingers through his, giving his hand a light squeeze of comfort.

"I tried to get her away. I swear I did. But on the night we'd chosen to sneak her away, Jason discovered and—" he pounded his free fist into her couch "—killed Sabrina."

"And you got Meggie?"

"Jason went to jail, and I appealed to the courts to be the next logical choice of kin. Though I was ready to fight tooth and nail to get Meggie. Sometimes I think she's my reason for living."

"And the reason I was so graciously visited by you regarding a donation," Glory said, putting the pieces together.

"That's right."

"I know you aren't going to listen to me, but I'm going to say it anyway. It's not your fault, Ethan. There was nothing you could do to change the events as they happened.

"You are, in fact, quite amazing. Not many

men would take on a toddler. And there's not a person alive who could fault you for your job parenting Meggie.''

Ethan winced, knowing there were probably many ways he failed in parenting that he didn't even know about.

''Moving back to happier subjects,'' she said with a silky laugh, ''Where's my surprise?''

''I'll go get him,'' Ethan answered promptly, trying to swallow around the catch in his throat.

''Him?''

He cringed at the slip of his tongue, and to Glory's could-be negative reaction to it.

''Uh...I don't think I want to try to explain him to you. Just stay put and I'll be right back. No preconceived notions, okay?''

He walked back outside and pulled in a deep, fortifying breath of air. The night was cool, but he'd broken into a sweat, which he carefully wiped off with his handkerchief.

''Oh, this wasn't a good idea, Wheeler,'' he said aloud in a rush of breath. ''In fact, I think this is the worst idea you've ever had.''

And that was really saying something.

He stopped before the shiny new silver

minivan he'd purchased earlier that day and grimaced, both at his predicament and the minivan itself.

What had possessed him to buy the quintessential family car? And the crazy thing was his answer—it was Glory every bit as much as it was Meggie.

Propping his elbow on the rooftop, he leaned his head against his hand and groaned.

What was he doing lately? And why? He'd never been more confused in his life.

Two months ago he was a tightly wired corporate executive putting all his time and energy into his law firm, with his only real touch to humanity being his sweet Meggie.

He'd known where he was supposed to go, what he was supposed to do, and how he was supposed to act.

Now, more often than not, his legal assistants pulled most of the weight in the firm, while he was off chasing his dreams.

And for all that, he'd moved into a state of chaos beyond imagining. He didn't know anything anymore, and it just kept getting worse.

He was leaning against a minivan, for crying

out loud. It was laughable. Except that he didn't feel like laughing at all.

He'd seen the greatest happiness of his life since the day he'd walked into the corporate office of Angel's Wings and proposed his wacky ideas for contributing computers. That one move had ended in his contributing nothing less than the total package—Ethan Wheeler, heart and soul.

He'd not thought to find happiness, not since the death of his cousin shattered all his illusions about finding happiness in marriage.

Then Glory entered his life and changed everything. Glory. And the shelter. The ladies and children there he was learning to love and who had given him a true sense of purpose and meaning he'd been direly lacking as they freely gave their own gift of love.

Battered. Wounded. But not broken.

And yet....

There was still something missing.

Not *missing,* exactly, merely hovering just out of his reach. He knew what it was. Or more precisely, *who* it was.

The workers at the shelter talked about Jesus

Christ as if He were a friend, someone with whom they had a very personal relationship—a daily, constant experience, in stark contrast to his own infrequent, clumsy prayers to the Father.

Father, Son and Holy Spirit. He knew God. He believed Jesus died for his sins. But the daily walk thing was a new concept.

He closed his eyes, but didn't pray, at least not with words.

Making a sound that was halfway between a sigh and a groan, he pushed himself off the van and opened the back hatch. "Hey, Bruno, how are you doing, boy?"

The pitch-black German shepherd inside the metal cage scratched eagerly at his confines and whined a happy hello.

"Yeah, I'll bet you'd like me to get you out of there."

He released the dog from his cage, slammed the hatch shut, and headed for the door, feeling as if he were walking the last dance before an execution.

Yet another harebrained scheme for Ethan Wheeler. And the crowd goes wild.

Glory opened the door when he knocked, and immediately exclaimed her surprise.

"A dog?" She took a shaky step backward, and Ethan moved forward to catch her elbow.

"I'm sorry," he apologized, his heart stricken. Why was he so impulsive? Just once, it would be nice if he thought things all the way through before he embarked onto one of his novelties.

"I didn't consider the possibility that you'd be afraid of dogs."

"Oh, I'm not," she said, crouching to the dog's level and allowing him to sniff her closely fisted hand before petting him. "I love dogs. You just surprised me."

Ethan pursed his lips and grinned crookedly. "That seems to be happening a lot lately."

"What's his name?"

"Bruno."

"Bruno? That sounds like a bulldog or a mastiff or something, not a German shepherd."

He winced. "I guess you're right. It is an odd name. But I'm not responsible. The name came with the dog."

"You got him from the pound?"

"Oh, no." Ethan shook his head. "I got him at—" he took a deep breath and pressed on "—at a professional dog-training center."

When she didn't scream in protest, he continued cautiously.

"You know, where they train police K-9 units and such."

That pulled a response from her. Her eyebrows hit her hairline, and then she frowned, her dark eyebrows scrunched endearingly together over her small, straight nose.

"What does that mean? That he is trained to be a fighting dog?"

"In a sense. He's been through several levels of training. He can track, run agility paths, sniff out drugs or people, and bring down a criminal, among other things."

Glory pinched her lips and looked away, but Ethan caught her expression before she did— like she wanted to cry. It ate him up inside.

Glory wasn't the crying type.

She cleared her throat and squared her shoulders. "I think I know where you're going with this. I'm sorry, Ethan, but I'm afraid I'm going to have to nix this particular idea right here and right now, before it gets out of control.

"I hope you understand, and that there will be no problem giving him back to his training center and getting a refund."

Ethan frowned, feeling as if he'd been punched in the gut. She was being totally unfair! And without even hearing the facts!

He'd expected resistance, but not an out-and-out refusal to even consider the matter. That was hardly reasonable.

Fortunately for him, he was a lawyer, and Bruno *was* a good idea. Glory just didn't know it yet.

But she would.

"Madame Director," he said in his best closing argument voice, "you have yet to examine the facts in this case. I'm sure if you'll consider the matter you'll see—"

"I won't see your point of view," she snapped, cutting him off.

"That wasn't what I was going to say," Ethan replied, confounded.

"No?"

"No. I was *going* to say that you haven't yet heard, much less examined, the facts in this case."

Glory blanched, then nodded apologetically. He was quite right. She hadn't let him say a word, much less explain why Bruno was here.

She owed him that, at least. He was a good friend, and she knew he had the best interests of the shelter in mind, however misguided his harebrained scheme.

"You've tried and found me guilty, sir."

A moment ago he'd looked hurt and angry, but in a wink, or maybe that was *with* a wink, his expression returned to the old, cheerful Ethan she knew and loved, accompanied by that sweet little pucker that suggested a smile.

"Does that make me the judge? 'Cause if I get to deal out the punishment..."

His eyes were shining, and there was no mistaking his meaning.

A blush rose up her neck and into her face. It was an unfortunate aspect of being a redhead; the light, smooth skin that beamed like Rudolph's nose whenever she was embarrassed.

Part of her wanted to run and hide at his implications. How could he tease her this way?

Then again, running straight into his arms wasn't such a bad idea, either, as ideas went. She fought to suppress a grin.

"Would you like a cup of tea?" she offered, resisting the impulse to flee, or something worse and infinitely more problematic. "I have several herbal blends to choose from."

Ethan shook his head. "I'm a coffee man, myself. Tea isn't my cup. Not manly enough for my tastes, you know."

He grinned. "But don't feel obligated to make coffee on my account. I'll do just fine with a glass of water."

"I would feel blessed to make you coffee," she said, then colored at the awkward language she'd learned from her mother.

His smile made it all worthwhile, as he sauntered out of the kitchen, looking as if he had the world in his pocket.

Glad for something to keep her occupied for a moment, Glory set about to make a pot of coffee for Ethan while he wrestled quietly with Bruno on the rug.

It struck her that there was something oddly domestic about the situation—a man, a woman, a baby and a dog, all happily, contentedly together on a Friday night.

She shook her head. Her woolgathering was

going to get her into trouble one of these days. She definitely ought to be thinking more about the big black dog, and less about the big, irrepressible man.

What in the world was she going to do with a German shepherd?

Because she was relatively certain Ethan was going to talk her into whatever outrageous scheme he had concocted. To her increasing chagrin, she found she couldn't say no to the man.

Who could resist him when he pursed his lips and cracked that crooked smile that made the sun shine?

And the dog was pretty charming, too.

Bringing a large mug of coffee to Ethan, she settled onto the sofa. Bruno immediately moved in her direction, placing his chin on her knee and looking up at her, pleading for attention with his big, black eyes.

"Oh, you men are all alike," she said, scratching the dog behind his ears.

"We all want attention?" Ethan asked, still crouching on the floor.

"No, I was thinking more about the puppy-dog look that helps you get your way."

Ethan sat down beside her on the sofa, his arm resting lightly over her shoulders. With his hand on her cheek, he gently turned her head until their gazes locked. His eyes were full of compassion and something else she didn't dare hope to recognize.

"I'm not trying to get my own way here," he said softly. "It's completely your decision, Glory, and I'll respect whatever you decide."

She sighed softly. "Remember, Ethan, whatever *I* think about Bruno, he has to be approved by the board of directors."

"How could I forget?" He grinned, his eyes sparkling. "I brought him here tonight because I wanted you to become acquainted with Bruno first. *Before* I made a formal proposal to the board."

Glory was ashamed of the way she had acted earlier, jumping to conclusions before Ethan had a chance to say a word. She prayed for forgiveness. She had an exceptionally hard heart. God sometimes had to take a jackhammer to it.

"Ethan, I am *so* sorry. I acted like a complete dumbbell earlier. Will you forgive me?"

He looked surprised.

"I know what you're thinking. Glory Weston, the world's number one Frost Queen, coming down from her icy throne to apologize."

"Glory, I wasn't thinking anything of the sort," he protested rather loudly.

She shook her head. "I saw your face. I'm not blaming you. It's true."

"Glory." He took her by the shoulders and turned her to face him. "Be quiet for a minute."

She laughed, struggling *not* to struggle in his arms. He was holding her gently, but her flight instinct had kicked in nonetheless.

"I admit I was surprised, but not by your apology. I've never met a woman with more honor, dignity, strength, character and love as you have, or a woman that I've admired more.

"I was surprised because I've never had anyone ask me for forgiveness before. I—it—"

With a huff of breath, he cut off whatever it was he was going to say.

His blue eyes were blazing, sparkling stars. The myriad emotions in his gaze were beyond reading.

Glory struggled for something to say, but Ethan cut her off with a look.

She found herself leaning into his hand, which had slid up her shoulder to cup her jaw. His other hand slid around her back, pulling her closer.

"Glory, I—" he said, his voice raw and husky.

This time it was she who cut Ethan off. The cool, brisk scent of his aftershave, the sweet smell of his warm breath, and the burning look in his eyes all melted together to send her head spinning.

His lips were mere inches from hers. She closed the gap in an instant, freezing just as their lips met.

What was she doing?

Passing the point of no return.

Kissing the man she loved.

Chapter Eleven

It was as easy as that, and every bit much as difficult.

As Ethan deepened the kiss, murmuring sweet nothings under his breath, he knew he'd passed the point of no return. Glory might not know it, but his lips were sealing his intent. His commitment.

His love?

It was worth exploring, he thought, grinning over her lips.

"What's so funny?" she murmured, cuddling into his chest.

"Funny?"

"You were smiling."

"Of course I was smiling. I just kissed a beautiful woman."

"Thank you." He barely heard the words, muffled as they were by his T-shirt.

"Heh, heh," he said, trying to sound like the bad guy. "Anytime, gorgeous. Anytime."

She swatted him with her hand, and their camaraderie was instantly restored. Ethan was glad. As much as he wanted to keep kissing and snuggling all evening, they still had to deal with the subject of a very active, pacing Bruno.

"We have to talk about the dog," he reminded her regretfully.

"Okay," she said softly. "Talk away."

She yawned, then gestured her apology with her hand. "I'm listening."

"Don't let me keep you awake," he teased, chuckling loudly.

She covered her mouth over another yawn. "Don't worry. I won't crash on you. I'm just so...*comfortable* at the moment."

He hoped so, as she hadn't moved out of his embrace. He had her right where he wanted her, in the best sense of the words.

"I bought Bruno for the shelter."

He could feel her chuckle into his shirt. "I suspected as much."

"Then why did you say it wasn't a good idea?" In for a penny…

"Um, can I *not* answer on the grounds that it may incriminate me?"

"Not in this court."

She stretched, reminding Ethan of a cat, then wrapped her arms lazily around his neck, kissed his cheek, and snuggled into his side.

"Ethan, you're a wonderful, kind, caring man. But you do—occasionally—have the tendency to run off half-cocked in your enthusiasm to help out."

"I can see how someone might *possibly* think that about me." He tried to sound wounded, but didn't think he succeeded very well.

He wasn't going to admit to anything if he could avoid it. He pursed his lips in an attempt to keep from smiling.

"But what does that have to do with you and me?"

"You, me and Bruno here," she reminded

him in a wry tone. "The fact of the matter is, we can't have a dog at the shelter, Ethan, no matter how much I'd like to accommodate you."

Why did he get the feeling she wasn't going to listen to his proposal? Her ears were closed.

He squeezed a tight fist in his frustration with Glory. The woman swung as widely as a pendulum in her emotions and actions.

"Why not?" he asked, after an extended silence.

He wasn't usually silent, especially when he felt as strongly about an issue as he did about Bruno. But he didn't know what to say, didn't know how to convince her to at least give it a try.

Maybe it was having to approach the board of directors that was holding her back. But then again, she knew there was very little Ethan Wheeler couldn't get around if he put his mind to it.

If he could win Glory to his side....

"Why not?" she echoed his question, sounding as if he'd spoken the question in a foreign language.

"Why not? Well, for starters, a dog would be unsanitary. I can't have a big, slobbery dog wandering around the shelter. I have hygiene issues to think about.

"Another issue is, of course, safety. We have a number of children at the shelter, as you well know. Many of them are too little to be around such a big dog. What if he bit someone? Can you picture some of these problems here?"

Ethan shrugged, but she didn't let him talk.

"If I brought Bruno in, I'm sure it would cause a huge ruckus among the women living at Angel's Wings."

He sighed. "Are you finished yet?"

She clamped her mouth shut, her eyes wide, then nodded her answer to his question.

"Okay, then. Let's take these concerns of yours one by one."

He ticked them off on his fingers.

"First, hygiene. Bruno is a dog, not a walking, barking germ carrier. He's no more dangerous than you or me. If there's a kid with allergies or something, we could make allowances accordingly. He'd only be allowed in some of the public rooms, and would mostly remain outside doing his duty."

"Hmm," she said, absently stroking his jaw with her fingers, making it awfully hard to think about the matter at hand.

"Second," he continued, trying to ignore the feelings she stirred in him with every caress, "we don't necessarily have to have an inside dog at all, if that becomes a monumental problem."

"I don't understand."

Ethan blew out a breath. Why hadn't he started with the rationale behind getting Bruno in the first place? Or had he tried?

He grinned. It was time to start out with another round.

"I've been going over and over the problem of security at Angel's Wings, and until Bruno, I hadn't been able to come up with a solution."

"Security," she said, sounding surprised.

Ethan cocked his head at her and raised his eyebrows. "Of course. It's the perfect solution, even if I do say so myself. What, you thought I bought you a full-grown dog without asking you about it first? He's on loan, you know."

She pinched her lips wryly, as if holding back a smile. "Explain, you big lug."

She pushed away from him and pulled her legs up on the sofa, wrapping her arms around them. She looked adorably mussed as she pushed her hair back over her head and wiggled her bare feet.

His heart swelled in his chest.

Her expression, however, was suddenly all interest, and all business. Too bad!

"The training center allowed me to interact with several dogs, and there were more that I saw and didn't mingle with.

"I picked Bruno because the two of us hit it off right away. He's a tough old fellow, but he's got such a kindness in his eyes."

He stopped talking, and then added as an afterthought, "But there are other dogs."

"You said that."

"What I mean is, Bruno is an inside-outside dog. He's been especially socialized to small children, though all the dogs are well socialized to people of all ages.

"Bruno's supposed to go to a family, or to the police, since police dogs usually go home with the K-9 officer at night. You know, the kind of dog a criminal wouldn't know was specially trained until it was already too late."

He chuckled, and it bothered him that she didn't join him. He cleared his throat and continued.

"The dogs trained to be more suited to guarding large businesses, the outside dogs, are usually sold as a group, so they have regular canine interaction, if not human interaction. Those are the ones you see on television action movies—the ones patrolling the grounds with a bite worse than their barks.

"Either way, they have training classes for you to learn how guard dogs work, and how to work with them. If you decide in favor of Bruno, I'll sign you and the rest of your immediate staff up for lessons. We'll want to be careful how many people we have working specifically with Bruno, for security reasons."

He stopped talking.

He didn't have anything else to say. His last sentence had been worded half as a joke, but Glory hadn't laughed. And it was terribly awkward to sit and watch Glory and not speak.

He rubbed his palms flat against the denim of his jeans and waited.

Her lips were tightly pinched and her brow

low. She looked much like a young girl concentrating on drawing a picture.

Only there was no picture. Just his knee, if he interpreted the direction of her gaze correctly.

"Glory?"

She looked up slowly, her lips still pinched. But her green eyes were wide and clear. "Well, I guess the best way to figure this all out is to have Bruno visit the shelter. The sooner the better. Tomorrow morning, I think. First thing. Is it a date?"

Ethan grinned so wide he thought his cheeks might burst. She was giving his idea a shot, probably against her better judgment.

In answer to her question, he stood and pulled her up into his hug.

"Thank you," he whispered into her neck, enjoying the feel of brushing his lips against her soft, fragrant skin. "You won't regret it."

Glory laughed and hugged him back. "I already do, you crazy, adorable man. I already do."

Chapter Twelve

"Cool. A dog," Ginger said as she met Ethan and Glory at the door. "What a great idea!"

Glory wasn't at all sure it was a great idea; in fact, she was inclined to think it was a pretty poor one, not to reflect badly on Ethan in any way.

It was simply a matter of bad judgment.

That, and the fact that she couldn't seem to say no to Ethan when she was face-to-face with him. He'd already pushed the envelope about as far as she would—or could—allow it to stretch.

She felt tired. She couldn't keep up with him.

Maybe that was the problem. How could she continue to focus on the day-to-day work and the worries of running the shelter if she was going to be continually distracted by Ethan's latest notions?

And Ethan himself, she admitted reluctantly. She grew weary just thinking about the innumerable possibilities.

"Yes, a dog," she answered in lieu of Ethan's satisfied grin, which made her distinctly uncomfortable. It didn't take much to figure out what her sister might be thinking, and probably was. "A *guard* dog."

"Cool," Ginger said again. "What's his name? Can we introduce him to the others?"

Glory sighed. "His name is Bruno and yes, that's the general idea."

"*Bruno?* That sounds like a bulldog or mastiff or something, not a German shepherd."

Ethan cracked up. "That's exactly what Glory said."

He turned to her with that wry purse of his lips. "See? You and your sister are more alike than you realize."

Ginger appeared to appreciate Ethan's comment, if her beaming face was any indication. Glory wasn't so sure it was a compliment.

Why would Ginger want to be like *her?* Given the choice...

"Well, what are we waiting for?" Ethan asked, eager and impatient. "Bring on the kids."

"Don't you think—" Glory began, but Ginger cut her off. "I'll go get the kids and sweep by the computer room. Glory, you holler at the gals in the den."

She sighed. This was obviously going to happen with or without her. She might as well do as Ginger said. At least then she'd have a moment to warn the ladies what they were getting into.

Warning appeared not to apply when she mentioned the fact that Ethan was bringing in a dog for everyone to meet, a possible new watchdog.

She hadn't seen such enthusiasm in the place since the day the computers arrived. It was almost a stampede as some women dashed for the front hall, while others rushed to the children's quarters to round up any stray kids.

Glory followed distractedly behind the chattering group of ladies, lost in her own thoughts. She wished she could run the other way and not face this moment with Ethan.

By the time she reached the front room, Bruno was completely surrounded by two-dozen clamoring people of all sizes and ages. Even the other shelter workers were joining in the fray. Little Meggie toddled around right in the center of the mob, with Bruno flanking her faithfully.

The dog didn't seem to mind the commotion at all. In fact, it appeared he was quite happy. His tail wagged enthusiastically as he turned every which direction, licking whatever child's hand or cheek was closest.

This was precisely the kind of sanitary issues she'd been talking about, among others, she thought, feeling self-justified even if the truth was she loved dogs and didn't really consider them unhealthy.

Besides, she doubted any words of warning, especially from her, would be heard above this din. She'd heard less racket at major league baseball games.

Another big score for Ethan Wheeler, and three cheers for the same.

She realized how unkind her thoughts were, and prayed forgiveness for them. Ethan was the best man she'd ever known, yet she directed her anger at him as if he were the root of the problem.

The worst part was, he wasn't. The dog wasn't even the real issue. Bruno wasn't why she was so cross and snippy this morning.

With a shake of her head, she backed away, slipping away to her office where she could be alone and regain her equilibrium.

Sighing, she propped her hands behind her head and leaned back in her chair, squeezing her eyes closed until she could see sparkling lights on the back of her eyelids.

This was going to be one very long day. And it didn't look as if it was going to stop any time soon.

She'd woken up this morning with nothing but wonderful, giddy thoughts about the evening she and Ethan had shared.

The way it felt to see sweet Meggie napping on her floor, content as if she were in her own little crib

The way Ethan made himself at home, making his way around her house as if it were his own.

Even the way that silly dog had curled up around the hearth and looked for all the world like the cherished family pet.

She chuckled at the memories. Last night wasn't something she'd forget easily.

Ever.

Ethan's kiss had been the highlight of an evening of highlights. There weren't words to express the fantastical discoveries she'd made in the brushing of their lips, the sharing of their combined breath, the way her heartbeat had matched his pace for pace.

She'd not known such bliss existed; certainly not here on earth. To find a place where there was, for as long as it lasted, peace, pleasure and contentment, with the added advantage of the complete repression of anything bad.

No past or future; only the moment at hand. A magnificent combination of elements, if ever there was one.

But of course that had ended when Ethan walked out her front door with Bruno and Meggie in tow. The house was once again empty and sterile.

Like her heart, she supposed.

Last night had been wonderful—which was exactly why it couldn't happen again.

She would simply have to tell Ethan it had been a mistake. She knew he wouldn't want to hear it, but he certainly couldn't deny it.

They were as different as night and day.

More to the point, they were working together at Angel's Wings.

She'd completely panicked this morning when she and Ethan had arrived at the shelter at the same time. All she could think about was that it might look to others as if they'd come together.

It probably had, though her sister hadn't seemed terribly surprised or shocked. If Ginger knew things had changed, she hadn't said a word.

But if she unintentionally hurt anyone....

She couldn't do her job as the shelter director if she was constantly worried about what other people were thinking about her and Ethan, wondering if they were spending their free time together. Wondering how their relationship was progressing.

Relationship? When had it become a relationship?

It *wasn't*.

She would just have to make Ethan see why what happened last night couldn't happen again. Not if they were going to keep working with each other, as she sincerely hoped they would.

Ethan got nothing out of his time at Angel's Wings beyond God's blessing and the satisfaction of a job well done. Yet he'd done far more than he'd originally planned, drawn in by a combination of his goodness and kindness, and of the guilt he bore from his relationship with his cousin.

Neither of them had known at the time that the computers had been just the beginning.

Lately, he and Meggie were practically daily fixtures here, with no sign of leaving. Everyone—and she meant *everyone*—knew and loved them.

And she loved them most of all.

She was still musing on the subject when Ginger knocked softly at her door.

"Everything okay, sis?"

Glory did her best to smile. "Of course. Why would you think anything was wrong?"

Ginger's blue eyes glowed with amusement and concern. "C'mon, Glory. This is me you're talking to."

She shook a finger under Glory's nose. "Maybe no one else noticed, but you lit out of the hall like your tail was on fire. Spill the beans, sis. What's the story?"

Glory scowled, then realized she was better off fading her expression to feigned innocence. "There is no story."

"Right."

Okay, so she wasn't buying it. Heaven knew her sister wouldn't give up, not when she smelled a *story*. Glory banked herself for the inevitable attack.

Ginger obliged her with a wry smile. "You walk in looking like you're about ready to jump out of your skin. You won't even glance at Ethan or me, never mind make eye contact."

Glory looked away, and Ginger snorted merrily. "I'm slow, but not stupid. There's definitely a story. And it is *definitely* a story I want to hear."

Her mind raced with what she might say. Anything except the truth—that Ethan had kissed her and she was wigging out, as the young people at the shelter would call it.

Ginger tapped her chin thoughtfully. "Is it the dog? Are you mad at Ethan because of Bruno?"

"I'm not mad at Ethan," Glory snapped, annoyed that she sounded annoyed.

Ginger threw her arms up and took a mock step backward. "Whoa. So that's the way the wind blows. Or should I say hurricane?"

"What are you talking about?"

"Ethan." Ginger hovered over her, not allowing Glory to break eye contact. Sweat beaded on her forehead and the back of her neck. Was this what the Inquisition had been like?

"Ethan kissed me."

Glory smacked a hand over her mouth, but it was too late. The damage was done.

Oh, her big mouth!

Mortified, she swung her chair around so she wouldn't have to see the smug, I-told-you-so look in Ginger's eyes. She gritted her teeth, preparing herself for the lecture her sister was sure to give—if she ever stopped laughing.

Except she wasn't laughing—not even a telltale chuckle.

Instead, a few silent moments after Glory's appalling revelation, she felt her chair being pulled slowly and firmly back around.

She tensed, then relaxed at the concerned expression on her sister's face. No hint of teasing, no amusement twinkling in her eyes. Glory's throat tightened in response.

Ginger knelt by her sister, reaching a hand to clasp Glory's two in her lap. She was smiling, but it was a kind smile, not smug at all.

Glory couldn't have been more surprised at her sister's kindness. Not that Ginger wasn't a kind woman—she was, and Glory had seen it many times at the shelter and elsewhere.

But the two of them shared a unique relationship, with Ginger playing the ever irascible little sister.

Since they'd been small, she'd been an incurable tease, always looking for something to torment Glory about. And naturally, over time, Glory had become defensive toward Ginger's constant prodding and joking.

The Glory-Ginger paradox defined their relationship now, and as backward as it seemed, Glory was lost without it.

"Glory?" Ginger queried softly, breaking into her thoughts. "Sweetheart? I don't want to pry."

Glory shot her a look that clearly revealed her disbelief.

"Really, Glory. Cross my heart. I *don't* want to pry."

"Hammer it out of me, then," Glory returned, unable to stop herself from bantering.

Ginger grinned, then put her hands flat under her chin and batted her eyelashes. "Who, me? I'm just confused. There's a very important piece missing from this puzzle of yours."

Her catty grin revealed her true intentions. "Why is Ethan kissing you a problem?"

In any other situation, Glory would have suspected Ginger's motives. But now, for some reason, she believed Ginger was sincere, despite the wicked grin. And she definitely needed someone she could share her dilemma with, someone who might be able to give her some much needed advice.

"It was wonderful," she confided in a whisper. "*He* is wonderful."

Ginger chuckled. "I'm not seeing the problem here, Glory. You like him. He obviously likes you. This has the makings of happily-ever-after, if you ask me, which you didn't."

"Oh, Ginger. That's exactly it. There can't *be* a happily-ever-after."

Ginger's eyebrows hit her hairline, and she shook her head in disbelief. "At the risk of repeating myself, I don't see the problem."

"Isn't it obvious?"

She grinned. "*Obviously* not."

"I can't run the shelter if I'm carrying on with Ethan."

"Glory, having a relationship with a man is hardly carrying on with him."

"You know what I mean."

Ginger sighed loudly. "Yes, I know exactly what you mean. You're embarrassed. As simple as that. Or, in my dear sister's case, as impossible as that."

"Impossible. Thanks a lot, sis."

Glory stood so suddenly her chair spun on its casters. "Look, I know you're trying to be

helpful. I do. But right now I need to be alone.''
She gestured toward the door to her office.

''Well, I'm not leaving,'' said Ginger stubbornly, crossing her arms for emphasis.

''Fine,'' Glory snapped back. ''Then I am.''

She followed her words with the deed itself, stomping out of her own office to find a place to be alone. If this wasn't the ultimate stain on her dignity, she didn't know what was.

Or maybe—probably—the worst was yet to come.

Ethan.

Part of her regretted her churlish behavior toward her sister. She knew Ginger was only acting out of the goodness of her heart, even if she completely misunderstood the situation, and more to the point, misunderstood how Glory felt.

She sighed deeply, feeling a deep, almost physical heaviness within her chest, a heaviness that pulled her spirits down as well. It seemed she was ever asking God for forgiveness for her mouth getting the best of her.

Her attitude wasn't exactly without fault, either. She could at least admit that.

It was just that she always panicked. And when she panicked, her brain shut off and her mouth ran away with her.

She might appear calm, cool and collected to the outside world, but on the inside, she was a quivering mess. Indecisive. Insecure.

Maybe that's why she tried so hard *not* to react emotionally at the shelter, no matter what the crisis or catastrophe. What she'd just displayed with Ginger—that open, emotional woman—was nothing less than weakness, in her book.

And she couldn't afford weakness. The shelter women and children depended on her strength.

Reminded of her God-given obligations, she stopped barreling down the hallway, leaned her arm against the wall, and squeezed her eyes closed.

Lord God, may I find strength in You, that I might be strong for those in my care. I know I've failed them, Lord. Give me renewed strength of thought, mind and spirit. I won't let You down again.

Fortified by her internal monologue and

prayer, she toyed with the idea of going back to the front room and welcoming the erstwhile and very hairy Bruno into the family, but upon turning into a kitchen full of dirty dishes, decided not to return. At least not yet.

A few more minutes alone wouldn't hurt. Ginger wouldn't follow her, not with her tongue-lashing so fresh. No one would find her here.

A feeling of internal peace encompassed her, now that she had her sights set back on the Lord and on the shelter, and had her decisions quite firmly and resolutely made.

She knew her spirit wouldn't stay serene for long, and she wanted to savor it while it lasted.

Donning an apron, she filled a sink with suds and began absently scrubbing away, her mind going over the many details she'd been neglecting while her head had been in the clouds with Ethan—*no*. She'd better not actually think about him by name, at least not for a while.

Until her heart got used to being alone.

Nonsense. She'd been alone before, and it hadn't mattered a bit. What made her situation now so very different?

It suddenly felt very empty in the vacant and echoing kitchen. The clang of the silverware she set in another sink to rinse suddenly sounded altogether too loud.

Deciding she'd quit after this one sink of dishes, she began humming a hymn, something to listen to besides the quiet. Before long, she was lost in the joy of praising God. She wasn't aware of her surroundings anymore, at least until she felt a gentle elbow nudge her in the ribs.

"Hey, gorgeous. We've got to stop meeting here like this. What would the help think?"

Chapter Thirteen

"Ethan!" She hoped she didn't sound as surprised and stunned as she felt, but even she could hear that her voice was squeaking.

"None other," he said with his usual purse-lipped, crooked grin. "Were you expecting some other devastatingly handsome man?"

"No, of course not. I mean…" She clamped her mouth shut.

She looked up to see he'd already slung a towel over his shoulder and was drying a dinner plate. Her heart did a double take, as it always did, at the magnificent man beside her.

She was making a muddle of this, and she

hadn't even started. She'd expected to be able to have the upper hand in her conversation with Ethan—selecting the time and place, at the very least.

This was neither the time nor the place, yet she couldn't just go on pretending nothing was bothering her, or that nothing had changed.

She owed Ethan the truth. He was a good man, and he deserved so much more.

"Hey, not a problem, gorgeous. You don't have to explain anything to me. Let's just say I noticed that you disappeared as soon as we got here. And when you didn't come back after a while…"

He cleared his throat. "I hope Bruno didn't run you off."

"No. I've been giving it some thought, and I believe you're right about a watchdog being a good idea for the shelter. Bruno stays if I have anything to say about it. A conference call to the board should seal the deal."

Feeling a little bit more in her element, she gambled making eye contact with him. "Do I need to go down to the kennel for the paperwork, or can you bring it to me? I probably need to go there, right? So they can check out the potential owner, and all that. That's just as well—I can sign us up for that training you were talking about last night.''

His eyebrows hit the ceiling, but she ignored his expression and continued.

''They'll be five of us—myself, Ginger, and three others,'' she continued, counting on her fingers. ''Oh, and you, of course. Please feel free to add your own name if you'd like.''

Ethan opened his mouth. She didn't know if it was a signal that he wanted to speak, or shock that she was rambling, but she just couldn't stop herself from talking.

''The first available date would be best. If we're going to do this thing, we may as well get on it and do it right.''

Finally, to even her own astonishment, she closed her mouth.

The ensuing silence was a mockery of her extraordinary speech.

Ethan looked pleased, but still very stunned. ''Whoa, lady, you never stop astonishing me. Tell me, when we've been together for twenty years, will you still spring stuff like this on me?''

She grimaced. Brace yourself, Ethan Wheeler, because I haven't even started.

"I prayed about it," she admitted in a mumble.

"Thank You, God," Ethan chimed in immediately and cheerfully.

Glory felt as if she would choke. "Please don't tease about God."

He shook his head fervently. "I'm not. I do thank God. Especially for you."

He was serious. Completely, absolutely serious. Over her, of all things.

Serious about God. The man who'd made light of the God of Angel's Wings. He'd obviously found that God here.

She wanted to cry with happiness and laugh in bitterness, all at the same time.

The knowledge that she would hurt him ached to the point of physical pain in the general area of her heart.

And she would hurt him. She'd known that even before his last words.

No man would like hearing what she would be forced to tell him, and Ethan was more kind and sensitive than most. And if he cared for her in more than just a casual way....

But surely after she'd explained, after he'd had a chance to think about it, he'd see the rightness of her convictions.

Perhaps he'd *already* thought about it. Ethan was an irredeemable flirt.

Besides, she rationalized, it wasn't like they wouldn't see each other at the shelter. That was the whole point, wasn't it—they had to *work* together at the shelter nearly every day?

Ethan hooted a laugh that made Glory stiffen and swing her gaze to him. He looked amused.

Sometimes that joyful twinkle in his eye drove her crazy, especially now. And at the moment, she'd rather wipe the characteristic purse in his lips—the one that lingered just short of a smirk—right off the man's happy face.

"Is something funny? My glasses are on crooked? What?"

"I asked you a question, and you didn't answer." He grinned incorrigibly. "Thus, my—ahem—laughter."

"Come again?" The knots in her stomach and shoulders were quickly turning into rocks. Why, oh why did Ethan's presence have to turn her inside out? Where was all her self-control?

"My question," he said, broadening the word dramatically in lawyerlike fashion, "was why on earth would I find you washing dishes on a busy Saturday? I mean, really. It's not like there aren't procedures for this sort of thing."

As tense as she was, feeling like a cannon about ready to go off, she couldn't help but chuckle, despite knowing laughter was a sure step down the hard road to tears. He was talking about their chore poster, which laid out the duties of the residents.

As Ethan had pointed out earlier, every new person she introduced to the shelter was a potential danger, so the women and teenagers mostly cared for the large household themselves.

Actually, Glory had found cleaning to be an excellent means to building back a battered woman's self-esteem. It was reassuring somehow, to take a messy room and make it neat and clean.

But that was hardly the point right now. Ethan was still talking, and she wasn't paying attention.

"So I asked myself," he said, rubbing his

hands on the towel at his shoulder and turning toward her, leaning his right hip on the counter. "What would a woman like you be doing in a place like this?"

Only Ethan.

"At first I thought you just wanted to get away from Bruno, of course, but you've just— and quite eloquently, I might add—explained that Bruno is not your problem."

He frowned and squinted at her. "So what *is* your problem?"

He made the question sound so inflammatory that someone coming into the kitchen at the moment would have thought they were having a fight. Glory knew better. Ethan was just be-ing...well, *Ethan.*

Once again, she reaffirmed her commitment to follow through with what must be. What if one of the more needful shelter women barged in on her shelter director having a "fight" with one of the shelter's most adamant supporters?

She sighed aloud. It was time.

"Ethan," she began, but paused, thinking through her words carefully. "You, um—might have noticed I sort of, well, *ignored* you when we came in to the shelter together this morning.''

Ethan cocked his head and tried to capture Glory's gaze. He'd heard her sudden change in tone, or maybe her serious tenor had been there all along and he'd just now noticed it.

Either way, something serious was going down.

He wanted to reach out to Glory, to hold her and reassure her against whatever was ailing her, but he knew better than to do that. She had her pride, and he wasn't about to step on it.

Not that his arms wouldn't be readily available when the time came, as he knew it would—the time when she was ready to come to him and accept what he offered.

Which, for a matter of record, was his whole blooming heart.

''Yes. As I said earlier, I noticed your posthaste disappearance from the front hallway when we first arrived.''

''Exactly,'' she said in a husky whisper.

He shrugged. ''I just thought Bruno—''

''It's *not* Bruno,'' she shouted, then clapped a hand over her mouth and dashed a look at each of the doors. Her expression was mortified, as if she expected to see someone leaning on the door frame watching her.

Apparently satisfied they were alone in the room, she narrowed her gaze on him and continued in a hiss. "It's not the stupid, silly mutt."

"I think we've established that point," he commented with a wry purse of his lips. "But you still haven't told me what's wrong."

She sighed, her hands tightly clasped in front of her. "Nothing's wrong, exactly. At least, that's not the word I'd use."

She paused and took a deep gulp of air. Ethan was beginning to get worried. Glory was usually tied up in a twist about something, but this seemed severe even for her.

"So nothing's wrong and we're doing dishes together. Works for me." He grinned and stuck his hands in the suds."

Glory's hand on his arm brought him up short. "You don't always have to be doing something for me—for us, Ethan, though the goodness of your heart flows all the way through Angel's Wings."

Ethan frowned; the deep guilt he'd been living with for so long reapplied itself with a vengeance to his chest and shoulders. "I could never, *ever* do enough for Angel's Wings. Not if I worked here every day of my life."

Glory was the only one he'd ever told of the situation with Sabrina. She alone would understand his desire to make amends, to somehow erase the stain of his guilt on the death of his cousin.

Still, he realized how abrasive his words sounded, and he backed off. "And as for doing enough for you, my dear, it would be my very great pleasure to be allowed to keep doing things for you."

To his frustration, Glory turned away from him and wrapped her arms around herself in what looked like a self-comforting gesture.

Why couldn't she find comfort in *his* arms?

"Ethan, we've got to stop seeing each other."

His breath rushed suddenly from his lungs, as if he'd been sucker punched in the ribs with no warning. As a matter of fact, that was *exactly* how he felt at the moment.

Shoving his fingers through his thick hair, he struggled to recover from the shock. He sucked in a big breath, ignoring the choking sensation that ensued when the air met his closed throat. Pressing his lips together, he tried to think through Glory's reasoning, to come up with why she'd made such an outrageous statement in the first place.

Why hadn't he seen this coming? Glory always went into a tizzy when situations went beyond her immediate control. It was one of the traits he adored about her, the crazy woman.

Guess that made him a little bit crazy, too. Crazy in love, that was.

"Is that all that's bothering you?" he asked lightly.

"What?" Shocked didn't begin to describe the high-pitched sound of her voice.

He grinned. He liked throwing her off balance a bit just to see her reaction. This time, it was a diversionary tactic—something to keep him in the game while he struggled to figure out what she was really saying.

He continued with a forced grin. "It's obviously a problem—that we're seeing each other, I mean."

Her eyes were dual round saucers, so he kept it up, pushed harder.

"Like you said," he reminded her. "But there's a simple solution, really."

"Really?" Now she sounded a little relieved and a lot bewildered.

"Really."

He knew she wanted him to explain, so of course he paused thoughtfully. "One of us will have to wear a blindfold."

He raced on, presumably oblivious to the strangled sound she made in her throat. "I volunteer, of course. The manly thing to do, don't you think?"

For all his efforts, he was rewarded by another strangled sound. He wondered drolly if he ought not perform the Heimlich maneuver on her.

His grin widened, for real this time. "Perhaps we ought to have it be ladies first? Oh, I know! We'll split the effort right down the middle. Half-and-half. Fifty-fifty."

He pulled out a quarter from his pocket and tossed it in the air. "Should we flip to see who goes first? Or do you prefer rock, paper, scissors?"

Her face had turned an alarming shade of red, and he realized belatedly that he'd gone too far, pushed her beyond her limit.

She apparently agreed with his assessment, because the next moment she pegged him in the chest with a very wet washcloth and whirled around, heading toward the nearest exit.

He went after her, grabbing her by the elbow, which she quickly shirked off. She didn't turn to face him, but she didn't leave, either, to his relief.

"Look...that was a really lousy thing I said to you back there. I'm—"

"Incorrigible," Glory snapped, turning around. Tears poured from her eyes, but other than that one word, she was completely silent.

He flashed her his best grin. "I was going to say sorry."

A wavering smile lit her face. "Yes. That, too."

"Why do I think you're using the second dictionary definition of the word?"

He raised his voice an octave to imitate Glory. "Ethan Wheeler, you're the *sorriest* individual I've ever met in my life."

She chuckled.

Feeling as if they'd regained their sense of equilibrium, he took her hand and drew her back into the kitchen, into a quiet corner where she could pull up a chair if she wanted to, where she'd feel safe, and where prying eyes might not see them.

It was time to get to the bottom of this situation once and for all.

Chapter Fourteen

Glory allowed him to pull her with him into the far corner of the kitchen, though she was suddenly quite dubious about talking to him. She'd realized the error in blurting out her feelings just after they left her mouth.

Of course Ethan would want to hash it out here and now, before God and everyone. A public kitchen was neither the time nor the place for such an effort. They risked much of a possibility of running into other people.

In all likelihood, Ginger would come looking for her after a while, though if she realized Ethan was missing as well, she'd probably drag her feet getting here.

As usual, Ethan asserted himself in such a joyful, carefree way that she couldn't help but give in to him.

It annoyed her that he knew the power of his smile, and used it to his advantage. She knew she should be angry with him.

She often was, but it never lasted long.

The crazy thing was, she was even more in love with Ethan for all his antics. She'd balked because she was afraid she'd blurt out that she loved him and would have to leave the shelter to fend for itself.

He'd thought she was angry, of course. She was, but not at him. She was mad at herself, for her lack of faith and courage in following her convictions. Mad about being a wimp of the first degree.

It didn't matter what her feelings dictated where Ethan was concerned. She had to look to the best interest of the shelter.

She'd told herself the same thing a thousand times, and it still didn't ring true in her heart. At the moment, all she wanted to do was throw herself in Ethan's arms and beg him to kiss her just the way he had last evening.

"Do you want to sit?" He shoved his fingers through the tips of his hair, leaving them at whichever angle they drew. This was as edgy as she'd ever seen him. Even his smile looked forced.

She looked away. She'd never get through this if she had to look him in the eye.

"What happened last night," she began, then paused. "Not that it wasn't, uh, wonderful. It…was."

Her speech was as choppy as her thoughts. She sat down, trying to relax and gather herself together for her next round.

Ethan leaned over and planted a gentle kiss on her forehead, his hand brushing lightly across her hair. "I thought it was, uh—wonderful, too," he whispered, close enough to her ear for her to feel the warmth of his breath, and to hear the trademark chuckle that followed his statement.

"Nevertheless," she continued determinedly, "it can't happen again."

He cocked his head, then shook it adamantly. "Glory, you—"

"*I* have thought over the implications of last night," she interrupted.

"You think I haven't been thinking about it? C'mon, Glory, all I've been thinking about since last night is *last night.*"

She sighed. He was being obtuse, and they both knew it. Why couldn't he just once give it a rest?

"It would not be in our best interests to continue our personal relationship in light of our relationship at the shelter here."

She could see he was struggling to keep his jaw from dropping at her outrageous statement.

"And that would be why?"

"These women are my responsibility, Ethan, and I can't afford to—I *mustn't*—let anything or anyone get in the way of that duty."

"No one's asking you to—"

"I know no one is asking. No one would. That's why I have to take it on myself to do what's right. As much as I love when we're together, I cannot forgive myself for not being there—*here,* at the shelter—when I'm needed.

"I sincerely hope you'll recognize your magnificent contribution to Angel's Wings. You have quite literally changed the atmosphere around here, and I hope you'll want to continue your work. We'll simply have to make ours a platonic, business relationship.''

Ethan was grinding his teeth so hard his jaw ached from the effort. If she'd let him get a word in edgewise, let him finish a sentence, maybe they could work this out. But as long as she continued to speak for him, they'd get nowhere.

He shook his head and tried again. ''But I'm not—''

''Distracting? Yes, actually you are.''

''Okay, that's it,'' he announced sternly, knowing she wouldn't know what to do with such a statement.

He knew he was right when silence ensued. Joy to his ears.

Gripping her firmly by the shoulders, he raised her to her feet.

''*Fatal Distraction,* indeed.'' He snorted and bent to remove her glasses, placing them on a nearby counter.

''The only distraction here, Glory, is you. You and your ideas of what the shelter requires of you. Open your eyes, gorgeous. Life goes on whether you're there or not.

"God didn't ask you to make such an outrageous commitment, and neither did the board of directors or the women themselves. They recognize even when you can't that you can't be refreshed to serve them if you never get any downtime yourself.

"It's a simple equation. You, me, Meggie and God. You can serve Christ better by being *with* me than without me. And you do the same for me—make me a better man than I could be alone. Can't you see that?"

When she tried to turn away from him, he slid his hands up to gently grasp her jaw. "Can't you?"

Tears rolled down her cheeks and over the backs of his hands. He squeezed his eyes shut, knowing the answer before it came.

"No, Ethan. I can't see it that way. I've tried, but I can't."

He heard the agony in her voice, but he couldn't find it in his heart to find sympathy for a woman who was throwing both their happy futures away.

He pulled her closer. She'd look him in the eyes this one last time.

"I have my limits, too, Glory. If I leave today without you, I won't be back to Angel's Wings."

She jolted in his arms, but he wouldn't let her go.

He closed his lips over hers, not really knowing why. But instead of the hard, passionate kiss he'd intended, he kissed her softly, tenderly.

It was his goodbye kiss, as well as hers. He might as well make it the best it could be.

A slam and a shout intruded, and they jumped apart like dual sparks as Stephen dashed toward them. "Miss Glory! Mr. Ethan! Hurry!"

Ethan took his model from Glory, who casually slid her hands across her tousled hair and squared her shoulders.

He didn't miss the shaded look she flashed at him. He wasn't really good at having to be told I told you so.

The boy was out of breath and shifting from foot to foot. He was obviously distressed, but he'd stopped dead when he'd reached them. No doubt from seeing the two of them kissing.

"What's up, Steve-o?"

Ethan asked the question, but Stephen directed the answer to Glory. "Dad's here, Miss Glory."

Glory's arm was around Stephen in a heartbeat. "Are you telling me you've seen your father here? At the shelter?"

The young man nodded vigorously, and then dashed a wayward tear away with the back of a dirty hand. Judging from his clothes, he'd been outside playing football with the other boys.

Ethan saw Glory's jaw tense, but other than that, she showed no sign of fear or dismay, only a calm concern. At that moment, Ethan was glad she was so strong, and saw just what that tough veneer meant to her, and to the shelter residents.

"Son, I want you to tell me exactly where you think your father is at this moment, and your mother, as well. Take your time. I need an educated guess."

The boy nodded. "When I left, Dad was talking to Mom in the main hallway."

"Okay. I want you to go back to your room and stay there, all right? I'll let you know when it's safe to come out."

Glory patted the boy on the shoulder, a gesture Ethan suspected the boy wouldn't have allowed from her four months ago when they'd first arrived at Angel's Wings.

Stephen merely nodded, eyes wide.

"It'll be fine, Stephen. You'll see."

As Stephen went the back way to find his room, Ethan's gaze rose to Glory's. "What about his sister? Will Mary be okay?"

Glory nodded grimly. "She's probably in the children's dayroom. Her teacher will have to be alerted, though."

Ethan reached his hand to Glory, and to his relief, she accepted and returned the gesture. "I'll slip through the back way and make sure the little ones are safely tucked away, then meet you in the hallway."

She nodded again. "Thank you," she whispered coarsely.

He pursed his lips and turned toward the back door.

"Ethan?"

He spun around, soaking in Glory's frightened but determined gaze. "Yes?"

She smiled softly. "Pray hard."

Chapter Fifteen

"Now, look, everyone," Mark said as he stood virtually surrounded by staff and Lena's anxious friends. He gestured persuasively with his hands.

On the other end of the hallway, stood Lena, looking small and mussed, her own arms wrapped around herself protectively.

"No harm meant," Mark insisted. "I only want to see my wife."

Glory's throat was so tight she thought she might choke. The only difference between this Lena and the one who'd come crawling into Angel's Wings four months ago was the fire of determination blazing from her gaze.

But would that be enough?

"Go home, Mark," Lena said softly, but firmly. "You know you have a restraining order out on you."

"Yeah, I know," he said, his voice at once soft and hard. He looked like a well-off businessman in his weekend wear—khaki slacks, grass-green polo shirt with the collar cocked up. A golf-yellow cardigan. Penny loafers. Well-tanned, blond and muscular.

Typical husband. Typical abuser.

"Baby, I've missed you," he half whined, half coaxed.

Lena dropped her head and didn't answer.

"I love you." He reached out to her and took a step forward, but the group around him squeezed against his progress. "You know I do.

"Come on, baby. I just want to talk to you." His gaze made a sweep of the company, lingering on Glory with narrowed eyes. She wondered how he knew, but he did.

Her skin burned. The face-off with the shelter's director was an inevitable part of what he was doing, breaking in like this. He had to know that, too.

"So talk," Lena said roughly. Her hands shook as she stood to her full height.

Mark shifted and waved his hand. "I can't talk here. Not with all these people around."

He swept a glance in Glory's direction and grinned like a cat, then took another step toward Lena.

And another.

Glory felt as if she were watching a movie in slow motion. She knew she needed to act, to step in and stop whatever was happening, yet her feet felt frozen to the floor.

She'd never felt so alone. If ever she needed help, it was now.

Where was Ethan? How long could it take to check the dayroom? Major fireworks were about to explode, and he wasn't here to help.

She needed him. Desperately.

"I know I did wrong, Lena. Give me some credit. I made a mistake. But I've changed. I swear it. I'll never touch you again. I'll make it up to you, baby, you know I will. Please. Just let me talk to you for a minute."

Lena wavered at his pleading drawl, then lifted her face, tears streaming down her cheeks.

"Ten years of marriage, Lena. You want to just throw it all away? Think of the good times we had, you and me."

Oh, he was smooth. Every word coming out of his mouth was a coy mixture of truth and fancy.

Glory knew she should be screaming, drowning out the words that made a woman turn and trust a man who could not be trusted.

"Lena?" Mark continued. "Just a few minutes. We can stay here. What harm could it do?"

To Glory's horror, Lena nodded. "Only a minute, though."

Glory had panicked, and now it was too late. What Ethan said had been right. She couldn't do it alone.

Still, she stepped forward. If Lena wanted to meet with Mark, she couldn't stop her; but she could set the parameters of the meet.

"Mark, I'm Glory Weston, the shelter director."

Mark nodded but didn't look at her. His gaze was wholly focused on Lena, and the look he gave her had Glory in chills.

"You have five minutes. I'll escort you to a hallway where you may walk and talk," she continued, thinking of the hallway on the farthest side of the shelter from the children's dayroom and Lena's living quarters.

Glory quickly gave orders to her staff, then showed the two down the hallway. She stepped out of sight, but didn't leave. She had no idea how she might help by hovering around, but she couldn't just leave Lena here.

She could hear them talking softly, him persuading, her disagreeing. Nothing to be concerned about. Yet.

Which was why she bowed her head in prayer.

One moment. One single moment was all it took to send a batterer into a violent rage, and Mark had proven himself persistent. Whatever he wanted, she doubted he'd leave before he got it.

Suddenly she felt something wet and sticky lick her ear. *Bruno!*

She'd forgotten about the dog until now. A serious-faced Ginger had him by the lead.

"I thought he might help," she whispered.

"He didn't come with instructions on his collar, though. Do you know how to command him?"

Glory shook her head. They'd have to figure it out. A *guard* dog. Surely Bruno would help if the situation between Mark and Lena got out of hand.

"The police are here," Ginger continued. "I'm keeping everyone back."

Glory nodded, wanting to hug her sister tight and knowing now was not the time. "Keep them back," she agreed. If Mark saw police uniforms, he'd certainly panic.

When Ginger withdrew, Glory clung to the German shepherd like a lifeline, the answer to her prayers. And somehow, cuddled in his fur, the danger of the situation seemed less imminent than it had earlier.

Voices had risen, so she told the dog to stay and hoped he wouldn't make any noise. Creeping on all fours, she peered around the corner.

Mark had Lena pinned against a wall, dangling her nearly off the floor by her neck. She was struggling and kicking madly, but he just laughed.

"Let her go." Glory launched to her feet and

barreled down the hallway to stand and face Mark off. *"Now."*

Mark immediately released Lena, who backed away slowly, delicately holding her neck. "Yeah, you're right. Okay. I got a little upset. But we were talking about my kids, okay?"

"Okay," Glory agreed, keeping her voice calm and even. The best thing to do was not to rile him any further. Just get him to agree to leave.

Somehow.

Her mind was a blank. Again. And time was ticking away Lena's chances of getting away clean.

"Aw, everyone's having a party and I wasn't invited. I have to say, I'm devastated. After all these years being neighbors...."

Ethan waltzed into the hallway from the opposite end, looking for all the world as if he *was* going to a backyard barbecue. He sauntered up with a cavalier attitude, hands casually tucked into his pockets, whistling under his breath.

But when his gaze met hers, she knew he was

totally serious. He'd obviously taken stock of the situation and was moving in according to some kind of plan.

At least, she hoped he had some kind of plan.

"Hot dogs, anyone?"

She could see where he was walking—covering the distance between Mark and Lena.

No one breathed. Mark looked around desperately. Lena looked horrified, frozen to the spot.

"No? Well, then, I guess it's time for everyone to leave." He looked straight at Mark.

Mark reached for Lena in such a lightning-quick motion that she was wrapped in his arms faster than anyone could do anything about, least of all Glory.

"I don't think so, buddy," Mark replied in his gravelly voice. "My *wife* and I aren't finished talking yet. And it sure isn't any of your business."

Ethan pursed his lips in the way he had that looked almost like a low, irritating smirk. She didn't think Mark needed to be egged on, but she didn't know how to communicate with Ethan short of speaking out loud, which would be fruitless.

Slowly, steadily, he moved toward Mark.
Glory held her breath.

"Is that a fact?" Ethan drawled, nearly mimicking Mark's voice.

"That's a *fact*." Surely Ethan couldn't miss that hard edge.

"Well, the way I look at it, Lena and me are good friends. And as a friend, I have the obligation to protect her from nozzles like you."

Where the handgun came from Ethan couldn't have said. He'd slid a glance at Glory, and when he'd turned back, the gun was there, being waved around by nothing short of a madman.

Slowly and deliberately, making firm, hard eye contact with Ethan, Mark pointed the gun at Lena's forehead and put pressure on the trigger.

"I don't want *you*," he barked huskily into Lena's hair. He tightened his grip and nearly pulled her off the floor with the force of his clutch.

"Let her go, Mark," Glory said smoothly. "You can't get what you want this way. Just let Lena go. Give her to me. Then we can all talk when everyone has regained their composure.''

She was very good at negotiating, with her soft, persuasive tone, but Mark was obviously not phased by it as Ethan was.

Mark jerked Lena around, trying to take both Glory and Ethan into his gaze. ''I didn't come here to talk. I didn't come for this little tramp, either.''

A wide-eyed Lena remained frozen with the gun pointed at her forehead.

Ethan slid sideways so he and Glory were facing each other across the hallway, and thus making it impossible for Mark to keep them both well in view. He watched the gun with care, and kept a close eye on Glory.

A couple of times, she gestured faintly toward the hallway and tried to tell him something with her lips, but even through his rushing adrenaline, he couldn't understand her charade.

Mark swung Lena around like a rag doll. Ethan could see the blue marks forming on her arms and neck. It was all he could do to keep a lid on his anger. Especially with Mark's continued rambling, which grated against everything Ethan stood for.

God, country and family. None of these meant anything to Mark, not if his constant, slurred cursing had anything to say about it. Mark was angry and frustrated, and at the moment, he was in control of the situation.

Ethan's blood screamed for action, but he knew he'd be foolish to act without thinking and planning. He would *not* put Glory or Lena into further danger by his actions, yet paradoxically he *needed* to act to get the ladies out of danger.

"I don't care about the court order, and I don't care about the divorce." Mark waved the gun around like a baton, using it to make his points.

Then his eye and his gun landed on Glory, and Ethan knew he had to gain control of the situation now.

He was here to save Lena, and he would. But his heart stopped beating altogether at the thought of losing Glory, especially to some crazy man with a gun, ready to unload on the woman Ethan loved.

No way. It wasn't going to happen. It *wasn't* going to happen.

Mark swiveled on his feet, almost as if he were drunk, though his gun remained firmly pointed toward Glory.

"I want my son, and I want him now," Mark demanded. "Man's got a right to his son."

"We can talk about it," Glory coaxed. "Just put down the gun."

Instead of following Glory's suggestion, he pressed his lips together and aimed the pistol directly at Glory's head.

Sweat poured down his face, dampening his golf clothes. "The way I figure it, if I shoot one of you, I'll get what I want. *Stephen.*"

Glory and Lena gasped simultaneously—not at being named as prospective victims, but at the idea of Stephen being sent away with Mark. And surely they were also thinking about little Mary in the dayroom.

Think, Ethan commanded himself, wiping sweat from his own forehead. *Think!*

Mark was caught like a wild dog in a corner, and he would use any means at his disposal to get what he wanted. He was also clearly delusional.

How could he believe he would regain his

parental authority over his son by killing Stephen's mother in cold blood? How could he believe he'd walk out of the shelter?

He had to know police had surrounded the place by now.

Delusional.

Ethan shivered. Mark's monologue gave him a pretty good idea where the man's state of mind was.

Mark was caught in a trap of his own making, and he knew it. He was probably open to making more mistakes, but that also meant a more volatile situation all around.

Any word, any movement, could set Mark off with fatal results.

Sweat pouring down his face, Mark finally looked at Ethan, and Ethan knew, as he made eye contact with the man, that this was the moment he'd been looking for.

Mark had turned the gun on him.

"If you want Stephen…" he said slowly, and then accelerated "…you're gonna have to go through me."

Ethan screamed like a banshee and plowed straight for the man with the gun with all the strength of his being.

Time slammed to a halt.

Mark let go of Lena and propped the gun with both hands, aiming straight at Ethan. But that didn't matter now. Ethan was beyond caring.

Glory pulled Lena away.

The women moved out of Ethan's peripheral vision.

Mark's, too, he thought.

The women were safe.

Something exploded.

Ethan thought the police must be closing in.

Still, he ran.

He must get to Mark. Must save everyone.

Glory yelled, "Bruno, come."

Bruno flew in from nowhere. A flash of fur.

Glory yelled again. "Bruno, *bite!*"

Ethan was confused. Off balance, as if in a dream.

He lunged for Mark, but Bruno beat him to the punch, wrestling the pistol away from the man.

Without a gun, the stakes were even, and Ethan tackled Mark and knocked him out cold. Even then, Ethan sat slumped over the man, pinning him down in case he regained consciousness.

He was taking no chances.

Lena was screaming wildly. Something about blood.

Blood. He was pretty sure he'd broken Mark's nose. There was blood.

Glory clucked around like a mother hen, directing people here and there. Counselors. Policemen. Someone called for an ambulance.

The mist fading, he was suddenly aware of a glaring pain in his left shoulder. He looked down.

Blood. More blood than on his knuckles.

For a moment he just looked.

Then he yelled, "Glory! I...think...need...sit...down."

Glory's face was pale. Worried. She looked like she might cry.

Ethan scowled, trying to think. Glory cry?

He gave her what he hoped was a smile, though it felt more like a grimace.

Suddenly he could no longer stand. He dropped to his knees.

"Gorgeous," he said with a coarse chuckle, "I think...that nozzle...shot me."

Chapter Sixteen

Glory paced across the room and back for the hundredth time. The doctor said Ethan was only sleeping, but he didn't so much as twitch in his sleep. She thought the effects of having his shoulder patched up was catching up with him.

At least the doctors said no permanent damage had been done. Still, she'd hated being away from him, even to tend to shelter details.

The first few hours after Mark had first entered the shelter, and then had shot Ethan had been a terrifying rush of activity, accompanied by a stomach-turning rush of adrenaline.

Mark himself had to be dealt with as a first

order of business. Bruno had taken good care of the gun, and Ethan had knocked the man clean out, so the police had no trouble hauling him off.

Between what he'd done to Lena and shooting Ethan, he was looking at some serious jail time.

There would be more than enough time for Lena and her children to move on with their lives.

Lena had already taken her children and moved into a new shelter somewhere in western Washington, but Glory didn't think she'd be there for long.

Oddly enough, facing Mark off the way she had, hadn't sent Lena back into her shell; instead, she was more determined than ever to make a new life for herself and her children, far and away from the influence of Mark.

Bruno was heartily welcomed into the Angel's Wings family, by the mothers as much as the children. They were already begging Ginger to discuss with Glory the possibility of the addition of another <u>dog</u> to their troupe.

Mrs. Bruno? Glory's lip twitched upward. She'd bear it in mind.

All this had happened in such a short time, and Ethan still slept peacefully and oblivious in his hospital bed.

To say she was anxious to get the old Ethan back would be an understatement. When the gun went off in the hallway, for one moment Glory had realized the possibility of losing him.

Not only as a friend, someone she worked with at the shelter, but as someone who could take a cloudy day and make it bright. Someone who could make her laugh when she was down, and fly on his fancy just by his words.

She sat down at the chair by his bedside, wondering, as she had many times that day, why they made hospital chairs so uncomfortable.

Hers was a big, vinyl armchair thing that she couldn't get pushed close to the side of the bed, but that popped up an annoying footrest whenever she leaned backward.

One of the many paradoxes of life, she supposed.

Settled, she reached out tentatively and began stroking Ethan's silky blond hair. She loved the feel of his hair. Someone had washed it free of the blood that had dried there.

How would he take it, she wondered, her sudden change of heart. Or would he have known it all along, and it was only her stubborn heart that needed to learn how to yield.

Stubborn? Like *he* could talk about stubborn?

Running into a gun, for pity's sake. What kind of sense did that make? And yet, at the very same time, it was the greatest sort of bravery, to run headlong into danger for the sake of your ideals and the people you loved.

"You've paid your penance, you big oaf," she said aloud, kissing him lightly on the forehead where her fingers had just been. "You ran right into the wrong end of a gun. How smart is that, Wheeler?"

He didn't answer, of course. His breathing pattern hadn't changed. She chuckled.

"You're a hero. I've brought a newspaper for you to read when you feel like it. You didn't make the front page, but page two isn't bad for a first-time champion. Big, close up shot of your ugly mug and everything."

She took his hand, the one that wasn't attached to an IV, and began a long, stroking massage she'd learned in a class once. She hadn't had much use for it, since she lived alone.

But now...now there was Ethan.

Her heart swelled until she thought it might burst. The man of the hour, and he wanted her.

She'd asked herself why, and then again, why she would ever have wanted to throw away what she shared with Ethan. But for every answer, there were a thousand more questions.

For one, did he still want her?

"You know, it galls me to have to say you were right," she whispered, softly stroking his hand. "I don't do apologies well. But when I saw you on the other side of that gun...."

She chuckled and held up a hand. "Okay. Okay. You don't have to say anything. I'm an idiot."

Brushing a tear away, she leaned as far forward as she could, given the chair and the handrails on the bed, and placed her head on his chest, listened to the beat of his heart.

"When you're right, you're right. I do need you and Meggie in my life. You do make me a better person, and better able to help others. And I think I do the same for you."

Suddenly Ethan's arm slipped around her, and she jumped, but she stilled when she felt the chuckle in his ribs.

He brushed the hair away from her face with his hand. "Tell me," he said, pursing his lips in that half smirk, "Was that a proposal?"

"Ethan Wheeler, how long have you been eavesdropping on me?"

Of course, he ignored her question. "Because if it *was* a proposal, I accept."

"What?" she screeched, jumping away from him. The man was crazy. Certifiably crazy.

He just smiled contentedly. "When should we get married?"

"Married? Ethan, I'm still trying to figure out if you're lucid."

"Glory, hon, come back on over here." He patted the mattress beside him.

She sat daintily to avoid hurting him.

"You aren't the only one who had a revelation last night, Glory. Try looking down the barrel of a gun."

He looked away for a moment, but when he looked back, his gaze was clear and full of amusement. "I almost lost *me* last night, Glory," he said in a high-pitched squeak.

Glory chuckled. She just couldn't help it.

"I'm not leaving, Glory Weston. You can throw me out or run away, but I'm just going to keep coming back and chasing you."

She smiled. "I'm glad to hear it."

He narrowed his eyes on her. "Well?"

"Well?" She looked confused for a moment, and then blushed from her chin to the tip of her forehead.

Ethan grinned like a cat.

"I do."

He leaned on his good elbow and cocked his head. "You *do?*"

"I do."

"Well, then," he said, pursing his lips once again as if he had a secret to hide, "I guess the only question is, 'How do we do?'"

Ethan wanted to stretch his arms behind him and clasp his hands behind his neck, but that was kind of difficult to do in a sling. He was feeling great, really. He had wanted to go home since the first night he was there.

But the doctors had said *one more night, one more night* consistently, until the mimic of those words echoed in his head. Finally, though, three very long days and longer nights later, the doctors had given their go-ahead.

And with their go-ahead was his Go For It!

He'd just made the call—to Ginger Weston, his partner in crime.

"Is everything ready?" he asked anxiously as Ginger walked into his hospital room laden with bags.

She barked a laugh and set her arms akimbo on her hips. "Since when did you care if everything was ready? To hear Glory tell it, you'd be classified as more of a free spirit."

Ethan rolled with laughter, which hurt his shoulder. Which, in turn, of course made him roll even harder with laughter.

"That's more like it," Ginger replied, tongue-in-cheek. "Now. I brought you everything you asked me to get, but I'm telling you right now, this is pushing too hard, too fast. Glory is never going to go for what you have planned."

Ethan just grinned and shrugged. "Maybe. Maybe not. Is my big brother here?"

"If you mean that good-looking, Stetsontoting, duster-wearing cowboy brooding in the waiting room, that would be him.''

''Yeah,'' he agreed. ''That would be him.'' His younger brother Rhett couldn't make it on such short notice, but Erik went out of his way, despite his surly exterior.

When everyone save Glory was present, they set their trap, putting it together piece by piece until it was perfectly assembled. Now all they— *he*—had to do was wait.

Wait. And sit and wonder if he was making yet another life-threatening mistake, just as potent and dangerous as running headlong into a bullet.

Maybe he could call it all off, on account of his shoulder hurting. Make it another day. They'd all understand.

And then the wait was over, and it was too late. For better or for worse, he was committed.

''Places everyone,'' Ginger pealed gaily.

Lights, camera and Hawaiian music.

''What is all this?'' Glory asked the moment she entered his room. ''Your music is loud enough to be heard down the hall. Don't you think you should be….''

Her sentence faded to nothing as, Ethan presumed, she suddenly became aware of her surroundings.

He held his breath, waiting to see if she'd play the nurse and have all these people gone. Waiting to see if she'd ban the party.

After all, she was in the middle of a luau.

It took her a moment. She gave everyone and everything a good hard look, from his cowboy of a brother to the red, fruity punch bowl covered with pineapple slices. The radio was blaring too loud. There were way too many people in the small room. She was certain there were health codes.

She crossed her arms as she turned to Ethan, and his heart nearly stopped cold. She didn't like his idea.

No, of course she didn't. She wouldn't.

What had he been doing, testing her? He opened his mouth to apologize, but never made it that far.

"You were having a party without me?" Then she whirled and she whooped and she blew Ethan a kiss.

"Believe me, honey," Ginger said, "this is one party that *can't* start without you."

"I've got a shirt for you, gorgeous," Ethan said, reaching his gift to her. "It's my second-best shirt—I'm wearing the best one."

He chuckled, then coughed and stopped for a moment. "I'd have bought you a new one, but I couldn't get out on time."

Glory brought the shirt to her face and inhaled deeply of Ethan's brisk scent. "Believe me, this is better than new."

As she threw the shirt on over her sweater, Ginger presented her with a lei. "Congratulations, sis," she said formally, with a tear in her eye.

Glory's throat caught. "If you're getting mushy, something bigger than a party is going on here."

Ginger's eyes twinkled. "I'll give you a hint. That deliciously good-looking cowboy over there who is bouncing Meggie on his knees is Ethan's older brother, Erik."

"His brother?" Glory's eyes widened. "Excuse me while I have a quick little rendezvous with Ethan."

Now that she noticed it, nearly everyone she worked with at the shelter was here, in addition to Ginger and Erik. The tone was clear enough.

Her panic instinct, that fight or flight, was setting off bells all over the place.

Sure, she wanted to marry Ethan. They'd sort of alluded to it the day after he'd been shot, and had talked quietly of their future together in the two days since.

But get married? In a hospital?

Wouldn't it be better to wait until he was healed, at the very least? Until they'd had more time to work on their relationship?

And then the picture of Ethan, Meggie and Bruno filling her tiny town house with warmth and love intruded, and she decided to play firefighter another day.

"Yes," she told Ethan as she approached. "I mean, I do."

"I do, too," he whispered huskily, leaning into her kiss for a moment. "But I've paid a lot for the band. Can we say it before the minister, already? I can't wait to be married to you."

"Your wish is my command," she said with a rolling bow.

Then, with a sly grin, she turned to the company and gave a sharp, two-fingered whistle. "Ginger and Meggie with me. Erik Wheeler, front and center. You're on."

She looked around, unable to account for one member of their party. "Has anyone seen the minister?"

"Present and accounted for," cried a small, bespectacled man standing up by Ethan's bed.

She took a second look when she realized the man was dressed in a flowery Hawaiian shirt over his clerical collar.

Ethan's doing. Would a lifetime be enough with that man?

She intended to find out.

* * * * *

Dear Reader,

I don't know about you, but I've been in Glory Weston's shoes a time or two. I fight the good fight, surround myself with what I believe is God's work and I strive to fulfill His will with all my might.

And sometimes, like Glory, I'm suddenly surprised to realize I can't see the forest for the trees.

I want to do what is right. I strive for what is good. But sometimes, in my zeal, I set up a target, pursue a goal or make a way for myself that isn't God's best for me, however good and right it may be in itself.

Today, open your eyes and watch for God's special blessings to arrive in your life. I'm praying He'll surprise you even today with His goodness, in ways you yourself never envisioned!

I love hearing from my readers, and would love to know what you thought of Ethan and Glory's story. I'm at P.O. Box 9806, Denver, CO 80209.

Surprises and Blessings in the LORD!

Deb Kastner

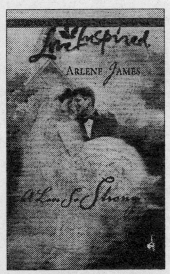

A LOVE SO STRONG
BY
ARLENE JAMES

He'd prayed to God for the perfect woman. What pastor Marcus Wheeler got was Nicole Archer. While she was kind and beautiful, Marcus Wheeler thought she was too young and unconventional to be a proper pastor's wife. Yet sometimes God's plan isn't what one expects....

Available September 2006 wherever you buy books.

Steeple Hill®

REQUEST YOUR FREE BOOKS!

2 FREE INSPIRATIONAL NOVELS
PLUS A
FREE
MYSTERY GIFT

Love Inspired

YES! Please send me 2 FREE Love Inspired® novels and my FREE mystery gift. After receiving them, if I don't wish to receive any more books, I can return the shipping statement marked "cancel." If I don't cancel, I will receive 4 brand-new novels every month and be billed just $3.99 per book in the U.S., or $4.74 per book in Canada, plus 25¢ shipping and handling per book and applicable taxes, if any*. That's a savings of over 20% off the cover price! I understand that accepting the 2 free books and gift places me under no obligation to buy anything. I can always return a shipment and cancel at any time. Even if I never buy another book from Steeple Hill, the two free books and gift are mine to keep forever.

113 IDN D74R   313 IDN D743

Name _____ (PLEASE PRINT) _____

Address _____ Apt. _____

City _____ State/Prov. _____ Zip/Postal Code _____

Signature (if under 18, a parent or guardian must sign)

Order online at www.LoveInspiredBooks.com

Or mail to Steeple Hill Reader Service™:

IN U.S.A.	IN CANADA
3010 Walden Ave.	P.O. Box 609
P.O. Box 1867	Fort Erie, Ontario
Buffalo, NY 14240-1867	L2A 5X3

Not valid to current Love Inspired subscribers.

Want to try two free books from another series?
Call 1-800-873-8635 or visit www.morefreebooks.com

* Terms and prices subject to change without notice. NY residents add applicable sales tax. Canadian residents will be charged applicable provincial taxes and GST. This offer is limited to one order per household. All orders subject to approval. Credit or debit balances in a customer's account(s) may be offset by any other outstanding balance owed by or to the customer.

LIREG05

Love Inspired CLASSICS

TITLES AVAILABLE NEXT MONTH

Don't miss these stories in September

FATHER MOST BLESSED
AND
A FATHER'S PLACE
by Marta Perry

Two single fathers each find
the woman of their dreams with a little help
from their children in two classic stories.

LOOKING FOR MIRACLES
AND
THE PRODIGAL'S RETURN
by Lynn Bulock

Love comes home in two beloved
Missouri-set romances.